SINNER

FEATHERS AND FIRE BOOK 5

SHAYNE SILVERS

ARGENTO
PUBLISHING

CONTENTS

Shayne Silvers

Sinner

Feathers and Fire Book 5

A Temple Verse Series

ISBN 13: 978-1-947709-18-8

© 2018, Shayne Silvers / Argento Publishing, LLC

info@shaynesilvers.com

IF YOU WANT TO GET TO HEAVEN, YOU'VE GOTTA RAISE A LITTLE HELL...

*C*allie Penrose is struggling to find her special purpose in life. Rather than allying with any of the powerful supernatural groups begging to sign her up—the Vatican, the vampires, the shifters, or the Armies of both Heaven and Hell—Callie has been picking fights with all of them.

But when she's abducted by a Host of Angels, and a Greater Demon begins hunting her through the daytime streets of Kansas City, Callie learns that her past has come back to haunt her.

Thanks to her actions in recent months, Solomon's Temple has been opened, and the estate sale is on a first-come, first-served basis.

To win her birthright, Callie is going to need Cain's help. Even then, she's going to have to cut some corners, cross some lines, to take a bite out of an apple...

But they say every Saint was once a Sinner...

~

OLLOW and LIKE:
Shayne's FACEBOOK PAGE

www.shaynesilvers.com/l/38602

I try my best to respond to all messages, so don't hesitate to drop me a line. Not interacting with readers is the biggest travesty that most authors can make. Let me fix that.

CHAPTER 1

$\mathcal{T}$he penthouse overlooked the glittering streets below. I watched the people walking from storefront to storefront, taking advantage of the cool evening air. Expensive cars cruised past, likely blaring music in an attempt to impress any single females walking by—like a bunch of hairy fishermen running a large trawling net across the ocean floor to pick up some crabs.

Pun intended.

Other cars cruised by shining with opulence and elitism, showing off the size of their bank accounts—or the weight of their monthly lease—as they struggled to compete with their uncaring neighbors in the never-ending contest played by most Americans.

I took a sip of my champagne, envying their ignorance. They had no idea that a horde of monsters in tuxedos and dresses was hosting a ritzy party high above their heads, discussing how best to slaughter the humans with impunity. That every single one of the attendees behind me was liable to rip their ignorant human throats out for the slightest offense.

Or just for fun.

And right now, I seemed to be the only one standing between the two parties—between the would-be Lords and their cattle. I grunted at the observation. Then I took another healthy sip of my champagne, hoping to absolve myself of the responsibility for at least a few more minutes. Like any good Catholic, I thought drinking was a sensible coping mechanism.

I sighed wistfully, realizing my glass was now empty. Before I could find some depressing symbolism in that, a waiter with a hint of Asian descent whisked by like a ninja to replace my glass and then slipped away so as not to disturb me too greatly. If he had been one heartbeat slower, I would have told him I preferred the champagne over the rosé he had given me. But I didn't want to be that girl, so let it go, resigning myself to accept the unasked-for new experience with the grace of a lady.

I gasped as the pink alcohol touched my tongue in an explosion of crisp, sweet strawberry. It was shockingly good, *much* better than the champagne had been. Bastard waiters, able to read into my alcoholic soul without even a word, broadening my horizons with their demon-juice.

I shook my head in begrudging appreciation of the posh service. The monsters knew how to throw a party—that was undeniable. The gentle sounds of violins behind me and the smells of the savory food lining the catered tables—raw oysters, lobster bisque, and dozens of other expensive dishes meticulously parceled out into bite-sized samples so as not to stall conversation from the tuxedo and gown-wearing crowd—was enough to make a girl momentarily forget about her problems.

I didn't want to be here, but it was an unfortunate requirement of my recent self-inflicted punishment—a small job I had undertaken. Rather than turning back to the firing squad of socialites, I continued staring through the wall-to-wall, floor-to-ceiling window before me, envying those fishermen and crabs on the streets far below. That was where I belonged. In the trenches. The front lines—

"Against stupidity, the very Gods Themselves contend in vain," a voice said from beside me.

I turned to see an exotic beauty studying me over the rim of her champagne flute. She wore a cute little black dress that hung below her knees and her black hair was done-up in a perfectly tight bun. She lowered her glass, smirking playfully. Her big brown eyes flicked over the room in a swift assessment, indicating the guests huddled in groups of three or four drinking, talking, and likely making deals.

"Friedrich Schiller?" I asked, surprised to hear someone quote the abstract German poet.

She nodded, giving me an impressed once-over. I wasn't that familiar with Schiller, but he was a favorite of my mentor, Roland Haviar. It was his favorite way to unwind after a stressful day of slaughtering monsters—seated in his favorite chair, reading Schiller by the fireplace at Abundant Angel Catholic Church. Well, it *had* been a favorite pastime.

Before he'd become a vampire and been relieved of Shepherd duty for his conflict of interest.

"It may have just begun, but I'm certain it will all be over soon," the woman added with a playful grin.

"What will all be over soon?" I asked, masking my instinctive trepidation as idle curiosity. Because I was standing in a room full of monsters, thank you very much—none were card-carrying members in my ever-so-small *circle of trust* club. Thankfully, the woman's playful tone appeared to be mocking but authentic, not setting off any rational reason to alert my mental alarm bells that she was really some sociopath casually informing me she had poisoned the buffet tables. But I remained hyper-aware just in case. Because paranoia *was* a card-carrying member in my circle of trust. The bitch hardly ever lied to me.

And one never truly knew what one faced with these types of crowds. And I'd assumed wrong before. Been played by an innocent smile.

Fuck happy, smiling people. That was a good mantra. They were often lying about something.

"Materialism," the woman replied with an easy shrug, showing off a delicate collarbone. I cocked my head at her answer and used the motion to quickly scan the room full of guests behind us. There was a lot of money represented here, but there was even more power. Magical power of several flavors.

Many of the guests had acquired other forms of power over the years, as well, hedging their bets—whether it was political, monetary, or a vast number of followers. And no one knew every single secret their fellows held up their sleeves. Like a game of poker, they were all bluffing, calling, raising bets, folding, and using social cues to feign ignorance, to mask their true machinations, or to find an advantage—a tell—to capitalize on.

Not a single one of them looked truly happy. Momentarily pleased, yes. But that was it. With all the power at their disposal, I still sensed a frantic desperation in their eyes, and a profound emptiness in their souls.

It was all so…trivial.

But I kept my face blank as I turned back to my new friend, the pretty scholar.

She was beautiful in a fashion, her black dress more professional than alluring. She wore delicate golden bands on her biceps that glittered with semi-precious stones. Her bronze skin seemed to glimmer in the light—likely some kind of lotion to subtly attract wandering eyes. Her face was long and narrow, and her harsh cheekbones stood out in the dim lighting, making it almost impossible not to stare. And her choice in makeup told me she had seen the dreaded *smoky eye* YouTube video.

"Materialism…" I repeated, neither confirming nor denying I agreed with her comment.

The woman jerked her chin out towards the street below us. "As above, so below," she said demurely.

"As above, so below. As within, so without…" I quoted. It was one of the seven principles of Hermes, and had been adopted in the Catholic arena, like most clever quotes had over the centuries. Roland had often used the phrase in my weapons training as well as my meditations.

The woman nodded appreciatively, the flash of excitement in her eyes telling me that I was now officially adopted into her nerd-herd where we would change the world with cryptic quotes, one bored college kid at a time. Her plan was flawed, though, because my ability to recognize her quotes was just a coincidence.

Or…

She was playing me, knowing more about me than she let on, tossing out specific quotes she knew would be familiar to me—like laying out a trail of small candies to lead me to her gingerbread house of death in the nearby woods.

Paranoia made a girl feel all warm and fuzzy inside.

"As above, so below," the woman repeated. "They just don't know it. Everyone competes in this unspoken game to prove how much better they are than their colleagues. Of course, there are different levels to the game…" she said, glancing back at the room around us. "Some more beneficial than others. But no one openly talks about those things. They just dance back and forth, back and forth, side to side, all along for the ride. There should be more to life than this."

I found myself nodding thoughtfully, wondering what flavor of power I was talking to. Some bored socialite looking for thrills? Or perhaps she was a powerful witch or shifter angling for a crumb of influence in Kansas City.

"You sound like a friend of Dorian Gray," I told her, taking another sip of my delicious rosé.

She scoffed gently. "Hardly. Different circles."

I watched her eyes for any sign of deceit, but all I saw was amusement. Dorian seemed to have good relations with the witches through the Hellfire Club parties he hosted, so if she was being honest right now, she likely wasn't a witch. "I'm sure he would love to meet you. Would you like an introduction?"

"It isn't necessary...but I wouldn't turn it down," she admitted with an interested grin.

CHAPTER 2

I realized I was still gauging her response, wondering if the entire purpose of our conversation was her angling for an introduction. Or maybe it was to avoid an introduction with Dorian. Circles within circles. I knew I hadn't met her before and I couldn't decipher what kind of supernatural—or Freak, as we were sometimes called—she was. She wasn't a wizard like me. And she wasn't from the Heavenly crowd. Maybe she *was* a witch of some variety and was lying about knowing Dorian. She could have also been a shifter.

That was the problem with a Come to Jesus meeting like this between the local supernatural families in Kansas City—the first of its kind, I might add, thank you very much. It had taken some heavy negotiating on my part, but it all seemed to be working out. I'd petitioned enough different groups to chip in that it truly was a collective effort to bring everyone together. Much better than having one party set it all up—which would have resulted in everyone else acting standoffish and suspicious of a trap all night. Because there were a lot of new faces in town. Maybe even a lot of old faces that had spent their many years working in the shadows and preferred to remain unknown.

And admitting that you didn't know who someone was could be the equivalent of opening a vein to weaken yourself before a potential enemy. Your ignorance seen as a weakness to be exploited.

Or it could be seen as disrespectful—immediate grounds for a *coincidental* violent crime to be inflicted upon your person on your way home after the party.

Couldn't have that, now, could we?

The entire point of the evening was to get to know each other, and since everyone had unanimously voted *no* on wearing name badges, it was a pond full of Great White Sharks.

Which led me to wonder. Was my new friend a potential enemy, an ally, or a third party just hoping to survive the tension between the various other families?

Because there was definitely tension, and I had caused a big portion of it. By now, most had heard of my activities in recent months—taking out a couple Demons and, allegedly, an Angel. The Demons had been subtly angling the families against each other to start a civil war of some kind. Or to unite the families against an enemy that the Demons had never specifically mentioned. I was personally of the opinion that any enemy of a Demon was probably a good drinking buddy to have.

The Angel I had taken out had made poor life decisions and had Fallen from Grace as a result. Fallen right onto my thumb, as a matter of fact. But I didn't want to draw attention to that, so kept the ring of shadows circling my thumb out of view as discreetly as I could. No one wanted to talk to the girl with a Fallen Angel wrapped around her finger. She was probably super creepy.

But since no one really knew what had been false, true, or anywhere in between, no one really knew where they stood with their neighboring families. Had the werewolves really done that thing that made the vampires so furious? Did the bears really hate the Vatican Shepherds? Were the witches really friends with the Faerie Chancery? Is that why they weren't attending tonight? To hide their backroom allegiances with the witches? Or was it the wolves?

Essentially, this was prom night for the monsters. And the kids were a'gossiping.

With a sigh, I smiled at my new friend. "My name is Callie," I told her.

"Oh, how precious. Everyone knows who you are," the woman said with a smile. "I like women who take a stand against our hairier, self-proclaimed overlords. The world could do with a mother to keep these children in line. You wear the mantle well."

I found myself smiling at her gibe at men, but also because it equally applied to monsters and Demons. Equal opportunity discrimination in action. I didn't entirely agree on the black and white comment, but I understood what she meant. I didn't think men needed to be in charge of everything. I didn't think women needed to be in charge of everything. As in all things, balance was necessary. It had nothing to do with what biological toolkit one was given at birth, but with what that person did with their tool.

Considering how that sounded, I let out a sigh, accepting my depravity with grace.

"Oh, my name is Cleo," she said, blushing slightly.

I smiled, but my heart might have fluttered a little. Cleo as in…Cleopatra? Or was that just some kind of coincidence? However, asking such a question could make me look either disrespectful, if she was Cleopatra, or childish, if she wasn't. "Nice to meet you, Cleo," I said, lifting my glass in cheers. "Let's go find the center of the moral depravity." I turned my back on her, wondering if this fit into my plan for the evening, or if it would hinder it.

"I thought you were introducing me to Dorian?" Cleo asked from behind me.

And that right there hinted pretty strongly that she did not know Dorian Gray.

Unless…she *was* playing games, feigning ignorance. I really needed to drink more. Otherwise I would soon begin avoiding people altogether to become some crazy cat lady. Severe inebriation sounded much more pleasurable as a lifestyle choice. Cats were assholes.

Speaking of…

"Have you ever visited the Great Sphinx?" I asked Cleo over my shoulder. I had recently met Phix, the actual Sphinx, and she had taken a shining to me—self-admittedly adopting me as her plaything. Spending more than ten minutes with her at a time left my brain feeling like swiss cheese because her every comment was cryptic, a riddle, or spoken in a tone that let you know she was leading you towards a specific conclusion or statement. That—in her mind—the conversation had already ended, and she was merely following the dance card for propriety's sake. Thankfully, she was out on some errand for Darling and Dear—the mysteriously powerful, self-proclaimed Armorers of the Apocalypse, as they'd taken to calling themselves.

I glanced over my shoulder to find Cleo enmeshed in a conversation with a great bear of a man who seemed to be introducing her to two other women in an overly animated manner. Cleo shot me an apologetic look from the corner of her eyes and almost imperceptibly shrugged her shoulders, as if to let me know she had been picked off and hadn't been able to deny the man introducing her to his friends.

I smiled in understanding. That was kind of the point of the evening—to network with our neighbors. "At least I won't have to babysit," I murmured under my breath as I turned away.

"Baby, you can sit on me anytime," a man's seductive voice whispered in my ears.

I rolled my eyes at the familiar voice. "Easy, Dorian. Kitty has claws." I turned to face him and couldn't help but appreciate the specimen of a man before me.

Dorian was undeniably beautiful. When he entered a room, spoke in your ear, or touched you in any way whatsoever, reality seemed to shift and flicker like he was some godling arriving to take away all pain in the world and to sing that Disney song, *I will show you the world...*while conveniently taking off your undergarments. Gender would not save you from his silver tongue; his fetishes were multi-faceted, and his appetite was multi-sexual.

Dorian was still smirking at my threat. "Why else would I try to seduce you? I *love* claws." I sighed, shaking my head. "Tell me, why is the most beautiful woman in the room standing all alone at the very party she orchestrated?" he asked gently.

I gave up, the compliment warming my heart. I slipped my arm through his to let him escort me across the room, which had the added benefit of preventing any interruption as we continued walking. Now that we were touching each other, I had to focus more intently, battling away the almost euphoric feeling of being in such close proximity to Dorian. But the benefit was that absolutely no one interrupted us. Sure, we received hungry looks from almost everyone we passed—one obvious couple was openly, longingly, staring at us, entirely unaware that their date was doing the exact same thing. I watched as the two snapped out of their daze to look at each other warily, only to realize they had both suffered the same wandering eye.

Then they smiled devilishly at each other. As if seeing their partner stare at us had been some great revelation that silently opened up new avenues for fresh, late-night games. Jesus, even *seeing* Dorian led couples into considering inviting others into their bedrooms. He was like a plague of depravity. But I had to admit…he did it with *style*.

He was immortal but looked to be thirty-something. His steel gray eyes were intense and, as usual, his shoulder-length light brown hair was meticulously styled. He wore red loafers, a sleek white suit with faint silver pinstripes, and his black dress shirt was open to reveal his muscular chest. He wore a flashy, diamond-encrusted medallion neckpiece like a rap icon that said *Lie've Portrait*. I rolled my eyes at the clever double entendre—that his beauty was a lie, and that he really was a walking, living portrait.

Because Dorian Gray only remained so beautiful because every sinful act he committed had zero effect on his physical body—any harm transferring instead to a portrait of himself that was locked away in a secret vault that he'd recently relocated thanks to my prying eyes. I'd found it and extorted his assistance by holding a butane torch to it.

We'd been friends ever since.

"You look delectable this evening," he said in a low, meaningful murmur.

I blushed, hurriedly and clumsily reaching into my clutch purse to pull out a compact mirror to check my makeup as I finally picked up on the accent of the French man speaking behind me. I'd been so entranced that I'd momentarily forgotten about my target tonight, but Dorian's careful use of our prearranged codeword *delectable* had snapped me back into action, letting me know I was within range. I used the compact mirror to distract anyone from noticing that I was actually pressing a button on one of the two phones tucked into my purse. After a few seconds, the screen flashed with green text: *Cloning complete.*

I snapped my compact mirror closed and grinned as I slipped it back inside my purse. "Thank you, Dorian," I told him, leaning in to kiss him on the cheek and slip the phone into his inner jacket pocket. "Let's get the party started, shall we?"

His smirk looked wolfish as he nodded, casually buttoning up his jacket with one hand as he touched his cheek longingly with the other. Right where I had kissed him. Then, like a good lead, he guided me through the deadliest dance of the night—to mingle a little bit so as not to look suspicious. My work here was pretty much finished.

The rest of the evening was about retribution—taking a moment to appreciate the fireworks. Maybe have another glass of rosé…

CHAPTER 3

*W*e meandered through the crowd, nodding and smiling at those we passed. I saw Starlight representing the local shifter bears. They had chosen to send their smallest, cutest, most mysterious—and possibly the most dangerous—member of their Cave. Starlight was perpetually in bear form, about the size of an adolescent black bear but with gray fur tinging his muzzle, proving that he was no young cub.

He'd once told me that he had been a wizard in his younger days and had purposely chosen to become a shifter bear. He'd also chosen to live in that form, not bothering with a human form.

He smiled widely at my approach, leaning closer to place a paw on my shoulder and whisper in my ear. "Be aware of never-ending explosions."

I reeled back to stare at him, noticing his eyes were slightly glazed over as if he had sampled some of his notorious shifter weed—a hallucinogen. Before I could ask what the blazes he meant, a sudden commotion in the crowd pulled him into a conversation with a group of witches.

I couldn't risk making a scene, so promised I would corner him about it later even if I had to use a pot of honey to bribe the truth from him. The bears were friends.

My best friend, Claire Stone, had joined their Cave—what they called their pack—and was currently at their retreat in the Alaskan wilderness, learning more about her new form. And probably spending quite a bit of time with Kenai, one of the bears she seemed to have taken a particular fancy to.

Dorian tugged me onward, not wanting to risk getting sucked—totally unlike him, figuratively speaking—into a lengthy conversation with anyone. He still had a job to do tonight.

We reached relative privacy and he let out a sigh of relief, turning to face me with a broad smile on his face for anyone watching us too closely. He reached out to flick my hair, smiling. "I love the dress," he complimented me. "White suits you. And those slits down the side will still let you murder and maim if the chance presents itself." I nodded with a grin, happy he had noticed. "I'm glad you have your long hair back. It must grow very fast..." he added in a suspicious tone.

I shrugged, not wanting to tell him about the magic hair straightener my hacker friend, Othello, had given me in Vegas not long ago. She worked for Nate Temple—the billionaire wizard, King of St. Louis—in a company he owned that focused on fusing magic with modern technology. They'd come up with any number of amazing products, and most weren't listed in their catalog, because they pretended to be just another tech company for the world at large.

For all intents and purposes, Grimm Tech was a spinoff from his parents' now-defunct company, Temple Industries. But to anyone who knew Nate or Othello...well, Christmas would very likely kick serious ass. Or he and I were going to have a long conversation.

Because I'd recently kissed Nate Temple and, barring all the other warm and fuzzy feelings associated with that decision and its impending consequences, my kiss better have put me on the very top of his priority list.

Or we would have a very short conversation.

"How was Vegas?" Dorian pressed, smirking devilishly at the unbidden smile on my cheeks.

I scowled at him, shaking my head. "Fat chance. I'm still cleaning mud out of my ears," I growled in a cute but polite enough tone to be suitable for a party.

He frowned disappointedly, but I wasn't falling for his sad puppy-dog eyes.

I'd been roped into a twenty-first birthday bash for some shifter dragon girlfriends from St. Louis, along with Othello and a new friend named Quinn MacKenna from Boston. I'd learned that she was a black magic arms dealer, and decided that we could be friends—again, thinking solely of Christmas. Quinn was one hell of a drinker, but she really excelled at brawling and cursing. It had been a night to remember. Or forget. A drunken shamble that ended in a bar fight with leprechauns had ironically resulted in only one fatality—a shifter stripper named Lucky had been ripped in half by one of their rainbows when they demanded we return the gold bar one of the birthday girls had 'accidentally' acquired from their vault.

Rest in pieces, Lucky, I thought to myself.

But Dorian had provided part of the entertainment, roping us into a mud-wrestling match while wearing his designer non-clothing—that had been perfectly sized to our frames—in one of the underground night clubs he apparently owned on the Strip. Mentioning where or how I'd obtained the hair straightener that could alter my locks in any number of ways—lengthening or shortening it—would only invite questions leading to any number of alleged felonies we had been involved in that night.

I realized Dorian was watching me closely and, for the first time, he looked truly hesitant. My shoulders tensed instinctively, and I risked a glance over my shoulder, wondering what had startled him. But I saw nothing. I turned back to him, suddenly anxious. "What is it?"

He let out an unsteady sigh. "I want to bring something up, but I don't want you to kill me."

I nodded, encouraging him to proceed. "I won't kill you. I'm not a monster, Dorian."

This didn't seem to appease him. In fact, it made him wince. "Funny you should choose that word…" he said softly.

I began tapping my foot, not bothering to hide my displeasure. A private argument might be even better camouflage for our night's activities. "Out with it before I change my mind…"

He held up a hand, stalling me. "Right. Know that I am being sincere and that I'm concerned for you. Truly," he said, locking eyes with me meaningfully. I nodded uncertainly, almost afraid to hear him out. "It's just…you've been kind of going off the books a lot lately. Like you're just looking for fights everywhere you go. Almost like you're lost and are searching for…a purpose?" he ventured hesitantly.

My breath caught in my throat because…well, I *had* felt that way recently. I'd chosen to not ally myself with the Vatican Shepherds—the group that had spent over a decade training me how to use my magic and hunt monsters on their behalves—because when my mentor Roland had needed their support, they had turned their backs on him so swiftly that I realized they only saw two colors.

Black and white.

Even for a man who had spent his entire life working for them as a Shepherd, one of the noblest men I'd ever met...he was now only a vampire. They didn't care that he had chosen his fate in order to protect them, to prevent a war. No. Since he'd become a vampire, he was no longer welcome.

I hadn't necessarily wanted to become a Shepherd anyway, but after that...yeah, as a group, they could choke on a string of rosaries. The Shepherds *and* the arthritic group of milk-eyed wizards—the Conclave—that commanded them. One Shepherd, a man named Fabrizio, had proven his loyalty, sticking his neck out to vouch for Roland, but it hadn't changed anything. Well, it had proven his friendship and that he was the only Shepherd with even a shred of decency to him.

But the rest of them...death by rosaries.

The Conclave had rewarded Fabrizio's progressive view on vampires by promoting him to Head Shepherd and then promptly shipping him off to Kansas City to fill the spot vacated by Roland and me, running Abundant Angel Catholic Church until a replacement could be found.

Knowing beyond a shadow of a doubt that I no longer wanted anything to do with them had left me strangely adrift. I had no other family in the magical sense. Roland was now a vampire and I couldn't really hang out with their kind without making them fidget. Like dangling a steak in front of dogs and expecting them to ignore it. The smarter vampires knew the steak would kill them, but that didn't help my cause either. Fact was, I didn't belong with them.

Same with my other friends. Dorian hung out at orgies with witches and Claire was lazing about with the shifter bears at their Alaskan nudist colony.

I was all alone. I had taken to sticking my nose in anywhere it wasn't welcome in the local supernatural community. Essentially, picking fights with anyone who looked at me crossly. I'd even had to kill a few lately, and I'd heard the whispered rumors about the *White Rose*—the apparent moniker I'd been given. I wasn't sure whether it was due to my white hair and last name Penrose, or if it signified a white rose cast upon a casket at a funeral. Either worked.

In fact, I myself had even been warned about "that crazy, white-haired lady rebranding the City of Fountains to the City of Blood Fountains." Direct quote, for the record. Although, the gossiper had quickly made the connection between my own white hair and that of Kansas City's newest supervillain, and had then promptly run away from me, begging for his life.

While we were in line at lunchtime in a deli downtown.

The rest of the wait for my sandwich had been particularly awkward after that.

This fear was evident in many of the wary looks I had received tonight. I'd chosen white for this exact reason, relishing the nickname I'd been given. But that was mere pettiness on my part.

Dorian's claim, bless his heart, was spot on.

CHAPTER 4

J nodded at him calmly. "You're not wrong," I admitted. "But why were you scared to tell me? We're friends, Dorian," I said, feeling slightly hurt at the fear in his eyes. To scare someone who couldn't die meant I was more than just a rumor. I was a force of nature in his eyes. And if he was thinking it, thousands were saying it.

He nodded slowly. "I'm concerned because the way you're running around town...I don't know if you might someday find a reason to take me out. I'm not the only friendly face to say this, by the way," he added in a whisper, letting me know I was even scaring my staunch friends and allies. That was a shock to hear. Then again, I hadn't really spoken to anyone recently, not after sending most of those I cared about away from town for a while.

Because I'd released a Greater Demon from his prison, and I was pretty sure he would personally come to thank me in the very near future, even though I'd heard nothing to satisfy that claim. I just knew how Demons thought. They thanked people by destroying them. They didn't like owing favors. It was much easier to 'accidentally murder' the one you owed the favor to and apologize after. Demons, by nature of existence, weren't that great on honoring their prior obligations.

Samael would come for me. Likely sooner rather than later. So, I had bought tickets to send my adopted father, Terry and his lady-friend, Raidia trekking across Europe for a few months. I'd purchased their return flight ahead of time to guarantee their extended vacation. Because his girlfriend and I had history that I didn't quite want to hash out with her yet, and she had been present when I broke Samael out of his cage. She would likely be a target.

The others who had been involved with that night had their own protection, so I hadn't been as concerned with them. Beckett Killian was spending his time smoking out any of the existing Templars and their Commander, Olin Fuentes. He hadn't found him yet but had surprisingly recruited many of the old Templars to his cause, becoming the de-facto Templar Commander to counter Olin. Which meant a civil war was brewing for the future.

Alyksandre and his Nephilim had been shaken to the core to see their Angel boss, Nameless, Fall from Grace. But they were even more horrified to see me catch the Angel and bind him to my service by wrapping him around my finger. I was still waiting for the consequences of that action to hit me and had advised the Nephilim to keep their distance from me in case Nameless' Angel brothers decided to pay me a visit for a...talk.

Recently, I'd pretty much spent time only around Cain—the world's first murderer—and Roland. Dorian, too, but he wasn't looking too honored to be my friend right now. He looked like a startled rabbit with his leg caught in a trap. And I was the trap.

Shit. Maybe I shouldn't have worn white tonight.

"Well," I said, taking a deep breath. "I'm not angry or anything. This isn't vengeance."

He grunted, unconvinced. "You bound an Angel, killed two Demons, have been seen in St. Louis for a whole mess of earth-shattering wars Nate Temple keeps starting, and you've single-handedly broken the Vatican, the Templars, and the Nephilim," he said in what sounded like a rehearsed speech. "You look like you are perpetually angry, Callie. Very, very angry. I'm glad to hear you say otherwise, but you need to know how everyone else feels. I think they are too scared to tell you," he said.

"Okay. I'll...temper myself. It's just..." I swept the room as I took a sip of my drink, suddenly feeling like I wanted to leave and abandon my mission. I noticed dozens of pairs of eyes flinch away, not wanting me to catch them watching Dorian and I talk. I gritted my teeth at the real-world example of Dorian's claims. I needed to go on a vacation. To run away to St. Louis and have Nate whisk me off to Fae where I could kill to my heart's content. Until this pain inside me was drowned in pools of blood—

I cut off the thought abruptly, surprised at my own vehemence; I was openly panting, for pete's sake.

Huh.

Maybe I did have a problem.

I met Dorian's eyes and, even though I hadn't said any of that out loud, his face looked like he had heard every thought. I lifted my hand, hoping he would take it—careful not to appear threatening. He didn't even hesitate, or I might have broken down in tears. Which really would have scared everyone—to see the terror of Kansas City have an emotional breakdown.

Like *Carrie*, but with an LL. And, as previously observed, this party *did* kind of resemble a prom night. On steroids…with grown-up monsters.

I squeezed Dorian's hand in gratitude. "I feel like I've lost my purpose, Dorian. Everyone has either betrayed or failed me…" I murmured, leaning into his shoulder as I guided him back into the party. "But right now, we have a job to do. Are you still on board with it, or is this a roundabout way of telling me it's a catastrophic idea?"

He chuckled, squeezing my hand reassuringly. "Oh, tonight will be fun. Taking out the trash is important." He grew silent as we walked past a huddle of conversation taking place between some vampires. Their eyes tracked us anxiously, their shoulders tense. I realized they weren't watching *us*…

Just *me*.

And I was friends with the vampires. Damn it. I hated when Dorian was right. He was arrogant enough without successfully impersonating Dr. Phil.

"Is it anything in particular, or…" he gestured vaguely to imply all recent events combined.

"I don't know. Probably a combination. I feel like I've lost my place in the world. Who am I fighting for? Why am I fighting? What am I standing for? One week it could be protecting a vampire, but the next week, one of the vamps murders a wolf and I'm staking him to a wall in a dank alley to collect his fangs like a trophy," I admitted softly. "I get so frustrated at all the injustice. All the backstabbing."

"Maybe you need to start a gang," Dorian offered. Of course that was his solution. To make the city's crazy lady a gang overlord. "I'm just saying that maybe you need a family. Something to fight for, like you mentioned. Right now, you're unaffiliated with anyone."

I frowned thoughtfully. "Is there anything wrong with being unaffiliated?" I asked, wondering if he was dancing around the topic for some reason.

He shrugged. "I'm unaffiliated, too, but everyone needs a buddy in the trenches. Friends and allies make you stronger and keep you safe when you need to rest. They give you something to fight for, something the rest of us can look at, understand, and know ahead of time whether their decision is going to cross that line in the sand. People need to know where you stand on things. What the rules are. Otherwise, they get scared. And scared dogs bite. Without friends to look out for you, eventually that dog will go looking for you. Maybe an entire pack of dogs."

I frowned. "Are you hinting at something specific?"

He shook his head adamantly. "No. Just a word of warning from someone with personal experience. Why do you think I teamed up with the Hellfire Club? That's my family."

I nodded thoughtfully, but something he had said really angered me. "I think my line in the sand is pretty obvious. Don't be a dick," I snapped.

He met my eyes, a flicker of a playful smile dancing in those depths. "Well, Callie, I don't mean to tarnish your delicate sensibilities, but there are dicks, and there are *dicks*," he suggested, complete with a colorful hand gesture portraying the difference. He grinned proudly.

I slapped his arm, opening my mouth to tell him that not harming innocent people wasn't a hard rule to wrap your head around. "Do unto others as—"

I was interrupted as the lights abruptly dimmed and the hum of conversation halted instantaneously. Damn. We were running out of time. Dorian had to get moving, fast.

CHAPTER 5

*T*he music changed to a livelier tune as we slipped back into position, angling our path to where we needed to be.

Members of each supernatural family had contributed something to the night's festivities. I'd even convinced Fabrizio to write a check for the food —after arguing with him for an hour that no, he wouldn't be welcome to attend, no matter how many jokes he prepared ahead of time. Inviting a Shepherd to the party would have gone off about as well as a fart during Sunday Mass.

He hadn't thought my metaphor as funny as the jokes he had already prepared in anticipation of his invite to the party. I'd agreed to let him read me the jokes instead, somewhat soothing his disappointment over the matter. But getting him to write a check had been a stroke of pure genius on my part—letting him do a good deed for the monsters without ruffling any feathers.

The crowd murmured appreciatively as the entertainment seemed to come out of hidden closets around the room, courtesy of Dorian Gray—his contribution to the party.

Waiters wearing only body-paint suddenly mingled through the crowd, some dancing, some laughing, and others carrying golden trays—can't have polished silver around shifters—full of fresh drinks. We dodged a trio carrying small sticks with crimson ribbons attached to the ends as they skipped and frolicked before us. They entertained the guests with their acrobatics and clever use of their harmless streamers as a playful whip, or as a rope, wrapped around a standoffish guest and then used to tug him closer to a lone woman. More often than not, their antics produced successful romantic pairings, and conversation soon grew from its previous sober hum into a playful buzz.

Some of the entertainers were actually doing cartwheels—both in pairs or alone—as they purposely mingled through pockets of conversation, giggling and smiling as they forced attendees to break up from their safe social circles and instead mix with new groups of guests.

Since Dorian abhorred mediocrity in all things, every one of the new servers was exceptionally pretty to look at. They even moved as fluidly as their silk ribbons, weaving through the crowd to ensnare the guests' attention with artfully choreographed steps.

The body-paint didn't hurt, and it was done in such a way that their nudity wasn't quite obvious at first—looking like tight spandex in the now dim lighting. The dancers were painted to look like skeletons wearing Candy Skull masks, the rest of their bodies liberally coated in black. Their Candy Skulls were a myriad of colors and unique designs, turning the party into a *Día de los Muertos* fiesta. Once you were close enough to really look, it became apparent that not a single thread was worn outside of their ribbon batons. The men were easier to point out and were causing the loudest hubbub among the guests.

Because they had chosen to paint an additional bone on their bodies.

The best part was that the 'costumes' were so artfully applied that I found myself actually having to stare at a few of them to confirm that they were actually nude. I wasn't the only one reacting, but where my giddy laughter was an act, the crowds' reaction was authentic.

All by design, thank you very much. As each guest began to realize and take a closer look, their attention was distracted as easily as if someone had flipped the fire-alarm switch.

Dorian touched my wrist with two fingers, subtly steering me in a different direction.

I followed, finding myself smiling at the extravaganza bubbling around me. Dorian was good at his job. I had initially been against the chosen face paint due to some past experiences in St. Louis with Nate Temple where we had run afoul of some actual Candy Skulls—wardens to the prison of Hell—

but most of the guests present had no reason to fear Candy Skulls and probably didn't even know there was a reason to be afraid of such an iconic look.

Still, if any had been wearing black cloaks, I might have thrown out a fireball.

The new servers were also each liberally dusted with pheromones to boost libido and inflame sexual appetites. I hadn't known that was actually a real thing, but apparently Dorian knew a guy named Michael Riley who had nefarious connections in the supernatural underworld. I wasn't sure how he had acquired the pheromones or how much they cost Dorian, and I was pretty sure I didn't want to know since it probably involved things that would make me blush.

If I'd had any doubts about the pheromones working, they were dashed against the rocks of my naivety as I saw guests' nostrils flare, their pupils dilate, and their postures change. Several sniffed at the air openly—likely the shifters with their hyper-aware sense of smell—but even they couldn't decipher if it was simply them scenting something very appealing or if it was some kind of danger.

In actuality, we didn't have anything dangerous planned. We just needed a lot of distractions to keep everyone relaxed and unaware of the clever maneuvering Dorian needed to pull off in the next fifteen minutes.

And sex had clouded male judgment for a good majority of human—and inhuman—history.

Many women, too.

So, even though the various flavors of shifter smelled something strange, none wanted to point it out lest it be seen as a weakness that they couldn't keep their instincts under control—and since the crowd consisted of almost every supernatural group in town, none wanted to show any sign of weakness that could later be used against them.

Which was a great opportunity for some third party to exploit a weakness. To consider creating one in the first place. Sensory entrapment.

I spotted my target only paces away and used the motion of setting my empty wine glass on one of the proffered trays carried by a smiling waitress to conceal my quick assessment of my quarry. Le Bone was a new vampire in town—a security representative for the Master of Paris, who was planning to visit Kansas City in a few days on behalf of the Sanguine Council, the ruling body of vampires—but the French vampire had already ruffled some of the wrong feathers in his brief stay. Back in Paris, he had a notorious reputation for drinking his victims down to the bone, emptying them of almost every drop of blood in their bodies. Hence the nickname he had proudly accepted.

And two bodies had recently shown up in my city, drained of all blood.

Haven—the Master Vampire of Kansas City—had sent some of his vampires to question Le Bone on the matter, but the French prick had denied all allegations, rudely informing them that if they had a proper accusation with corroborating evidence, Haven could take it up with Le Bone's Master when he arrived in a few days. In the meantime, he had more important matters to attend—like confirming that *this backwards city was safe enough for his Master to visit in the first place.*

His words.

That hadn't gone over well, and Le Bone had since refused meeting with anyone else without his Master present.

Le Bone had also made the grave mistake of forgetting to request permission from Haven to enter the city in the first place and had shown exactly zero remorse when confronted about it, once again redirecting all further inquiries to his Master. Since I felt like I owed Haven a favor or two for his agreement to sign the lease that paid me back for Roland's new home —a decrepit old church I had purchased—I'd offered Haven my non-existent investigator services.

Le Bone was currently too busy ogling a female ribbon dancer to notice me brushing past him. Then again, he also had two looming security guards shadowing his every move, which was why I arched my neck in their direction as I slipped past their boss, momentarily distracting them with the pale, vulnerable flesh over my jugular vein, since they were also vampires. I waved my hand at someone behind them, conveniently clutching my compact mirror in that palm so my gesture turned into an impromptu strobe light to flash directly into the guards' eyes. It worked as planned because their eyes flicked away from my throat at the sudden flash of my mirror long enough for my other hand's motion—signaling Dorian—to go unnoticed.

For a single moment, both guards regarded me, assessing me for any sign of threat...and I was somewhat disappointed to realize that they had no idea who I was.

But then, Dorian 'accidentally' nudged Le Bone with an elbow, following my signal. Le Bone grunted, drawing the guards' attention away from me—the apparently non-threatening woman in the white dress. I watched from the corner of my eye as Dorian mumbled an apology and then picked out the entertainer Le Bone seemed fixated upon. "The best five-thousand you'll ever spend," Dorian encouraged, chuckling good-naturedly.

Le Bone grunted, the comment calming his initial anger from Dorian's elbow. "Is she yours?" he asked Dorian, eyeing the ribbon dancer with a visible hunger.

Dorian scoffed. "Oh, I thought you were admiring *Tyler*," he said, jerking his chin at the male server currently smirking at Le Bone. The vampire stiffened, finally turning to face Dorian as if only just now realizing who he had been talking to. Dorian shrugged innocently, discreetly eyeing Le Bone's attire. "I thought you played both sides against the middle."

Le Bone didn't find that humorous at all. "No. I do not, Mr. Gray. Not all of us share your appetites. My Master will be here soon—"

Dorian clapped his hand over his mouth in a show of flamboyant embarrassment, simultaneously managing to interrupt Le Bone's comment about his Master—but done so cleverly that Le Bone didn't even appear to realize it. "That's the thing about immortality," Dorian said with a smile. "Plenty of time to sample all the fruits. Try Tyler. I won't tell anyone…" He winked, tipped an imaginary hat and walked up to kiss Tyler full on the lips. They took their time extricating their faces from one another and, surprisingly, no paint was smudged. Only the best makeup for Dorian Gray's Dance Squad.

The guards were so baffled that they hardly even noticed as I awkwardly slipped past them with a murmured, "Excuse me," as I brushed their arms with my fingertips. They were tall but had looked lanky, and I hadn't been sure if they had any muscle to speak of since I was more familiar with shifters who were typically built like powerlifters. Vampires, on the other hand, typically had that old-man muscle—tight and tough as coils of wet rope but not as flashy.

I was still surprised to learn that they didn't recognize me—especially after all of Dorian's talk about the rumors flying around town about me. I had needed to know—before the figurative bullets began flying—if my cover was blown. If they had been keeping a close eye on me all night, we would have had to switch to Plan B.

But it looked like we were good to go—which was why I had signaled

Dorian to proceed as planned. If I had given him a different signal, he would have pretended to trip into Le Bone rather than bumping the vampire with his elbow—giving me enough time to slip away from the guards as they rushed to protect their boss from the clumsy-footed Dorian Gray.

The feeling I couldn't seem to shake was that Le Bone was frequently heard speaking of his job as the equivalent of the Secret Service for his Parisian Master, verifying that Kansas City was secure and safe enough to host his boss in a few days. Which meant he should have been digging into every player in town, making sure they weren't a threat. And with my newfound reputation, I should have been at the top of his list of people to watch out for. His own guards hadn't even heard of—or recognized—the resident, white-haired psychopath when she was only inches from their faces. I was like a flashing neon sign for any security group keeping tabs on local dangers for the impending arrival of their boss. Any real security force would have heard of—and taken appropriate action against—Callie Penrose.

Now, thanks to my investigation, I knew Le Bone had projects on the side, but I hadn't expected that his entire cover was a blatant lie. Le Bone's Thugs—*heh*—weren't doing what they claimed to be doing and weren't the prestigious group they declared themselves to be.

None of this showed on my face as I moved seamlessly towards the man I had waved at behind the guards—the only other partygoer privy to the details of my operation tonight.

Cain, the world's first murderer, was currently suffering the amorous affections of two rather senior, rather handsy, women who stood only as tall as his chest, forcing him to have to look down at their flaunted décolletage every time they asked him a question. He looked panicked and a little wild around the eyes.

CHAPTER 6

*C*ain smiled at me like I was a life preserver in the middle of the ocean after his ship had sunk two days ago, extending a hand to grasp my outstretched palm tighter than necessary. He bowed, kissing it dramatically. The Playboy Grannies paled in fear, seeming to recognize my white hair. I quickly decided there was only one way out of this, killing two birds with one stone. I slapped the back of Cain's head playfully to let them know he was still on the market for them.

And that maybe I wasn't as deadly as they feared.

Cain shot me a knowing scowl, reading into the real reason for my slap and not approving of being offered up as the sacrificial hunk of meat for these two women to gnaw on. The fear in their eyes faded somewhat and they exchanged a brief, thoughtful look. I instantly began lavishly complimenting their dresses...that they simply *must* tell me who did their hair, and *oh, didn't Cain look so handsome in his fancy gray suit?*

I risked a glance over my shoulder to verify Dorian had left to do his part for the night. Thankfully, he was gone, so all I had left to do now was wait.

I leaned in with a mischievous grin, speaking loud enough for Cain to hear clearly. "He's like an older brother to me, and I have to tell you that I can't remember the last time any woman—let alone women—held his interest for so long. He's not an easy one to pin down. He must really enjoy talking to you two."

The women were too busy blushing, giggling, and fanning themselves to notice Cain's face. I could actually *feel* his immortal soul snarling at me as he smiled with his teeth.

My charm solidly slipped me into their good graces. They hadn't seen me murder anyone in the last thirty seconds, and I obviously wasn't competition for their prize, claiming to be like his younger sister.

I was awesome in their eyes.

They doubled down on their efforts to flirt outrageously with Cain, and I watched the train wreck in slow motion, smiling and nodding my head agreeably every now and then as my mind began to wander, hoping Dorian was almost finished with his part of the plan. I found myself considering Cain's harem, wondering what supernatural family they belonged to. Judging by their obvious age and that I couldn't sense any wizard or shifter tendencies to them, I was leaning towards witch.

Which—*heh*—seemed to be a common occurrence tonight. There were a lot of witches here, and they were likely all members of the Hellfire Club— Dorian's family, as he'd told me earlier. He was practicing what he preached, bringing an army with him everywhere he went. It brought his earlier points about my lack of purpose and affiliation into perspective—

"Can we get a picture?" one of the two women asked, snapping me out of my thoughts. I blinked, wondering if I had missed part of her question.

"Oh! She would *love* that!" Cain chuckled, ushering me between them before I could come up with a polite reason to decline. I found myself smiling crookedly as Cain snapped a few pictures from three different phones in rapid succession. Wait a minute...three phones? The rat bastard was sneaking in some from his own phone!

The two clucked excitedly, thanking me as he handed their phones back. It took me a moment to finally process what had just happened. They were...fangirling. Over *me*. Maybe they just wanted proof to later show their friends that they had drank it up with the infamous White Rose at a ritzy downtown party—and had lived to tell the tale.

The night was young, though. And things might be getting hairy soon. If Dorian would hurry the hell up.

Cain tactfully stepped up beside me, draping his arm over my shoulder.

"I need to speak to Callie in private for a few minutes. Can you excuse us?" he asked with a warm smile.

"Oh, don't be so proper with us, young man!" Then the two began giggling as they made their way over to the bar, shooting playful smiles back at Cain.

He squeezed my shoulder meaningfully. "Not cool."

I rolled my eyes. "You took your own blackmail picture. We're even."

He grunted, muttering under his breath.

I scanned the room thoughtfully, wanting to ask Cain about Dorian's conversation—whether he had heard similar rumors about me. I spotted Cleo sipping champagne beside an attractive blonde woman, both smiling at one of the male entertainers. I discreetly pointed Cleo out to Cain. "She's smart. Maybe too smart. Said her name is Cleo. Know anything about her?"

Cain followed my gaze, his eyes catching the light looked like early-morning mist. "No. Want me to go talk to her?" he said, eyeing the two women appreciatively.

I elbowed him in the ribs, eliciting a grunt. "No, creep. Keep an eye on her for me."

"Fine," he sighed in disappointment. "Is everything going according to plan? Any way we can make it less boring for me?"

I thought about it, understanding his frustration. He had only been a lookout so far, keeping tabs on Le Bone. "What if everything was on fire? Lots and lots of fire. Fire everywhere," I suggested, under my breath so as not to be overheard and start a panic.

"That could work," he said thoughtfully. He patted the pockets of his linen suit, looking crestfallen. "I don't have a lighter, though."

I sighed. "If it comes to it, I am the lighter. Idiot."

He grunted. "Right. Wizard stuff. Cool."

Cain was definitely not the brains of our fearsome duo, not by any stretch of the imagination.

I stared across the room to see Roland, my old mentor, staring back at me with a pensive frown. Being a vampire, he was keeping his distance in such a public setting, but he knew me well enough to know when I was up to something. His past experience as a Shepherd meant he was more inclined to kill threats first, and ask questions later, so I hadn't shared details on my mission regarding Le Bone. Also, because I knew he wouldn't approve of me involving myself in vampire drama.

I was surprised I hadn't spotted Paradise and Lost—his two pet werewolves. Well, not really pets, but self-proclaimed protectors of the vampire who had single-handedly saved them from Vatican persecution when they were framed for the murder of a Shepherd. The same drama that had forced Roland to become a vampire in the first place.

It shouldn't have to be said that Roland did not *single-handedly* save them, but that his assistant played a *small* supporting role. But I still found myself reminding the two about it at every opportunity since they couldn't seem to get it through their flea-brained skulls.

Anyway…the two werewolves hardly let Roland out of their sight— especially if he was stepping into danger or any kind of public forum. They were attention whores and loved hanging off his arm in public to remind everyone that Roland was the only vampire with two werewolf groupies. Their eyes even matched his—blood red. So, despite them choosing to stand by his side, it was apparent that there was actually something magical about their relationship.

For them not to be here with Roland…was strange. Unsettling. I hoped everything was okay, telling myself they were probably still trying to get a grip on their ragtag group of werewolves, determined to rebuild the Kansas City pack that had fled a while back.

If successful, they would be the first female, dual-Alpha werewolves I'd ever heard about.

Go Team Estrogen!

I let my concern fade and flashed Roland a reassuring smile, waggling my fingers playfully. The skin at the corners of his crimson eyes tightened dubiously, but he was nodding his head as he listened to Haven beside him. They were having a little business trouble with Haven's string of night clubs. A new player had come to town in recent months, opening newer, flashier dance clubs a block away from all of Haven's clubs, offering cheaper drink specials and cover charges to steal Haven's customers. He'd been unable to discover who was behind it all, but it was too much of a coincidence for a competitor to open near every single one of his establishments.

I'd done a little digging and learned that Le Bone had frequented each of the competitors' businesses during his brief stay in town, and that he had been shoveling money to the new club owners for quite some time. The worst part was that the new club owners were just a consortium of pawns, knowing nothing about vampires or the very real turf war they had unwittingly stepped into by accepting Le Bone's cash and cutting into Haven's profits. They'd met a friendly French investor who wanted to finance opening up a night club—and he was willing to grant them ownership if they would manage it and give him a percentage of profits for his investment.

I had considered going straight to Haven with the information but wasn't sure whether Le Bone had informants in Haven's inner circle. How else could it have gone undetected for so long? Haven wasn't incompetent, so he had to have a traitor in his midst.

I'd also considered giving the information to Roland but hadn't wanted anyone to see it as Roland making Haven—his Master and Maker—look unfit for his throne.

The local vampires were still not entirely comfortable with having a once-vampire-hunter-priest turned wizard-vampire as part of their flock. No matter how the cards fell, it probably wouldn't have helped Roland if he officially had anything to do with taking out Le Bone.

I'd also considered the salted-earth policy of inviting my Shepherd pal, Fabrizio, over to take out the Eurotrash vampire. But that would have only turned all the supernatural families firmly against the Shepherds, and in effect, Roland and I since we both had past ties to the Vatican.

I wanted to show Fabrizio that there were subtler ways to handle complicated matters. Basically, to guide them into taking out their own trash. Since I was impatient, I hadn't wanted to wait until Haven and his crew finally realized what was happening on their own.

And I won't lie. Setting up traps like this was fun—probably more fuel for the fiery rumors blazing through the streets of Kansas City about me. Callie Penrose. The White Rose. The wizard kissed by Heaven. The Freak Hunter of Kansas City.

I watched one of Haven's vampires urgently lean in to give his Master some unpleasant news and hand him a phone. Haven's face darkened into a thunderhead of rage...

And the White Rose bloomed with pride.

CHAPTER 7

*H*aven snapped a terse command to one of his men, and then Roland leaned closer to speak in his ear. I hoped it wasn't to cast suspicion on me, because I hadn't decided whether or not I wanted to take credit yet. It would be best if the vampires handled this internally. Better for them. Whatever Roland said calmed the Master of Kansas City. Somewhat.

He was still furious but looked composed. And he didn't look my way, which was a plus.

Four vampires began snaking towards us through the crowd. Le Bone was still standing a few feet ahead of us, busy trying to flirt with the server he'd had his eye on earlier—not poor Tyler, like Dorian had suggested. She looked politely disinterested—the bane of a server's life—batting off unwanted affections while trying to earn a tip.

Le Bone only had one tip in mind, though, and it was apparent to me, a fellow woman, that she didn't want it. I knew she also wouldn't appreciate the tips of his fangs if she was too vehement in her denial. But this was a party of monsters, so I was betting Dorian had trained his employees well and that she could probably handle herself if necessary.

Le Bone's Thugs must have sensed some change in the atmosphere, because they were squinting at the parting crowd as Haven's enforcers headed our way.

Le Bone—either because he was a coward or a very wise man—had been careful to maintain his distance from the local vampires throughout the course of the evening. I silently stepped up behind the guards, placed the knuckles of each hand on their lower backs, and whispered evenly. "If you even *breathe* too deeply, my silver blades will sever your spine. It won't feel too nice for you and it will stain my dress. That's when my friend will get upset. He *really* likes this dress."

The two vampire guards froze obediently as Cain stepped into their view. "It's a very nice dress," he said in a soft voice. "I'm sure you've heard all about the White Rose, so let's not waste time with overly messy introductions."

By their stiff nods, it turned out they *had* heard my nickname—they just hadn't connected it with me, the pretty girl in the dress. I wasn't sure whether to be flattered or annoyed.

Le Bone was completely oblivious, reaching out to the arm of the server who was artfully skipping from his grasp. *Good girl*, I thought to myself. That's when he finally noticed Haven's four enforcers surrounding him. He risked a glance over his shoulder to find his own two guards incapacitated. He snarled defiantly, but one of the enforcers cleared his throat.

"Haven demands your presence. Let's not make a scene."

Le Bone's lips curled back. "*Demands?*" he sputtered incredulously in his utterly *non*-intimidating French accent. "You subdue my two guards and tell me not to make a scene? The Sanguine Council will hear all about—"

"I'm sure they will love to hear the story," the enforcer interrupted drily. "But that depends on if you survive long enough to tell them. For now, please accompany me."

Le Bone shot a furious glare at Cain. Then he shared that look with me, seeming surprised to discover that I was the one keeping them in line. "Release my guards."

I shrugged and stepped away. "I just wanted to pinch their asses, but they were so coy about it, not wanting their boss to see."

The two guards stepped clear from me with their chests puffed out, attempting to deny my accusation with their aggressive body language—but it was so overdone that it only seemed to lend credibility to my claim, making several in the crowd openly chuckle. The enforcers encircled them, and then promptly escorted the trio towards Haven. I glanced around to make sure Dorian was nowhere nearby. I found him near the bar, preparing to do a body-shot off of a particularly buxom troll's belly button. Cain's Playboy Grannies were leading the chant for the small crowd cheering Dorian on. It looked like the Chancery had sent a representative, after all. And I was going to miss meeting the big beautiful woman! The small crowd around Dorian roared as he knocked back the shot and held out a hand to help the beastly broad to her feet—which was hilarious, considering the incredible size difference between the two. He seemed oblivious to the drama regarding Le Bone.

But the rest of the party had noticeably hushed, snapped out of their party cheer as they sensed the sudden tension in the air—the apparent prisoners being escorted through the crowd by vampire Moses parting the party's Red Sea. Perfect.

I followed in their wake, tugging Cain along with me but keeping out of sight of Haven. Roland discreetly tracked my movement with a tightness around his lips, but I ignored his judging look. I was experienced at evading it after more than a decade under his tutelage.

Le Bone stepped up to Haven with a furious scowl. "What is the meaning of this, Haven? Is this how you treat guests in your city?" he demanded.

"That's *Master* Haven to you, venereal disease," a female vampire abruptly hissed, darting through the ring of enforcers to jerk Le Bone's head backwards by the hair.

Christ! Where had *she* come from? And to call Le Bone a venereal disease…that was just rude. I realized none of the enforcers looked alarmed that she had broken through their protective ring. My eyes slowly widened as it hit me. She had been *additional* security for Haven's enforcers, hiding in the crowd but always close enough to support them from the shadows.

That was definitely Haven's style. Secret backup plans.

Despite evidence to the contrary, Haven was incredibly intelligent. Which was why the whole club fiasco had surprised me. How had he not known about it? He was ruthlessly clever, always had a backup plan, and even when he appeared to fail in some venture, it was often later realized that it benefitted him in some significant way.

Haven's face was entirely too calm, making me wonder what Roland had said to him, what was really happening right now.

"Thank you, Anita. I think he feels properly emasculated, now," Haven said.

She managed to shove him away, knocking him into his guards before slipping back out of sight in the crowd. Le Bone didn't even get a chance to see what she had looked like—also intentional, I was betting.

Haven cleared his throat, his features a cool mask. "*Guest* implies that you reached out to the Master of Kansas City and requested permission to enter. That you then abided by *His* rules." Haven's face slowly shifted into a cruel smile that seemed to take about thirty seconds to complete. "I'm suddenly overjoyed that I happened to miss that meeting," he added.

"When my Master arrives—"

"He will request *my* permission to enter *my* city, as per custom. Since none of that has taken place, I must treat you as a rogue vampire in my territory. And it seems you've been quite the nuisance, killing indiscriminately and playing at being a businessman."

Le Bone grew very still. "What do you mean, 'playing at being a businessman?'" he asked.

Haven sighed in mock disappointment. "You confess your crime with your own words. Why didn't you ask about the killing as well? Are you truly that stupid, or just that arrogant?"

Le Bone's face paled as he realized he'd messed up, and that his powerful Master wasn't here to save him.

"You see, we are quite civilized in this...*backwards city*, as you called it." Haven said, using the exact quote Le Bone had used to describe Kansas City. The crowd growled threateningly. "I offer you the chance to come clean on your business ventures, for what good it will do you..." he gave an easy shrug, not providing a benefit to sweeten Le Bone's decision.

The crowd was eating it up. Haven's decision to make this public also served as a subtle message to the supernatural community that the vampires would keep their side of the street clear of any trash. Allowing them to witness the vampires' dirty laundry was a sign of goodwill.

"There is nothing to come clean about," Le Bone growled defensively. "What evidence have you fabricated to frame me? Do you even *have* any?" he demanded, growing bolder.

If I hadn't been privy to the evidence, I might have even believed his denial. Damned vampires perfecting their ability to lie over centuries of practice. No such thing as an impartial jury when many of the older vampires could talk their way out of most anything.

Haven sighed. "So be it." He turned to the crowd, surprising everyone.

"Would anyone like to claim responsibility for the evidence I just received? I don't want this to look suspicious..."

I scooped an apple off a nearby table as I considered outing myself. He had a point I hadn't considered. It did look like a typical vampire frame-job. They were notorious schemers, and it was important the city saw they could be trusted. Everyone was already terrified of me and would likely attribute this to the White Rose's growing list of atrocities by tomorrow, no matter what I did. I may as well get out in front of it. Own it.

I stepped forward, clearing my throat to get everyone's attention. "That would be me, Haven. You make a good point, though..." I scanned the crowd with a thoughtful frown, feeling the tension bubbling up with each passing second. Then I nodded distinctly. "This whole crowd looks suspicious. It's all dudes in here...except for *these* bitches." And I ended by pointing my finger directly at Le Bone and his thugs.

Cain choked loudly on his wine.

And the rest of the crowd burst out laughing in one thunderous explosion, openly pointing and laughing at Le Bone. None took offense at me referring to them all as *dudes*. I wondered if anyone recognized that I had just quoted one of Eminem's battle-rap lines from *8 Mile*.

Le Bone snarled as he lunged towards me, but Haven's associates gripped him firmly before he could take more than a single step.

Haven masked his smirk like a pro, but I knew him well enough to recognize it was a struggle. "Thank you. Eloquent and ladylike, as usual, Miss Penrose." I curtsied with a bright smile as if he had meant it as a compliment. He turned back to Le Bone, holding up the phone I had given Dorian earlier tonight. The infamous playboy was as stealthy as he claimed, because no one had brought up his name so far.

"It seems Miss Penrose cloned your cellphone at some point. It shows time-stamped GPS coordinates matching two recent murders that you previously denied involvement in. It also has a convenient bank statement, downloaded earlier tonight, that shows all recent transactions as of..." he glanced down at the phone, tapping a few times on the screen before looking back up, "yesterday."

Le Bone seethed, pointing at me. "I'm being set up. Even I've heard about the crazy bitch—"

"I have an idea," Haven said, typing a phone number onto a second phone in his hand. "I'm going to make a quick call and see who answers," he said, lifting the phone to his ears.

Le Bone looked incredulous. He opened his mouth to respond—

The room suddenly wavered like a mirage and I gripped a table beside me in confusion.

Simultaneously, my thumb pulsed with such a bone-deep cold that I actually hissed. The ring of shadows encircling my thumb was about to make the White Rose lose a petal to frostbite.

RUN...FLY...OR DIE! a weary, disembodied voice wheezed from within my mind, sounding as if it had used the last of its energy to warn me while hanging suspended in the deepest, darkest pits of Hell. Which might not be that far off base.

Because the voice belonged to Nameless, the Fallen Angel I had bound to my finger.

CHAPTER 8

I wasn't sure if the shifting shadow ring *was* the Angel or if it *contained* the Angel. But it hadn't been there before I trapped him. I gritted my teeth against the pain as I glanced down to find the shadows spinning faster than usual. And my thumb was almost entirely purple. No one in the room seemed to have noticed, still staring transfixed at Le Bone, waiting for him to respond. But...no one was blinking.

Like apparitions, I saw a host of winged, robed creatures racing towards me from the furthest edge of the room, ripping through people like they were mist—but causing them no harm and seemingly unimpeded by their physical bodies. In those hooded faces, I saw only glowing white eyes and outstretched fingers like pearl claws as they whisked closer, eyes locked on only one thing.

Me.

It seemed the Angels were finally ready to chat with me about their little brother, Nameless.

I didn't even hesitate to question the lack of reaction from the crowd. I spun and sprinted as fast as I could towards the giant glass window over-looking the streets below. I flung my hands out ahead of me in a concussive vortex of air like a horizontal tornado—knocking everyone in its path safely to the side and creating a clear tunnel for me to run through. Since they were still frozen, my real-time vortex struck them to create a cinematic marvel that would have made Netflix drool—if they ever decided to call me about a documentary on my life.

Or the end of it, depending on the next few minutes.

It was the most bizarre sight to see the party-goers completely motionless, and then suddenly flung back as if hit by a truck. My blast of air hit them so fast and hard that I could see the skin on their cheeks quiver and ripple upon impact, sending them immediately out of my way before they slowed back down again, drifting through the air like dandelion fluff. I hoped the time-distorted blow hadn't broken their necks.

I sprinted down the tunnel of still-rotating air, angling my shoulder forward as the tornado shattered the glass. I hadn't been sure if the glass would need an extra little nudge in addition to my weight.

I flew out into the night sky, the slits of my gown ripping as I called upon my wings—only now considering what might happen if they didn't respond. I was still learning how to control them and hadn't perfected their use yet. They seemed to work best on instinct.

Thankfully, my wings also responded well to *panic*—because I wasn't sure I had ever felt so startled and caught off-guard as I was to suddenly have Angel assassins gunning for me. Maybe it was because I couldn't think of a reason for Angels to suddenly want me dead. Well, there was the ring, of course. But I hadn't heard anything alarming from the Biblical side of the fence—Angels or Nephilim or Demon—since the night I had trapped Nameless and freed the Greater Demon, Samael. An accidental twofer.

My wings flared out from my shoulders, chips of ice, stone, and blue vapor crackling around me as they caught the air in powerful sweeps to either slow my descent or take me away from my pursuers. Preferably both. Shards of glass rained down around me, seeming to blend with my wings.

I thought I was going to pull off my escape before I felt one icy claw grasp onto my shoulder. Another grabbed my leg. Then another gripped one of my wings. But rather than climb up my body to pummel me midair, they seemed to work like a single hive mind, and collectively threw me *straight down*.

Wind whistled in my ears and the sounds of the street—laughing people, honking cars, and jazz music from a street musician—mocked my plight. My eyes watered at the unbelievable speed in which the dirty sidewalk raced closer. Several rapid blasts of power struck the ground in a ring, flaring to life in a circle of unfamiliar runes on the pavement. The concrete between the runes rippled like a pond, the ground no longer solid below me.

I struck it like a rock hitting wet newspaper, the sounds of screaming wind and nightlife ceasing in a single moment.

My wings caught the air, finally, and I landed in a crouch upon cracked, dry earth. I panted in relief to be alive, but my wings abruptly flickered out as if they had run out of batteries or been damaged by the Angels. I scanned the area to assess my battleground, wondering where the Angels had sent me.

Maybe they had whisked me off to Heaven. If so, they had probably deposited me conveniently outside the Pearly Gates, since they hadn't given me a security lanyard yet.

I frowned to find that I wasn't even in a distant, twice-removed *cousin* to a paradise.

I stood in a desiccated world of dehydrated plants, husks of skeletal trees, bleached bones, and discarded weapons that looked to have once been the finest blades ever created.

An ancient battlefield where the war had been so profound that even now, generations later, nothing dared grow back to life...almost like—

"What is *Blockbuster Video?*" one of the Angels asked from above, catching the idle thought that had briefly flickered across my mind. I blushed in embarrassment, pretending I didn't know what he was talking about. I looked up at the flapping sounds that heralded the arrival of the rest of the Angel gang. They circled above me like vultures, but I let out a gasp when I saw that the semi-transparent ceiling above them showed the streets of Kansas City—it was like looking at a reflection of my city in a puddle.

Three of the Angels remained circling me in the air, sweeping their wings to watch as their brother landed about a dozen paces away from me. He lifted his hand to flash them a few unspoken commands, and then turned to face me, his wings evaporating. His fellows continued circling us, but in ever-widening arcs, eyes outward as if determined to make sure my execution remained unwitnessed.

The Angel before me flung back his hooded cloak and tossed it to the ground dismissively, obviously not sticking to the unwritten—but universally accepted—Eleventh Commandment, *Thou Shalt Not Litter.* He seemed content to stay put and study me with his white eyes from a safe distance, possibly wary to get too close and catch the human contagion I carried.

His face was merciless and beautiful, harsh and perfect in every way—but it was an entirely different type of beauty from Dorian Gray. The Angel's beauty enticed no sexual hunger or fiery passion of any sort in the beholder—only the frozen, untouchable perfection of an ice sculpture. A mold of what mankind *should* look like.

I realized my eyes were watering, but not from the dry air of this place... it was at the sudden acceptance of how starkly flawed I was in comparison to the blonde Angel.

However...

Despite his millennia of existence, his face looked lifeless, showing no sign of wrinkles from the thousands upon thousands of laughs or tears he had to have spilled over his long lifetime. Like a new pair of boots that had never been worn, eternally stiff and crisp and painful.

He wore crystal armor straight from a videogame—ridiculously embellished to the point that it looked more grandiose than functional. It was similar in looks to the interior of those seemingly ordinary rocks sold in gift shops near mining towns that had been cut in half to reveal an inner beauty of raw, uncut, vibrant crystal. The Angel and his armor looked to have been pulled from the exact center of a planet after fermenting the Holy Spirit for about a billion years.

I had met two Angels in my life on Earth—Nameless and Eae—and it had been eerily difficult to spend too much time around them because of the raw power emanating from their bodies and their utter lack of empathy or emotion. Still, they had managed to blend in with us humans after much practice. Like a wolf among dogs.

This Angel would never—ever—blend in with mankind. Not a chance.

Witnessing this stark difference in the three Angels I had met up close, I was reminded that Angels had hierarchal classes—a pecking order, if you will.

And this Angel was obviously a significantly higher rank than Nameless or Eae, judging by the incredible waves of power rippling around him. I could tell he was holding back so as not to strip the flesh from my bones as a result of simply standing too close to him.

Reading my mind, the Angel gave me a very slow nod, confirming my analysis.

I stared up at a sudden pounding sound that seemed to echo like distant cracks of thunder. I gasped to see Cain in that strange reflection of Kansas City, beating his fist into the center of the street—but to me, it was the transparent ceiling to this place. Our two worlds brushing against each other like two soap bubbles. From the near-sighted look of rage on his face, he couldn't see us, having decided to beat his fist into the concrete where I had last been seen.

The anguish I saw in his eyes made me fall partly in love with him. That look wasn't simply anger from battle, but a deep, inner pain. A personal wound. It wasn't any kind of romantic love on my part, but akin to seeing a brother-in-arms weeping over your dead body on the battlefield.

You know, because it was totally normal to comprehend such macabre visions as that.

Another thought hit me. If Cain was that upset, wearing a look that screamed that all hope was lost—a look of total despair...who, exactly, did he think had taken me? I had the presence of mind to glance down at my feet—at my shoes. They had been made by Darling and Dear and had the ability to change shape and design to match my outfits.

But they also pinched my toes when pointed in the direction of a nearby demon.

I wasn't sure if I was relieved or concerned they weren't pinching my little piggies right now.

I noticed a scythe embedded in the ground to my immediate right with a flag hanging limply from the base of the blade. The partly scorched ribbon said *Non Serviam.*

A spear was embedded in a nearby boulder, and a shredded ribbon on the tip said *Defiance.*

It tickled my memory, but I didn't know why.

If I had to name the place's overall style, I would call it *Old Testament Chic*—a trend that had died long ago. Husks of large trees peppered the landscape as far as the eye could see, but they were burned and skeletal, as if the bones had refused to die centuries ago. I shivered, turning my head slightly to digest the rest of this dead world. The entire place looked to have been scorched to ashes, but white, lumpy pillars rose from the ashes like mounds of melted candlewax. Even though I didn't see any sun to speak of, the sky was a burnt orange, and the pillars glinted here and there.

Salt, not wax. They were pillars of salt.

I had somehow missed the gargantuan—but worn down—rock wall surrounding a forest of sorts a hundred yards away. A massive golden gate stood in the center of the wall, but it was pitted and bent as if having survived a great battle and a thousand years of acid rain. The gate continued up into a giant, battered arch that read *The den of Ed*, but the spacing between the words and letters was inconsistent.

I glanced back at my abductor, deciding to speak before he got any fresh ideas about taking me on a romantic walk. "I make it a point to never enter a place referred to as *The Den*. Only people who like shattered rainbows, lost puppies, pissed-off cats, and broken dreams willingly enter a Den. Not the kind of place a respectable human would enter by choice."

He didn't smile, and he didn't frown. "The Garden of Eden," he corrected, seemingly unwilling to look directly at the gate.

I stared at him for about ten seconds, my mind rebooting like an outdated computer.

Holy crap.

This was where Lucifer had turned against God, where Angel had first fought Angel.

And God decided to place the Garden of Eden, *here?*

I'd once heard a comedian say *if you're not laughing, you're learning*.

I'd learned something today.

CHAPTER 9

I slowly turned back to the wall itself, realizing much of it also looked as damaged as the gate and the arch. Scrutinizing it closer, I saw it was at least the same scope as the Great Wall of China, but the passing centuries had blown hills of ash, dead brush, scorched bones, and other rubble up against its base until sections of it appeared level with the land itself. Time had buried or concealed much of its grandeur, like some of the oldest castles in Europe where Mother Earth had reclaimed her surface.

Now, I wasn't an arborist or anything, but beyond the wall looked decidedly rough and overgrown. It *was* green—relatively speaking—compared to the desert-like side of the wall we currently stood on. It wasn't remotely pretty or impressive, though. Nothing like I had dreamed it would be. Not only did it look overgrown, it didn't even really look like it had a lot of vegetation in it. If there had been skyscraper-sized trees covered in flowering vines I totally would have sympathized with a lack of beauty, seeing it was obviously too large and wild for anyone to maintain.

But this…

It had been *neglected*. Since…well, since Cain's mom decided to eat an apple, perhaps.

"It is time you handed over the Spear of Longinus," The Angel said in an utterly calm tone. "It is not safe in the hands of mankind, let alone one such as you."

I wasn't even surprised at the demand. I'd been expecting something like it for quite some time. I'd found the Spear of Longinus—or the Spear of Destiny, as some knew it—when a Demon named Johnathan had attempted to destroy it. He'd made the mistake of inviting me to the party and it hadn't ended well for him.

Ever since I'd killed him, the Spear had somehow resided somewhere deep inside of me. I'd only been able to draw it out a handful of times, and only after a full day of calming meditation with exactly zero interruptions. Even then, I'd only managed to call it for a few seconds at a time.

Knowing that I had the Spear, that stabbed Jesus while on the Cross, hidden inside of me had not been the transcendent experience most would expect. Because I hadn't been given a choice in the matter—*it* had chosen for *itself*. My stomach curdled even thinking about it. Not in disgust or anything but...it was just a lot to process. It made me feel unworthy.

A fraud.

And I hadn't even wanted it. But you play with the cards you were dealt.

And now this Angel wanted to take my least favorite toy away. But it was still *my* least favorite toy, and I'd failed the sharing exam in preschool.

"You are not worthy of it. Hand over the Spear or die. Your choice," the Angel pressed, reading my thoughts as clear as day. I decided I was about finished with that nonsense, so I used a trick I'd recently learned to wall him out, blocking him from reading my mind.

I waved a hand distractedly, letting him know I'd heard him before he grew upset and pulled an emotion muscle that might disqualify him from the Den of Ed's upcoming annual flag football tournament with his siblings.

I thought about my earlier conversation with Dorian—how he believed that I was acting out as a result of feeling like I didn't belong anywhere, that I didn't have a purpose to guide me, that my lack of purpose was making everyone fear me as the new boogeyman of my city.

Then I thought about the Angels being hardwired with a purpose *and* a family and how they *still* somehow managed to fail on such an epic level.

I realized that, more than anything, I felt disappointed. With all of it. The Angels. The Demons. The Garden. The carnage in my city. The hatred in the world. My own actions.

I was fed up with it.

This wasn't how it was supposed to be. I knew I was no Saint. I had no reason to try to be one. I had yet to meet an Angel who had lived up to their reputations—a being that exuded poise, promise, and goodwill. One who made you weep with understanding.

Instead, I felt...nothing. No love. No hate. Just...a screaming emptiness. An eternal, rattling, death wheeze. Exactly like me, these creatures had forgotten their purpose, broken their family.

And instead of admitting it—deciding to fix themselves—they pointed a finger at me.

To bully and tell me how unworthy I was to hold and protect their precious Spear.

When it was pretty apparent, judging by our current locale, that their track record of protecting sacred things and places...

Was abysmal.

That, as a family...

They had turned on each other to such a degree that their future rematch promised to be Apocalyptic.

That, as shepherds of mankind, tasked with guiding and protecting their flock...

They were even *worse*. I'd run into—and killed—two Demons before an Angel ever deemed me worthy of a meeting, and then that Angel had ended up Falling from Grace not long after.

And now an *Angel* dared to point the *Holier than Thou* finger at *me*?

By some miracle, I was still clutching my apple from the party. I smiled absently, turning back to the Angel. Then I took a big, fat, juicy bit of the red fruit.

Let me put it into perspective: a *woman* took a bite of an *apple* while standing before the dystopian *Den of Ed*. I was very likely the only human being to ever set foot here since Adam and Eve—and for good reason. A few bad apples had ruined the barrel. Literally.

The Angel really didn't like my choice in fruit. Not. One. Bit.

His armor abruptly snapped, crackled, and popped—Vice Krispies—growing larger and spikier like one of those puffer fish, and his fist shot to the crystal hilt of his sword. His white eyes flared brighter, but he remained in place, staring at me.

"You dare to call me unworthy of keeping something safe?" I asked in a cool, measured tone. Then, with a mirthless chuckle, I indicated the Garden behind me and the war-torn landscape surrounding us. "Why would I give *you* the Spear?"

To both our surprise, I was suddenly gripping the crackling white spear in my fist. Two black bands encircled the haft, cutting the weapon into thirds, but it remained one solid piece despite this weakness. I stared down at it. Then I let out a slow whistle. "Speak of the devil…" I chuckled darkly. "And she will appear," I said, turning my wicked smile on the Angel.

If I was about to die, at least I'd managed a good one-liner.

"Foolish Angel…I *am* the Spear."

CHAPTER 10

The Angel had gone entirely still, staring at the Spear incredulously. Then, like a glacier calving, the new spiky growths on his armor cracked and slid from his body, crashing to the earth in a chiming pile of diamond grit. He never broke eye contact with the Spear.

I could tell he was trying to decide if I had spoken truly, but I was still blocking him from reading my thoughts, so he was instead trying to read or talk to the Spear. And it didn't appear to be answering his repetitive, desperate phone calls—sending them straight to voicemail, like a needy boyfriend after a breakup.

He finally shook his head and turned to look me in the eyes. I ground my feet into the earth, ready for anything, gripping the Spear in preparation of a very short fight, hoping I had my affairs in order back home.

The Angel abruptly flung out a hand and an orb of white fire erupted on the ground between us. It wasn't any kind of attack, because it looked like a simple, mellow campfire, but I could sense the raw power within. It was like my own white magic but on crystal meth. Or perhaps Angel Dust. Was this a glimpse of my future potential—the answer to why my magic would occasionally turn white when I made flames? I wasn't about to ask him, not wanting to further lower his already low opinion of me. The Angel took a deep breath, walked up to the fire, and then calmly sat down on a short pillar of salt.

I grimaced. That was just...distasteful. Hadn't that been a brother, once?

The Angel reached into the fire and withdrew a brilliantly glowing coal of pure light. He stared down at it in silence for a few moments, his face blank, but his hand shook in either pain or strain from the raw power. He finally looked up at me with his piercing white eyes and they flashed as if he had absorbed some of that fire. He gave me a nod, letting me know our argument was over. Obviously, a card-carrying member of the *man club*—maybe their first member—he didn't apologize or admit that I had been right.

It was good enough for me.

I released the Spear and it winked out of existence. The campfire flared brighter—as did the coal in his hand—before returning to normal. He considered this in pointed silence.

But the set of his shoulders let me know it had been both significant and unexpected.

"Sit with me. We have much to discuss..."

I sighed, realizing I really didn't have any other option. Cain continued to rail against the sky, mouth open in a silent roar, fighting to send his haunted, chilling music into his mother's garden.

I should have brought another apple...

The Angel watched me, his fist still shaking from the coal. I waited in silence, pretty confident in my decision to not play *follow the leader*. "This is my first time," he said in a tight, cautious voice. Well, for an Angel, it was practically screaming. I rose above my inner urge to pounce on the obvious laundry list of jokes and waited.

He eventually lifted the stone to his face, let out a breath, and set the coal against his forehead. He hissed and grunted, and I watched in disgusted fascination as his face...changed.

The beauty burned away, revealing the same face below, but...terribly, permanently scarred.

I leaned closer, my eyes wide as I picked out the same features from the previous mask, horrified to see the nasty scars that had marred such perfection. Like seeing *before-and-after* pictures in reverse. What remained was a rugged, raw, haunting beauty.

This face had seen war. His eyes were no longer as closed off, and I could see they were haunted and full of...loss—the first emotion I had seen here. As I stared at him, I realized his entire face now showed signs of life, emotion, sympathy, and fear. Not as naturally and easy to read as a human's face, but the potential was there.

I leaned back, letting out a breath as he met my eyes and nodded. He had experienced at least one bad Monday in his existence.

I very carefully considered my response. He had admitted this was his *first time*. This seemed ritualistic. A gift. A baring of blades. The first sign of honesty I had seen from him. Something real. I relaxed my shoulders and let myself show a genuine smile I hadn't realized I'd been holding back from him.

"You are still beautiful," I breathed, making sure to look into those white eyes as I spoke.

His face—I hadn't even realized it was tense and apprehensive—softened. Barely.

But his eyes glowed with appreciation. They were still hard and merciless, but a little humanity lurked in those depths. We weren't friends. I knew that. Beings like him didn't have friends. He only had brothers—and those brothers had earned their place at his table.

In his eyes, I was likely some yapping dog with a bad attitude. A dog he had taken on a walk to his Father's Garden. Then I had bit at my leash, begun barking at everything, and peed on their things. Out of the blue, I had then looked up at him and wagged my tail politely.

Something along those lines. Now, I needed to prove that I wasn't a temperamental Yorkie.

I hadn't been railing against God with my previous disrespect. The Angel seated across the fire was solid proof that He existed. In what capacity, I had no idea. But there was obviously a source to the Angel's creation. But until the big guy sat me down for a chat, I wasn't about to devote myself to Him.

Call it what you will, but it wasn't in my nature. I knew it was wrong, and that I was supposed to simply have Faith. I could have chosen to sit beside everyone else at church, singing the songs, reciting the prayers, but... it wouldn't have been genuine.

Accepting that fact, I had chosen to be brutally honest. Because I wasn't happy with how management had handled things. I was leaving a bad review.

I was showing this Angel—and his Father—that their actions had consequences. It wasn't bravery on my part. I knew I had an ace up my sleeve—

that if this Angel had truly wanted to end me, he would have already done it. He was powerful enough to snap his fingers and end me. Which meant he wanted or needed something from me.

"Why have you brought me here?" I asked him, folding my hands together in my lap, studying the white fire between us.

His gaze latched onto the shadow ring circling my thumb and his scarred face tightened angrily. "You bound an Angel."

This was shaping up to become one of those sensitive conversations. One where someone got their feelings hurt...

CHAPTER 11

I let the statement settle between us for a few moments, knowing it hadn't been what he originally intended to say. I slowly lifted my thumb, displaying the band of shifting shadows. "What choice did I have?" I asked softly. "Let him join your Fallen brothers and sisters?" I shook my head firmly.

He studied my finger in silence, a troubled look replacing his anger. "I do not have an answer, but it has been a long time since one wore an Angel on their finger," he admitted, sounding sickened.

I glanced up sharply. "I'm not the first?" I asked, surprised.

"Your ancestor, Solomon, son of David, also bound the Fallen into a ring. He had the wisdom to not let them touch his flesh. But to risk them so close to clawing away at your true soul..." he shuddered at the thought, staring at my thumb.

I twisted away from him to reach my fingers into the top of my bra and withdraw the tiny silk pouch holding the Seal of Solomon that I had tucked inside—not having wanted to risk it out of quick reach at the party. Good thing, too, because I had no idea where my clutch purse had ended up. It had only held my phone and some cash, thankfully—I hadn't bothered putting my driver's license in there. I smiled absently, wondering if it was lying somewhere here in the once-beautiful Garden of Eden.

That would really confuse some Angels.

I turned back to the Angel, dumping the silver ring into my palm and showing him.

He leaned back instinctively. I closed my fingers over it, shielding my mind in case any of the residents inside decided to reenact a Jerry Springer episode of family drama. Luckily, they were quiet. "I don't know how to put this one inside," I admitted, holding up my shadow ring. "Or what that even means," I admitted.

"It is not for me to know, but you should find out how to extricate him from your flesh."

I sighed tiredly. "No argument there."

He leaned forward, staring into the white fire. "It saddened me to feel him Fall…" he breathed. "We wear these scars like broken hearts for our siblings who chose wrongly on that fateful day," he said, holding his hand palm up as if to indicate his entire face with his fingers. "I have never shown a human this," he reminded me.

I sighed at the raw pain that briefly flickered across his eyes at mention of his scars. "Thank you for the gift. The scars do not negate your beauty, though. Why hide them?"

He let out a breath, shaking his head. "They see it as tiny victories, knowing we are just as scarred from our broken family as they are—even if it is a different type of scarring. They embrace their transformations, their grotesque visages, their self-inflicted mutilations, making a mockery of the perfection given to them by our Father. As a balance, we conceal our pain."

My heart broke a little at that, not having ever thought about it. He was speaking of Demons. Both literal and his own internal demons. Cain continued to pound at the sky, managing to emphasize the potential harm siblings could inflict upon each other.

I wondered if Abel's demise bothered Cain more than he let on. If he, too, felt like this Angel.

I smiled consolingly at the Angel. "Masks don't heal pain. Pretending otherwise simply means you continue to carry guilt on your shoulders. The scars are a *part* of you." I pointed at the landscape around us—at all the unmasked scars. "Pain is a lesson one shouldn't ignore. Embrace it. Understanding and accepting is healing."

He looked up at me, staring into my soul for a few moments, considering my words. "Perhaps." Then he smiled faintly, as if at an inside joke, but it was gone as swiftly as it had appeared, like a blown-out candle flame.

I frowned, wondering what I had missed. "But I'm just an ignorant human," I admitted.

He nodded seriously, turning back to the flame so he missed my responding scowl. He'd taken it literally. Bastard. "It's been thousands of years since I've spoken with a human. Ignorant, perhaps, but you see much. Experience much. Hurt much." He shivered as if shaking off a potential contagion. "It's terrifying."

I blinked a few times, and then a throaty laugh bubbled out from my lips. Soon, I was clutching at my sides, my eyes watering. He cocked his head, frowning. I waved a hand, laughing harder. "It's not terrifying. It's *existing*."

"I exist," he argued.

I forced back my laughter, knowing it wasn't helping. That this was a genuine opportunity to perhaps teach him something. "What have you learned in all your years?"

He thought about it. "Love. And War. Good and Evil—"

I nodded soberly but held up a hand to cut him off before he began reciting scripture. "I understand that, but you had one taste of *true* existence…" I again motioned at the war-torn land around us. "And your solution was to run from it, lock it away, hide it from sight as if it never happened. You won't even show your own face…" I added softly.

He stared into the fire, thinking silently. I gave him a few moments, but he seemed to be struggling with a response. "It was…bad," he finally said. I waited for more, because hearing that his family had been ripped apart, that a vast group of his siblings had rebelled and then been banished to Hell… well, that was a few million miles past a bad day.

Silence settled over us, and I realized that was the extent of his opinion. Wow.

"What use is there in reliving it? The battle is over until Judgment Day."

I nodded, a part of me jolting at the sudden realization that our conversation was entirely literal. I kept that from my features, attempting to address the topic in a rational, dispassionate way—trying to understand it from his point of view—speaking his language.

"And without learning from your past mistakes—and those of your Fallen brothers—what kind of result do you expect from that fateful day?

From my opinion, I would expect no different an outcome than last time. Perhaps a worse outcome. Those who do not learn from history are destined to repeat it."

"The same can be said of Sin, yet here you are," he challenged.

I nodded, understanding that he wasn't insulting me. Again, he was being literal. There was no room for emotion in this conversation. Maybe a little bit of humanity, but not too much. "That is true. We each have much to learn," I admitted.

He was silent for a time, thinking Angel thoughts. Finally, he pointed his finger at my ring. "May I embrace my Brother?" he asked hesitantly, his voice shaking slightly as if it had cost him something to ask me such a personal question. The passion in his voice moved me, making me reconsider just how much an Angel knew about love. Maybe they knew more than I thought. Or had a better capacity for unconditional love than humans. Which made perfect sense, really. God had hardwired it into them, after all, not giving them the ability to have *Free Will*.

"Of course." I lifted up my shadow ring—which was entirely silent in my head. Still, the shifting shadows seemed to vibrate like a child on the verge of tears. I realized it was shame. And hatred. And despair. And hope.

I hesitated. "I don't know how to take it off," I admitted, frowning.

"You do not need to." He waved a hand, and suddenly a smoky apparition hovered before us, making my heart drop into my stomach with a big splash.

Between us, directly over the fire, a somewhat transparent—like a hologram—Nameless hung suspended from millions of glittering, silver chains as fine as fishing line. They stretched out from him in every direction, the ends sewn into his very flesh—even his earlobes, nostrils, and lips.

There were so many silver chains that he resembled an exploding sun. I cringed at the agony on his face. He was nude, and his body was covered in thousands of runes, all throbbing with a pitch-black light, even though the wounds seemed to simultaneously eat up the very light they emitted. Gray, grimy blood oozed from his wounds like tree sap, never actually falling from his flesh. He stared at us with black eyes, his eyelids peeled back by yet more chains.

His face didn't seem to register pain at the piercings. It was cold and unyielding.

But his eyes showed a storm of emotions. He was...

Crying…

Laughing…

And silently screaming.

"My brother…" the Angel breathed. Then he stood uncertainly, approaching Nameless in a hesitant shuffle. He paused for a moment, shaking his head longingly. Then he enveloped him into a fierce, heart-wrenching hug that made my own eyes water. I could see that the simple contact threatened to destroy both of them with the emotions they so adamantly denied.

Nameless wilted into it, gasping out a rasp for the first time—as if the mere touch of his brother had filled some yawning, gaping chasm in his soul. A flame in the dark. A spark of hope in his torture.

Nameless whimpered in a soul-crushing shudder that rattled his chains like windchimes.

The Angel finally stepped away, his shoulders also shaking. He opened his mouth to say something further, closed it, and then finally hung his head as he jerkily waved his hand again. Nameless vanished, and my ring suddenly throbbed twice. I felt Nameless retreat deep within me, my ring no longer threatening to freeze my bones to crushed ice.

The shadows shifted more sluggishly now, like syrup around my thumb.

The Angel sat back before the fire, his face blank, but his eyes on fire. "Thank you," he whispered after a few moments. I nodded, unable to formulate a proper response. "Hopefully, that will quiet him for a time. Lessen his impact on you…" His voice trailed off, sounding numb.

The wasteland was silent for a time, other than the distant sweep of wings from his patrolling brothers and the crackling fire before us.

"Regarding the reason for your presence," the Angel finally said, regaining his composure.

"Abduction," I corrected.

His white eyes narrowed as they shot my way, but he found me smiling and let out a grunt. "There are three reasons you were…abducted," he said. I nodded, leaning forward expectantly. "But I will not explain them until you stop blocking my ability to read your mind. It is disrespectful to mask one of my many senses. Like me placing a blindfold on you for the duration of our conversation."

Then he gave me a look he must have learned from his Father, because it made me wilt.

How open and honest did I dare to be with the Angel? I didn't want him flying away in horror or turning me into one of the pillars of salt decorating their front yard.

He continued giving me that look, his white eyes roiling like swirling milk.

CHAPTER 12

I hadn't really thought about it the way he described. Reading minds was one of his natural senses—like touching, tasting, hearing, seeing, or smelling for humans. I didn't want to comply, but he made a valid point. And he had shown me his face, first—a sign of trust.

I let out a breath, released my control, and felt suddenly naked.

He dipped his head and let out a relieved sigh as his sense of telepathy came back online. "Thank you. I will not abuse your trust," he told me, wasting no time in reading my mind.

I nodded woodenly, focusing intently on clean, wholesome thoughts like a good little human.

I saw a flicker of a smile cross his face and instantly blushed, but he didn't comment on whatever he had sensed in my mind. He took a breath, his face growing serious. "Firstly, you are broken inside. And broken chains cannot hold a soul intact. It is a weakness you cannot afford."

I frowned, wondering if he was speaking about humans in general or specifically about me.

"To dare hosting an Angel on your finger, you must be strong. You must have Faith." He held up a hand, already stalling my obviously anticipated argument. "Faith in *yourself*. You are aimless right now. And power without aim is an explosion in slow-motion."

I nodded, recalling my conversation with Dorian.

"I do not know how to fix you. How to make you less pathetic," he said pensively, not acknowledging my mental hackles rising up. He continued in a clinical manner. "Maybe I am not *permitted* to aid you in this—that you must fix it yourself," he said in a frustrated tone.

I gritted my teeth to prevent a feather-plucking party, knowing he meant well. All I really wanted to do was walk away. Toss in the towel. I wasn't made for this level of crap.

The Angel shot me a dark, disappointed look. "Apathy is the gentle embrace of the deceiver. One cannot simply do nothing and hope to survive, let alone thrive," he chastised.

I scowled back. "Was that supposed to be a pep talk?"

"Take it as you will," he said in a frosty tone. He glanced down at my shadow ring—at Nameless. "Attempting to unbind him here could be catastrophic. He is *yours*. You claimed him—and responsibility for him—the moment you decided to catch him as he Fell. You must learn to control him or transfer him to the Seal of Solomon."

"Okay," I admitted, having no idea how to do such a thing. Since he didn't either, I felt marginally better.

"Secondly, it is now apparent to me that the Spear of Longinus—or Spear of Destiny, as it is also known—has somehow bonded to you, specifically. Attempting to take it from you or kill you—as I originally intended when I took you—would have almost certainly destroyed it." He shuddered at both the thought of it breaking and the fact that it meant he had to now leave it in my care. "But it is severely damaged. As its custodian, you must repair it or at least keep it safe until a solution can be found. The Spear is vital to Judgment Day, and if it is destroyed or falls into the wrong hands…"

I shivered both at the thought of it breaking and the fact that I had apparently just been tagged in to fight in the Apocalypse—because if the Spear had to be there, and the Spear was bonded to me…I would need to pick up a team jersey from Darling and Dear. "I understand," I said.

"Do not risk breaking it further, under *any* circumstances," he warned fiercely, refusing to avert his eyes until he was confident I comprehended the significance of his words. "Perhaps the solution to repairing it can be found in your bloodline—in the Seal of Solomon. Or maybe the circumstances that led you to the Spear in the first place." He didn't sound too confident, more like he was grasping at straws. Which was strange. If the Spear was so vital, and he had been willing to kill me to take it from me…

shouldn't he have had a pretty good idea how to fix it or what to do with it?

I nodded quickly, seeing my thoughts were only frustrating him. Which meant that my questions were valid. So far, this was not going well, but better than I had expected.

"Thirdly, Samael has been freed. This is what finally forced my hand. You—through no fault of your own—unleashed a Greater Demon." I flinched at the comment. Through no fault of my own? What did that mean? I'd pretty much admitted that it was *entirely* my fault. "He must be put back in the Seal. No matter the cost. Unless that cost is the Spear of Destiny."

I had no idea what to do, and felt the tension growing in my shoulders.

"You see my dilemma. You are full of a wild, unpredictable anguish, and you are tasked with guarding Demon prisoners. I cannot kill you for risk of destroying the Spear, forcing you to be its protector. And Samael must be stopped, or all hope may be lost, yet neither of us know how to accomplish this. Even now he works in the shadows to unravel my battle plans." The way he said that sent goosebumps down my arms for some reason.

"What is he doing? Where is he?" I asked instead.

He gritted his teeth. "Samael is hidden from me, but I see the ripples in the pond, the rumbling storm on the horizon. I believe all our answers can be found in the same place—a place I hope you will find very soon. The fate of mankind could very well rest on your shoulders."

"Mind explaining that?"

His eyes pulsed brighter for a moment, and he looked frustrated. "I quite literally cannot..." he watched my reaction, reading my mind. "I have not been commanded to silence, I simply do not *know*. Something is preventing me from seeing as clearly as I should," he admitted angrily.

Oh. That didn't sound good.

"I *do* know that whoever holds the Spear will find the answers," he told me, meeting my eyes meaningfully, subtly admitting to me why he had been willing to kill me earlier—so he could use the Spear to save the world, apparently. "Thus it is written: *The white blade must find its sheath, or all mankind will cease to breathe*," he quoted reverently.

Well, that wasn't Hallmark Card appropriate. But it seemed fairly clear—my Spear was a white blade. But I'd rarely seen a Spear with a sheath, and if it was as simple as *me* being the Spear's sheath, I would have already saved mankind and the Angel wouldn't be so concerned. "Maybe it's because any other solution would make for a crappy plot," I muttered.

"I speak not of land holdings," the Angel said, frowning. "Perhaps I am not speaking clearly."

I waved a hand. "No, I wasn't talking about a plot of land. Never mind..." I said, seeing the confusion on his face.

He suddenly cocked his head as if hearing something. Then he climbed to his feet, looking flustered. "Our time draws to a close," he said, staring out at one of his brothers circling a tree in the distance. "It is almost time for you to leave. My brothers will keep the patrol away for a few more moments. I fear Cain has attracted attention with his incessant hammering," he growled. "Impudent child."

I smiled, glancing back up at Cain and the vision of Kansas City above us. "He does that."

"He loves you like a sister. Like I love my brothers," the leader said, glancing up at Cain. The crazy bastard was still pounding on the pavement, not seeming to lose any energy in his relentlessly futile defiance. "I knew him as a boy. He and Abel were inseparable..."

"Family can be dangerous," I said, considering his words. Abel had received the short straw on sibling love. As had the Angel's siblings now in Hell. "But they can also be a strength," I said, smiling as I indicated one of his brothers circling us, high in the rust-colored sky.

The Angel nodded, matter-of-factly.

Wondering whether or not I would ever again get the opportunity to sit down with an Angel, I changed topics to ask a random question. Something to brag about to Roland later. "What is it *like* to be an Angel?"

He thought about it for a few moments, seeming to consider and then discard a million responses. He finally met my eyes, and his scarred, beautiful face was entirely slack, looking one-hundred-percent certain of his answer. "Like a never-ending explosion," he said in the same tone one might say, *that stone is hard.*

I watched him for a smile, a frown, any sense of exaggeration, humor, horror, disgust, anguish, uncertainty...anything my mortal mind could comprehend.

And I realized that he was being entirely literal. He wasn't telling me how awesome it was. He wasn't telling me how frightening it was. He was literally telling me how it *was.*

I knew, with that single statement, that I would *never* understand an Angel. Especially one who had been sheltered from mankind his entire life. And now I was expected to control the one stuck to my thumb, not even counting those inside the prison that was the Seal of Solomon.

I feared for humanity's future on the fateful day the Angels came to play.

I also had a newfound appreciation for the Biblical Four Horsemen.

And the new Fifth Horseman, Nate Temple. The Horsemen weren't just judges. They were mankind's elected representatives.

That thought both terrified and excited me.

"Think back on this conversation, Miss Penrose. I fear the Last Day soon approaches. The Fallen rail at the walls, the Four Horseman can now act in limited altercations, and a new band of Horsemen have been born..." He locked eyes with me. "That was *never* spoken of, and that concerns us. *All* of us. For if our Father never mentioned a second band of Horsemen...what else was he too afraid to tell us? He spoke in exquisite detail of so many things..." The Angel leaned forward, eyes terrified. "Yet he spoke *nothing* of Nate Temple's Horsemen. Of *Hope, Despair, Justice,* and *Absolution.*"

I stared right back into those immortal eyes, instantly clamping down my mind to block him from reading my thoughts.

His eyes narrowed as he felt me blocking him out, suddenly curious what I was hiding. Because I feared I might know the answer to his question about Nate and his new Horsemen—even though this was the first time I had heard any names other than Hope.

Maybe Nate's Horsemen rode to protect humanity from...*Heaven.*

God save us all.

I had also blocked the Angel out because I had suddenly remembered Starlight's warning from the party. To be aware of never-ending explosions. Even if he had been high on some mind-altering substance, it was too much of a coincidence for me to dismiss.

"I guess we will soon find out..." I told the Angel.

He grunted, glancing back up at one of his brothers who was anxiously urging him to get me out of here before we were discovered by...whatever was coming that had them all anxious.

The Angel wrapped his arms around me in a hug. Then we were racing up, up, up into the sky, back to Kansas City.

CHAPTER 13

*W*e had broken through the bubble, and Cain was suddenly battering at the street in slow motion, a line of cars behind him. He had halted traffic, and I saw slowly pulsing blue-and-red lights in the distance, but everything was still moving like molasses.

The Angel deposited me in a nearby alley, setting me down on a plastic crate. He again wore his hood and fake beautiful mask, even though I hadn't seen him don it.

"Godspeed, Angeling."

I gripped his arm before he could leave. "Angeling?" I asked quickly. "Why did you call me that?" I demanded.

He stared down at my hand clutching his arm with a pregnant silence. I released it and he visibly relaxed. He turned to look up at me and touched me on the center of my forehead. "Do not think that because I did not mention it, I did not see this."

I shivered in understanding. Phix had told me about the Enochian script branded on my forehead, and that only some beings could see it. A very short list. But since it was written in the language of the Angels, my abductor was well-versed enough to read the single word.

Despair.

"Why did you call me Angeling?" I repeated, staying on topic.

He considered me from only inches away. "Something was done to you after your birth. Something that makes you unique. Something hidden from even *my* sight..." he said, still not answering the question. Or maybe he had.

"And what makes you so important?" I asked instead, noticing the emphasis he had placed on the word *my*. He had done that a few times in our talk. "Who are you?"

He hesitated, possibly considering answering me only in exchange for whatever thoughts I was currently blocking him from seeing. I waited, keeping my mind locked down.

"Michael, of course," he admitted. The sound of slowly screeching tires made him glance over at Cain. "You don't want him arrested, do you?" he asked, sounding annoyed.

He didn't even notice that I was still reeling from his name. Michael, as in the General of God's Army against Satan? One of the Seven Archangels?

I looked over at Cain, not sure what else to do with my brain. "I'd rather he wasn't arrested."

Michael nodded, snapped his fingers, and then he abruptly disappeared.

I gasped to find the passage of time abruptly returning to normal, making my head spin for a few seconds. When I glanced up, Cain was no longer kneeling in the center of the street. There were also no police sirens and no traffic, and the city seemed eerily quiet for a little after midnight.

I felt like I'd just stumbled out of a bar. I didn't feel drunk, but my mind was beyond scattered, and I felt dizzy and weak from the jet-lag of hopping back and forth between Earth and...The Den of Ed.

I was also hallucinating, because I had been the alley's only occupant a few seconds ago, but now I saw Cain napping on a stack of newspapers a few feet away, the sleeve of his linen jacket submerged in a questionable puddle. I squinted, fearing there might be some side-effects for a human hanging out with an Archangel.

"Hey!" I snapped at the hallucination.

He sat up in a blink, eyes wide as he jerked his head back and forth, panting anxiously. He spotted me, and his jaw dropped. "Callie! We need to get out of here! The cops are coming!"

Then he grabbed a bundle of leather at his side, shambled over, scooped me up, and proceeded to use his enhanced speed to flee the scene of the crime before I had time to tell him that the cops were long gone. The super speed informed me that it was in fact, Cain, and that Michael must have done something to get the cops off Cain's back.

"I thought you were dead!" he snarled, leaping over something in his way, but landing easily on his feet. I closed my eyes against the blurring scenery, feeling suddenly exhausted.

"I'm fine. I just fancied a stroll through a garden," I told him.

"Don't go dying on me, now," he commanded.

"I'm just disoriented," I assured him, keeping my eyes closed. After a few minutes, he finally slowed, setting me down on the ground. He checked me over as I finally risked opening my eyes. The world no longer tilted or spun crazily. Cain's eyes were bloodshot, and his jaw was clenched so hard I feared he was about to crack a tooth.

I placed a hand on his wrist. "I'm fine, Cain. Really."

He stiffened at my touch, shuddering noticeably. "You scared me, Callie. Almost to death."

I nodded guiltily. "I know. We saw…"

And I told him everything, sparing him no details. Especially about the Den of Ed.

He listened with a grim, troubled look on his face. He was silent for a time, processing it all. Especially which Angel I had spoken with. Then his attention drifted to the pile of leather he had grabbed before picking me up —he had tossed it to the ground behind him as I told my story—and he smiled, climbing to his feet. He shook it out before holding it up and posing dramatically. My coat!

"Picked it up on my way out," he said, draping it over my shoulders. "Your purse thing is in the inside pocket."

I smiled at that. Clutch purses were a mystery to the male brain. Was it a wallet? Or was it a purse? What secrets did it hold? At least I didn't have to worry about an Angel patrol finding it outside the Den of Ed.

I nuzzled the collar of my jacket with my cheeks, practically purring.

Cain grunted in surprise and I looked up to see him frowning down at his phone. "That's impossible. It says we have a few hours until sunrise…"

I blinked. "How long were you beating on the street?" I asked warily.

He shrugged. "About an hour, maybe?" I heard the cops approaching and then…" he scratched at his head, turning to look at me with an uncertain frown. "You waking me up…"

And I suddenly realized what Michael had done. He had sped up the passage of time, somehow hiding us in the alley long enough for the cops to lose interest in their manhunt for the nut-job who'd been reported pounding the middle of the street with his fist.

No wonder I felt so disoriented. At least Cain had been allowed to sleep through the experience.

Cain pocketed his phone, still trying to make sense of it all. "You were taken from the party about an hour ago. I'm sure of it. It should be just past midnight..."

"I think Michael gave us some help. But before I talk any further, we need to find some coffee," I told him. "Lots of coffee."

He nodded stiffly, still wrapping his head around the time-shift. "Let's go, then."

And we went off to hunt down the elusive beast, caffeine.

CHAPTER 14

I stared down at the silver charm I had taken out of my jacket
pocket, smiling absently at the memory of a kiss as we walked
through the pre-dawn streets of Kansas City. While I was still wearing my
ruined gown from the night before, I now had my jacket to keep me warm
from the cool breeze. Thanks to Cain. It was also nice to feel like I had more
protection, since the coat was essentially armor, of sorts.

Nate Temple had recently given me the silver butterfly charm, probably
not considering how much it meant to me. Not just because the man I liked
had given me a gift, but because I had a newfound magical affinity with
Silver—capital S. I had more questions about this Silver magic than I had
answers, but I'd found myself using it more than my wizard's magic lately.
Often, without consciously choosing to.

I could call up Silver claws stronger than any metal.

I'd once used it to alter my vision into a chromatic landscape that had
allowed me to see things that would happen a few moments into the future.

I'd called up a swarm of living, razor-winged, Silver butterflies—and
been able to control them with my mind, to some extent.

I'd bound Nameless to my thumb, using liquid Silver to encase his body
from head to toe, transforming him into a chrome statue—currently located
at Roland's church.

I'd recently even had a realistic dream—more like a futuristic vision—

where I was crying Silver tears. Nate had been in the dream and we had kissed. I had later visited him in St. Louis and he had given me the butterfly charm, hinting heavily that he'd had the same exact dream as me. Creepily romantic, on both our parts.

Beggars couldn't be choosers, so I had taken what I could get.

And we had finally kissed for real—our first.

Despite the cool breeze as I walked beside Cain, the memory made my face flush and my toes curl in my boots. Now, the little butterfly felt like a kiss in my hand. Always close to me. But I could sense a hidden power inside the little charm. It wasn't just pretty. It had magic of some strange kind. Something wild and faint, but with the potential to ignite a figurative forest fire.

Cain walked beside me in silence, oblivious to my romantic thoughts as his eyes darted about, like my own private security detail. I noticed he kept his palm close to his hip, making me curious about what kind of weapon he was packing.

A car slowed beside us with the windows down, and I caught a snippet of talk radio as it stopped at a red light. "*...murder suspect was last seen fleeing into the Penn Valley Park, and is considered armed and dangerous...*"

The light turned green and the car took off. I frowned, hoping it had nothing to do with Cain.

"You didn't murder anyone while I was gone, right?" I asked him in a stern tone.

He tripped, rounding on me with a startled look. "Of course not!"

I nodded, the matter settled. But Cain was now shooting baffled looks my way as we continued on. Hadn't he heard the car radio? And let's be honest, it wasn't like it was a wild leap for me to consider that Cain had killed someone. It was kind of his thing.

I wasn't that far from the park, but I was more interested in coffee, and already had enough on my mind as it was. I'd thought about Starlight's *never-ending explosion* warning, but realized that I had no way of calling him. Bears didn't have pockets to carry cellphones. Even if they did, I didn't have his number. And calling the bears in Alaska would also do me no good because Starlight was here in Kansas City. He was probably still high out of his mind anyway.

And I really didn't want to think about meeting Archangel Michael. It made my brain hurt.

I continued walking towards the coffee shop, realizing that we had kind of turned the place into a regular part of our weekly schedules—meeting up at least once a week to grab coffee and maybe a pastry together. But we had never made the morning commute together, and it felt mildly strange, like we'd had a one-night stand and were now trying to maintain some semblance of normalcy. Well, an Angelic abduction was stranger than any one-night stand. Our usual was coffee with a few extra shots of espresso, courtesy of my two favorite baristas, Emily and Ramses.

We walked by a homeless man sleeping in the doorway of an accounting firm. He was using newspapers as a make-shift blanket, and this morning's newspaper rested on top, the headline catching my eye, *King Solomon Moves to Penn Valley Park*. I flinched involuntarily at the mention of King Solomon, recalling my own recently discovered heritage—that I was descended from the infamous king—the wisest, richest man in the history of ever.

A picture below the article showed a snapshot of the exquisite new fountain—a large empty throne, complete with six steps leading up to it with a different pair of animals on each step. I averted my eyes as the homeless man stirred, not wanting him to think I had been staring at him.

Cain had dismissed the homeless man as a threat, knowing I could handle a mere human.

I saw the coffee shop ahead and smiled. Coffee would soon be in my belly.

We waited at a crosswalk even though no one else was on the streets. Kansas City was full of terrible drivers and I knew it was better not to tempt fate. Also, I wasn't in a rush.

In the last fifteen minutes, I'd decided to change my life.

To focus more on living in the moment, relaxing, and fully taking the happy parts of this thing called life deep into my soul. Because my night had proven that things could always get worse.

And my talk with Dorian had shaken me.

Not even considering that Archangel Michael had pretty much said the same thing—that I was a wild, unpredictable, tainted soul held together by broken chains. Oh, and I was *pathetic*.

I needed to find my special purpose like Steve Martin in *The Jerk*. I needed to find my favorite lamp. But first, I needed to relieve the stressors in my life.

Step one, not risk getting run over by a commuter after my life-altering epiphany.

Step two, coffee.

Step three...

Feeling suddenly anxious, I decided to take my new life journey only *two steps* at a time.

A bus drove past, the driver not even pretending to hide the fact that he was checking his phone as he drove, proving the wisdom of my choice to honor the Patron Saint of Pedestrians.

"Doesn't he know how dangerous it is to text and drive? Idiot could have killed someone," Cain cursed, shaking his fist at the bus driver—who obviously didn't notice.

The side of the bus was plastered with another image of the fountain in Penn Valley Park. Kansas City was known as the City of Fountains, so it wasn't surprising to hear about a new one, but it *was* surprising to see it so heavily advertised. It wasn't like anyone in the city cared.

Tourists might care, but the locals couldn't care less.

The bus disappeared around a corner, the green walking man appeared on the crosswalk sign, and life rolled on. I led the still cursing Cain across the street, spotting the coffee shop ahead.

A few minutes later, I strolled inside the coffee shop, waving as I saw Ramses and Emily behind the counter. Ramses arched a brow at my torn, stained dress, and then grinned like a lecher upon seeing Cain stroll in behind me in his rumpled linen suit. I scowled, shaking my head, but I wasn't about to defend my virtue from across the lobby of an open coffee shop. Cain strolled past me, pointing at a table near the window as he pressed on to the counter to pick up our drinks. "Morning, robots," I called out to Emily and Ramses.

"Greetings, human scum," Emily replied, smiling at my comment even though she didn't look up from the espresso machine. "We put extra tar in yours."

"Thank God."

I made my way over to the chair and sat down with a sigh. Two businessmen were speaking about the fountain in a desultory fashion, something to lube up the old brain muscle before they kick-started their mental faculties to get down to real business. I saw today's newspaper before them, cringed at the image of the fountain, and turned to look out the window at the street. Cain strolled up behind me a few minutes later, setting a cup down before me. For the first time, I noticed his cuffs were blood-stained.

"Your friends gave me quite the silent ovation," he said, rolling his eyes.

I glanced over my shoulder to make sure he hadn't murdered them. "Can't blame them. I mean, *look* at us," I said, indicating our tattered evening attire. "Must have been a helluva romp."

He waved a hand dismissively, sitting down. "I don't see you like that. You're beautiful and all, toots, but after last night..." he trailed off, noting how close the two businessmen sat to us. "Well, you're like a sister to me."

I didn't say the obvious—that sibling love from Cain might not be that reassuring—but the pain in his eyes let me know he had already considered the dubiousness of the statement and was trying to be serious.

The businessmen behind us were commenting on the apparent manhunt at Penn Valley Park. I frowned absently, turning my chair slightly to face Cain.

"Did you get anywhere with those women at the party?" I asked.

"They never had a chance," he replied, rolling his eyes. "Before this morning, I was bored. Now, I'm wondering if I should have stayed bored."

"You've been bored? Why?"

"Dorian has been too busy to hang out and I'm dying inside."

I rolled my eyes. "I'm sure you'll find a reason to continue living. Try focusing on the positive," I suggested. "I need to make some phone calls about last night. People are probably concerned about me."

Cain made an awkward sound. The look on his face told me he needed to hit me with some truths I wouldn't like to hear. "That's a little complicated..." he began, fidgeting slightly with his cup. "You see, no one actually saw what happened. Well, they noticed the gaping hole in the window, but no one actually saw you jump. They just freaked out, thinking you had thrown your magic around, knocked a bunch of people down, and then blown out a window before running out the door."

I blinked at him, remembering how time had slowed while everyone was busy staring at Le Bone, waiting for him to speak. "Then how did you know?"

"I caught a glimpse of you right as you jumped. And I recognized *them*," he said meaningfully, implying the Angels. "It wasn't hard to put two-and-two together..." He took a sip of his coffee. "I was the first to look down at the street, and I recognized the runes. And the still-rippling concrete..."

I gave him a crooked, thankful smile. "Thank you."

He smiled back faintly, shrugging off the compliment. "I asked around, but no one saw you leave the room, and by the time they looked out the window, there were no runes or bodies on the street, just debris."

I tapped my cup with my fingernails, frowning. "They think I snapped, blew some shit up, and then ran away? So, I'm a crazy person..."

Cain sipped his coffee loudly, refusing to comment.

I scowled at him, letting out a breath. "Wow," I finally said, leaning back in my seat. "So, what do I tell everyone? Sorry for crashing the party? I had some bad lobster bisque? And what about you punching the street like a crazy person? I'm sure *plenty* of people saw *that!*"

Cain's cheeks flushed. "Well, you see, there's a story to that. A long story..." he quickly averted his eyes under my sudden glare. "I...acquired a potion—the how doesn't really matter, per se—that could throw up a flawless, but temporary, veil. All anyone saw was a stalled truck blocking the center of the street..."

I grunted doubtfully, not knowing which question to ask first. I was mighty curious to hear how he had gotten the potion, but also how the potion had made him look like a truck, of all things. By the way he was acting—still blushing and not meeting my eyes—I began to wonder just who he had gotten the potion from. And why he was embarrassed about the acquisition.

"Why are you blush—

He shook his head and immediately cut me off. "Nope. I'm not going to talk about her—" he coughed outrageously in a poor attempt to cover up his slip, causing the businessmen to turn and look back at us to make sure Cain wasn't choking to death. They looked more annoyed than concerned, though.

I grinned at Cain's discomfort, waving off their concern absently as I leveled Cain with a predatory smirk. "Oh, I think I *really* want to hear about *her...*"

His cheeks were almost purple as he took another long drink. "All that matters is that no one saw me losing my shit in the middle of the street, and no one saw the...saw *Michael* take you. Haven was already shouting to arrest Le Bone when I grabbed your coat and ran to the elevator. He didn't want to wait to get Le Bone in chains in case he was behind the chaos somehow.

Everyone else was too busy whispering about...how you went postal," he admitted with a wince.

I slumped in my chair, both disappointed that he hadn't spilled the beans and that my already scary reputation had taken a turn for the worse.

"Damn. Those are going to be some awkward phone calls..." I finally said.

I took another sip of my drink, wondering which two steps I wanted to tackle next. The phone calls would wait. I wanted to think about my story, first. I knew I couldn't delay too long, but the sun wasn't even up yet. I had time.

Cain cleared his throat pointedly. "I think you should call Roland first. Maybe don't delay..."

I frowned. "Why do you say that?" I asked, not liking the uncomfortable look on his face.

Cain thought about it, frowning himself. "The minute he saw you were gone..." he trailed off, shaking his head. "Something inside of him snapped, Callie. It was a subtle thing. Like a frozen pond's first crack in the spring. It was like he was standing in an empty room, staring at nothing. If Haven hadn't snapped him out of it to help with Le Bone..." He watched me, gauging my reaction. "I've seen that look before, Callie. It usually prefaces a massacre. Trust me. You need to call him before you call anyone else."

Crap. "Looks like we're heading to church," I sighed, feeling nervous. "This isn't something I should do over the phone."

"I'll call an Uber," Cain suggested, pulling out his phone.

I placed a hand on his wrist, halting him. "Let's walk. It's not far, and I could use the fresh air to collect my thoughts before talking with Roland."

He looked uncertain about my decision, but finally shrugged. "Your call. But we should get going. We only have about two hours before sunrise, give or take."

I climbed to my feet and began walking towards the door, wondering what the hell I was going to tell Roland.

And what the look Cain had seen on his face had prefaced.

CHAPTER 15

*W*e exited the coffee shop and I pulled a scarf from my jacket pocket, wrapping it around my neck. I straightened it, careful to keep the emblem concealed from casual view. Cain noticed, and his lips thinned. "Are you sure it's smart to wear that out in public? Pretty sure the Templars are still hunting you."

I thought for a moment before turning left to walk down the street. "That's exactly why I'm wearing it. In case they hired a wizard hitman. But I'm pretty sure they left town with their tails tucked between their legs." Cain grunted, neither agreeing nor disagreeing as he walked beside me. But he was paranoid—a good trait to hold close these days.

A Cross Pattée was emblazoned across the center of my black scarf, and it nullified magical attacks—part of the uniform for Knights Templar, keeping them safe as they hunted down the big bad supernatural folk of the world in the name of God. All Freaks were evil in their eyes.

"Beckett's been searching all over town for Olin and his renegade Templars," I told Cain. "Every single one of their old hideouts has been found abandoned, showing no signs of recent activity. I'm pretty sure Olin and his ilk fled Kansas City to regroup elsewhere. But they will be back someday. That's for sure."

We continued walking in silence for a few moments before Cain spoke again. "Outside of business, have you talked with Beckett?"

I sighed. "You know I haven't."

"You used to be friends, once. Kind of kicked some serious ass together a few times," he reminded me. I didn't say anything. "It's a shame that he fell for Olin's lies. But Olin tricked a lot of people, didn't he? Not telling his own Templars he was a werewolf—"

"Do you have a point?" I growled.

"Just a shitty way for a friendship to die."

I grunted, kicking at a chunk of gravel on the sidewalk. It hit a trashcan, pinning a flyer announcing a music festival in Penn Valley Park a few weeks from now. Someone had put some serious money into the park to advertise it so widely.

"Is it working?" Cain asked, sipping his coffee loudly.

"What?" I asked, tearing my eyes from the flyer.

"My subtle hints. Are they working?"

I was silent for a time, biting my tongue. "Have I told you I'm trying to become a better person? Calm. Serene. Less violent—"

"So, it's not working," he interrupted, chuckling. "But the fact that Beckett is now a tiny teddy bear must be a nice karmic kiss."

I finally laughed, shaking my head. "A sun bear! It helps more than you know." My smile withered after a few moments. "What he did...it cut deep, Cain. I know he was deceived by Olin, but he made some personal choices that put people directly in danger. My people. And he did it knowingly, not accidentally. That's not something I can easily forgive." I let out an angry sigh. "A lot of bad stuff happened that night, and some of it was a direct result of Beckett's actions."

Cain chose not to comment further.

My thumb cooled noticeably as Nameless overheard me mention the night I had caught him and trapped him. Michael had said he'd quieted Nameless somewhat, but I wasn't sure what that actually meant. Michael was adamant that I needed to get the Fallen Angel off my finger and into the Seal of Solomon, pronto. I sighed, shaking my head.

Release me... Nameless pleaded from somewhere deep within me, like an echo of a whisper. I shuddered. His voice was fainter than usual, but still too loud for my liking.

The random commentary was one reason I wasn't entirely fond of my new buddy, even though he was sometimes helpful—like when he'd tried to warn me about Michael abducting me. Another reason was the constant chill. I'd been forced to keep my thumb in my pocket a lot more often to keep it warm, but also so no one saw the moving shadow circling my finger like smoke. So far, I hadn't noticed any boost in power or anything, just a whole lot of angst, suffering, and begging.

I had never learned Nameless' real name and hadn't thought to ask Michael about it. I found myself idly wondering if changing his name had been the first step towards his Fall from Grace.

I shook my head and clamped down on the voice. "You hear about the manhunt at Penn Valley Park?" I asked, looking both ways before I crossed the street. The park in question was just ahead of us.

Cain frowned. "Manhunt?" he asked. "No. Where did you hear about that?" he asked, just now spotting a sign with the park's name stamped into it just ahead of us.

I glanced over at him. "How have you *not* heard about the manhunt? The car that stopped next to us on our way to the coffee shop was blaring the news from his radio. And those suits at the coffee shop were even talking about it." I gave him a look of disappointment. "Not very perceptive."

He blinked a few times, as if trying to recall our walk. "The guys behind us were talking about investments. I remember because one of them mentioned Grimm Tech. They didn't talk about anything local."

I shook my head. "I heard them when I sat down." I waved a hand at the peaceful, tranquil, moonlit park ahead of us. "Anyway, if there's a manhunt, why are there no police or reporters?"

Cain scanned the park, his forehead furrowing. "Maybe they already caught him."

I nodded absently. "Well, we can cut through the park. There's a new fountain I want to see." I shot him a significant look. "Solomon's Throne."

He stiffened slightly, glancing at me from the corner of his eyes. "Oh?" he said warily. "How...serendipitous."

"Easy, champ," I warned. "Save your big words for the witches. They pay in potions."

He muttered something less than flattering under his breath, making me grin.

Even without Michael urging me to learn how to use the Seal of Solomon, I was very aware of the cosmic coincidence at play. But curiosity killed the cat, and all of that. And technically, visiting this fountain was paying homage to my distant ancestor. What kind of descendent would I be to *not* go see it?

I entered the park and knew we were the only ones here. It just had that feeling about it. Maybe they really had concluded their manhunt. The entrance to the park revealed a moonlit clearing with an elaborate fountain depicting two nymphs blowing a fawn's pipes.

I thought about how that sounded, realized Archangel Michael had been right about me being broken inside, and continued on with a resigned sigh, motioning for Cain to follow.

Cain caught up with me, matching my stride. I'd already told him all about my ties to King Solomon and the Seal. He had listened intently to my story, asked to see the Seal afterwards, nodded once or twice, and had then asked—with a big grin—if the princess commanded him to bring a tiara to our next coffee date. That was the best kind of friend. And yes, he had brought a cheap, plastic tiara to our next coffee date.

I think they called this type of friend an enabler.

I didn't see any signs for the new fountain, but after about ten minutes I noticed a freshly beaten trail leading off into an area surrounded by tall trees. The path wasn't paved yet, but I heard gurgling water on the other side of the trees. Cain cleared his throat pointedly as I was about to round the bend for a closer look. "Didn't you say your fountain was on the front page?"

He was holding up a copy of today's newspaper and the front depicted a Kansas Senator doing something either heroic or scandalous, I couldn't tell. It definitely wasn't about a fountain. I had been sure the homeless man's paper had been from today. I shrugged. "Maybe I misread the date."

But Cain was studying me suspiciously, knowing how good I typically was with details. Coupled with the other facts I had mentioned that he couldn't recall—and the coincidence of those facts leading us here to a fountain in honor of King Solomon, his alarm bells were likely ringing. To be honest, mine were, too. But I was still going to take a peek. It was right around the corner from me. I had a feeling. Cain cursed and gave chase as I dashed around the bend.

Ten feet further, I skidded to a halt, my eyes widening as Cain caught up to me. We stood on the edge of a clearing holding a massive fountain with an exquisite throne in the center—the type of fountain that should have probably stood outside the Bellagio in Vegas. My mouth hung open as I stared at it, feeling calmer by the moment. The full moon illuminated the fountain, making it look like it had been formed from fresh milk, rising up from a pool of water.

"Wow…" Cain breathed. "You weren't kidding. But what's something like that doing tucked away back here? And why haven't we heard anything until now? This had to take forever to build…"

I nodded absently, walking over to it. My ancestor's throne…it suddenly felt a lot more personal to me. Reading about it in books was one thing, but to see the man's throne? I pulled out the Seal of Solomon, holding it in my palm, feeling like it was the right thing for the man's descendent to do. Paying tribute. The Demons typically only bothered me if I put it on my finger, but I remained alert, ready to shove it back in my pocket if necessary.

"Something feels wrong about all of this, Callie…" Cain warned.

I placed my hand on the slick ledge of the pool, staring up at the ornate throne. Six wide steps led up to the royal seat from the water's surface, a different pair of meticulously carved animals facing each other from either side of each step: a lion and an ox, a wolf and a lamb, a tiger and a camel, an eagle and a peacock, a cat and a rooster, and a hawk facing a dove. Above the throne itself, a dove held a hawk in its beak—which was definitely bizarre.

But the attention to detail was stunning. Cain was right. This had to have taken a long time to build. They hadn't just slapped some concrete forms together. In fact…I leaned forward, rapping on the ledge encircling the pool. It was marble.

I grunted in surprise. This was way too nice to have out in public. It was going to be covered in graffiti in a few days, tops. No question.

I leaned closer, placing both palms on the ledge and shaking my head. "Cain, you need to see this up close. It's beautif—"

"Get back, NOW!" Cain roared, and I heard him unsheathing something metallic.

CHAPTER 16

I spun to confront the threat, instinctively shoving the Seal of Solomon back into my pocket. It had remained entirely inert, but Cain didn't jump at shadows. Nor did he draw steel on them.

Except…this time he had, because we were entirely alone.

Cain abruptly grabbed me by the shoulder and shoved me behind him as he held out a long, wicked dagger, keeping me away from…

The fountain.

I stared from over his shoulder to see what had alarmed him, and immediately gasped in disbelief. Where I had touched the marble, glowing text was slowly appearing in a flowing, elegant calligraphy. I peered over Cain's shoulder, struggling to read it while he fought to keep me back with his free hand.

Solomon's Temple has opened at last, to be found by the one who discovers the path.

Many will seek, but only one may find, as the Doors to such wisdom, can shatter the mind.

From corner to corner, from East to West, the Temple is calling, your trial, your test.

To find her location, to find where she hides, is for you to decipher, for you to decide.

Two ways one can enter, two ways one may find. One lies on the earth, one lies in the mind.

The Doors on each path, so vast and so varied, like wounds to the heart, are oft deep buried.

Go forth, my children, be daring, be bold, Solomon's Temple is calling, with treasures untold.

"Motherf—" Cain breathed, but I cut him off by shoving him to the side, eager to get a closer look at the message. Because the letters were slowly fading.

Remembering the signs that had led me here, and how Cain hadn't seen them, I whipped out my phone and took a hasty picture, shaking my head in disbelief. At first, I had thought it was some elaborate light display built into the marble. But I could hear and feel a faint hum in the air, like the beginning of a distant song. As I focused on it, goosebumps prickled down my arms.

That song practically screamed *magic*—but it was unlike any magic I had ever experienced before. It was taunting and enticing, like a Siren's call. I checked the image on my phone—because one never knew with magic being involved—and let out a shaky breath of relief. I had a good memory, so wasn't concerned about forgetting the words, but this way I had proof. Unlike the other signs that had led me here.

I made sure to save the picture to my cloud storage account, so I could check it later from a larger screen if needed. I wasn't a tech nerd or anything, but perhaps there was more to the message than could be seen on my phone's small screen.

I glanced up to find Cain looking like he was on the verge of vomiting. He immediately began to shake his head. "No way, Callie. This is a terrible idea, and that's coming from the guy who made one of the first bad decisions in human history—preceded only by my mother."

Eve chomping on the apple. Right. Not really much of an argument there.

"Do you know something about this?" I asked. Because Cain looked suspiciously aware of exactly what this was all about. He was shaking his head too adamantly. "Cain…" I warned, using my mom voice.

"Callie, this is bad. Very, very bad. I don't care what ideas Michael put in your head about finding answers. If this is what he meant, it's not worth it."

"It doesn't seem to matter whether I participate or not. Someone is going to go after the Temple. It's a foregone conclusion." I pointed at the fountain. "It said *many will seek*."

He gave me a stern look. "And *only one may find*," he said, completing the quote.

I waved off his concern, pulling out the Seal of Solomon to remind him that its contact with the fountain was what had revealed the message in the first place. "I've got a ticket to play. I was led here with the newspaper, the flyer, all of it." He sighed in defeat but seemed adamant to not give up in his opinion. "Come on, Cain," I added, huffing as I placed my hands on my hips. "I'm kind of guaranteed to win anyway. I'm blood-related to the guy! And this seems like *exactly* what the Angel was talking about."

He was shaking his head adamantly. "You don't want to do this, Callie. Only one person can win. All the others die!" He looked about to explode with frustration.

"So, you're saying there's a chance..."

He took a deep, calming breath, staring at the fountain. Then he frowned suspiciously. "Maybe none of this is even true. Maybe *no one* has ever won the damned thing. I don't recall ever hearing about a victor. Just because—"

"The fear of the Lord is the beginning of knowledge..." a man's voice interrupted Cain from behind the fountain. Cain spun with a feral snarl, gripping his dagger with white knuckles.

The man strode out into the open, wearing jeans and a flannel. He was a fit, middle-aged man, and almost boringly handsome, if that makes any sense. The kind of guy you'd be *satisfied* being married to when the other polo-clad husbands were lined up at the grill for a neighborhood block party. "You should heed your friend's advice," he said, studying us.

"Unless you want to get baptized, you should take your preaching else-where," I warned.

The man smiled—a sad, disappointed smile. "Fools despise wisdom and instruction," he said. "The Sons of Solomon will pray for your soul."

Then he pulled out a pistol and began firing.

I flung my hand up instinctively and a black fan materialized between us, shielding the bullets even as I gasped in surprise. What the hell? We were in the heart of downtown and Father Tombstone hadn't even batted an eye at unloading his lead sermon on us.

"I told you!" Cain snarled, hurling his insanely large knife at the man. It struck him in the throat, almost decapitating him as it knocked him into the fountain. The crystalline water bloomed crimson almost instantaneously. "We're leaving. *Now.*" Cain commanded.

I nodded stupidly, still stunned at the drastic escalation of the preacher. "Right. We'll talk about it later."

"Wrong," Cain snapped, gripping me forcefully by the bicep and steering me towards the trees. "We won't be talking about it. We're done." He raised his voice loudly. "You hear that? We're done! We're not playing!"

"Who are you shouting at?" I hissed as Cain dragged me closer to the path that had led us here. I cringed at the sound of incoming sirens from the nearby police precinct. "I'd like to get away *without* letting the police know we were here!"

"He wasn't talking to the police, child," a woman said, stepping out from the trees. I skidded to a halt, blinking in confusion. Because it was Cleo, the beautiful, black-haired scholar from the party last night, and she held a sinister vial in one hand, poised to hurl at us as she walked closer. Cain glared at her and the vial like a caged dog, and I wondered if he recognized her from the party as the woman I had warned him to keep an eye on.

Men never listen.

Unfortunately, Cleo had an entirely different look on her face than she had last night. It was the suicidal smile of one so devoted to their cause that nothing could sway them.

And the way she was gripping her vial let me know it was a hairline fracture away from being crushed—and that none of us would survive the result. Clenching a fist was faster than Cain drawing a blade, and I couldn't see a way to use my magic to simultaneously lock up all five of her fingers without breaking the glass myself.

Cleo nodded, seeing the comprehension in my eyes. "If air touches the contents of this vial, we all die. And I put a drop of my blood inside, so if my heart stops, we all die."

We nodded carefully so as not to startle her.

"It's a shame, Callie. I had such a pleasant time speaking with you at the party. We could have even become friends, perhaps."

"Still can, Cleo," I suggested.

She shook her head sadly, but her eyes were feverish. "You should never have concerned yourself with Solomon's Temple. It is not a prize for the uninitiated. This has been my life's purpose, preparing for the day the

Temple reappeared. I've spent *decades* of my life studying Solomon lore, preparing for this ultimate trial, this test of knowledge...The Song of Solomon. I even mastered potions to extend my years in the hopes I would live to see this day. I've walked the earth where the Temple once stood, tasted the air, dreaming I would one day walk in the Temple Gardens..." she said wistfully.

"Well, it's open, now. Why don't you just book a flight since you know where it is?" I asked.

Cleo cast me a very condescending look, one that almost made me wither in shame. "It never reappears in the same place twice. Everyone knows that." She checked the clearing and the trees to make sure we were still alone.

"Waiting for a friend?" I asked, sensing a potential opportunity.

She scoffed. "The Sons of Solomon pretend to be a family, but everyone knows only one will enter the Temple at the end. It's a game, using each other to progress, but not so far as to risk losing the ultimate prize to them."

Sons of Solomon? I'd never heard of them, but they sounded like a pretty deadly book club.

"Which brings me back to you. I don't know how you discovered the fountain in the first place, but I saw you take a picture of the message, so I'm going to need your phone. I'd rather not risk walking down there myself. All sorts of crazies sneaking around here this morning."

"Give you the phone and you'll let us live?" Cain asked carefully.

She shook her head. "I'm afraid this is the end to your quest. I cannot allow the Vatican to take my prize."

I frowned openly. "The Vatican? I no longer work for the Vatican."

She gave me a very dry, pointed look, indicating my scarf with a quick flick of her eyes. I cursed inwardly, remembering that my scarf had a big Cross Pattée on the front, and it must be showing. I didn't bother arguing about it because, based on the conversation thus far, I was pretty sure she would have simply justified another reason to kill us for her precious Temple.

Long story short, she had no intention of letting us ever leave the park.

CHAPTER 17

*C*ain cleared his throat gently. "Give her the phone, Callie. We aren't playing, remember?" He glanced at Cleo with a calming look. "Just the wrong place at the wrong time. We will even swear an oath not to search for the Temple."

I nodded to Cleo, trying to look sincere. "I will swear to it. You can have the phone." Cain was up to something, probably picking up on the fact that Cleo had no intention of letting us leave, sworn oath or not. But taking an aggressive stand was a great way for all three of us to die for our pride.

I slowly reached into my coat pocket, watching Cleo's eyes as I withdrew my phone using my first two fingers, not my thumb—also the best way to pick pockets, believe it or not. My reason for using the grip was simple. It looked precarious and awkward, drawing the eyes.

It worked.

Cain had been watching for it, too, and was a heartbeat faster than me.

I didn't even see him move. But I saw the spray of blood as he neatly severed her wrist and shoved us both clear of her potion. Cleo shrieked in agony, her free hand reaching up to grasp her stump before she even considered the potion falling to the earth.

"The Sons of Solomon will hunt you to the ends of the Earth!" she screamed. Cain and I rolled away frantically to escape the blast radius and I flung up my hand. A wall of liquid silver rose up between us, shielding me from the blast as the ground around her erupted with purple flame in a ten-foot-wide circle so hot that I felt the skin of my face tighten, despite my shield. I had never used my Silver magic to do that before, but I'd learned it was based on raw need, so my subconscious must have decided I needed some added protection from her potion.

Cain stared down at his dagger, frowning momentarily, but then he was tugging me to my feet. "Get us the fuck out of here!" he snarled, eyes scanning the woods around us for the next threat. I saw two more silhouettes racing our way, probably drawn to the blast, so I gripped Cain's hand and focused my mind on Roland's church to Shadow Walk us the fuck out of this crazy park.

I felt a tug of resistance like someone had bumped my funny bone, but my magic still seemed to work, yanking us away to safety—

I gasped in confusion to find that something had gone horribly wrong with my Shadow Walking, because I was somehow perched atop the damned fountain. And there were about a half-dozen new people in the vicinity, all keeping a cautious distance from each other.

Cain, still gripping my hand from Shadow Walking, had unfortunately appeared above the water rather than the fountain. The undefeated champion named gravity immediately grabbed him by the ankles and yanked him down, taking me right along with him. I snapped my lips shut at the last minute, remembering the pool was now spiked with blood from the flannel guy Cain had killed.

We struck the crisp water loudly enough that if any of the people around the fountain had failed to spot us appearing out of thin air above it, they had most definitely heard our splash at its base. They hadn't been attacking each other, so were apparently all hesitant allies—Sons of Solomon, as Cleo had called them. Which sucked, because we were not an ally, and now had a dysfunctional family to stand up against.

I breached the shallow water and flung up my hand, calling upon my magical fan to catch the anticipated barrage of bullets as I tried to understand what had gone so wrong with my Shadow Walking. It hadn't felt like an attack from a fellow wizard, but like something in the air itself had resisted my use of Shadow Walking. Maybe it was a ward to prevent some thieving wizard from jumping in at the last minute to steal the message they thought was a treasure map to Solomon's Temple. They were going to be sorely disappointed if they ever read it, because the message had been totally unhelpful. Definitely not directions on how to find the Temple.

Cain, apparently not trusting, or not seeing, my defensive fan, abruptly tackled me back into the water just as bullets began to fly. He dragged me—unconcerned with my spluttering and choking—behind the massive throne as the bullets pinged and whined off the beautiful marble.

He gripped my shoulders, staring at me with a frantic expression, likely wondering why the hell I had sent us to the top of the fountain rather than Roland's church.

"It wasn't me!" I hissed. "Something's messing with my magic," I told him, feeling slightly panicked at my sudden failed magic. What the hell was going on?

The realization that our escape now rested firmly on his shoulders turned his face into a grim, determined mask. Like he had rolled up his sleeves for a day's work. He was a warrior, not a sneaky wizard. Which meant blood would soon flow if our escape plan was solely up to him. And with the number of guns and potions just around the corner—and my magic unpredictable—one of us might not be making it to Roland's church.

"We're going to have to kill them all. They won't listen to reason," he growled, eyes alert to either side. "You ready?" he asked, shaking me to get my attention.

I nodded woodenly, understanding that he was probably right. These Sons of Solomon were freaking insane. Whoever they were. I frowned suddenly, realizing the guns had stopped firing.

Cain gritted his teeth, taking it as a sign of worse danger. He shoved me flat against the marble throne and peered around the corner quickly. Almost immediately, he jerked back, his face pale and disbelieving like he had just seen Abel's ghost.

"Shit," he breathed, eyes dancing wildly. I stared at him, waiting for something more helpful. But that was pretty much the extent of his analysis.

"What?" I hissed, glancing over my shoulder to make sure we weren't being flanked.

"The *Last Breath*," Cain whispered in a haunted tone, holding his finger to his lips for me to be silent. "Maybe he didn't notice us."

Seeing the raw terror in Cain's eyes, I didn't argue or badger him with questions. As a rule, Cain never got scared. He actually relished the fight.

Even the fear of death—if such a thing was possible for the immortal murderer. But this *Last Breath* person had him shaken.

He slowly crouched down into the shallow water, motioning for me to do the same after pointing out the drops of water falling from my clothes. I didn't point out that the sound of the gurgling fountain probably masked the sound of a few drops, and instead obeyed his request. We sat in the shadow of the throne, and I was suddenly grateful that the moon didn't reach us.

Cain leaned in close, his face almost unclear in the darkness as he pressed me against the wall and literally *breathed* an update into my ear, softer than a hummingbird flapping his wings. "They are all dead."

My hair might have climbed off my scalp at that. Half a dozen people murdered without a sound? What the hell? Cain nodded and slowly lifted a finger to his lips. I tried to calm my racing heart, the gentle lapping tickling the base of my chin as we sat in the bloody water, eyes dancing about for any sign of threat. Michael had warned me that an answer to my three problems was imminent, that I needed to learn how to use the Seal of Solomon to lock up Nameless, among other things.

Right before a deadly quest leading to Solomon's Temple plopped into my lap. I wasn't sure how any of it actually tied into his warnings, nevertheless it seemed to be related. But how in the world was I supposed to find the Temple before these Sons of Solomon—who had spent their entire lives researching Solomon lore, waiting for this exact day? I knew pretty much nothing about Solomon, even though I was his descendent, and the message on the fountain had sure seemed to confer that a whole lot of wisdom and mental acrobatics would be needed to win.

But none of that mattered right now. Because some psychopath named *Last Breath* was here.

And I couldn't Shadow Walk us to safety. Either my quest was over before it had begun...

Or we stayed silently sitting in this dark pool, hoping Last Breath wasn't smart enough to walk around the back of the fountain. Overall, this was a very unique experience for me. To sit in the dark and hide from a monster, like a Regular. I almost cried out as I saw a form silently stalking near the tree line, its back to us.

Last Breath.

It seemed to be sniffing the air, moving in utter silence on two legs like a man, but it was significantly larger than any human I had ever seen. Since it kept to the shadows of the trees, the moon did not illuminate it clearly. But it seemed to be wearing all white, almost smoking with white vapor of some kind. A concealment spell?

Cain gripped my arm tighter, drawing me lower into the water so that only my eyes were above the surface. I held my breath and watched as the silhouette abruptly darted closer in a white blur, trailing along the ledge of the pool now. His sapphire blue eyes seemed to sparkle despite no light hitting them. Like two tiny blue flames. But...he wasn't in the shadows any longer, so why was the moon not illuminating him?

Those eyes locked directly onto mine for a few heart-stopping moments and I fought not to move or even blink, hoping that the shadow of the throne was dark enough to hide us.

Those blue eyes held death like an old blanket. He *was* death. He was *all*.

I had never felt so small in my entire life. When I had seen Nate Temple step out of literal Hell, his eyes hadn't been that cold. Not by a long shot.

Then the figure was gone, completing his circuit of the fountain. Cain squeezed tighter, meeting my eyes. He slowly lifted his lips above the water. He opened his mouth, not even breathing the words, just moving his lips. *Deep breath. Long time.* Then he mimed taking a deep, silent breath, and lowered his head entirely underwater.

I did the same, as quietly as possible, trying not to disturb the water in the slightest. I was beginning to feel the cold settling into my bones but judging by the look in Cain's eyes I didn't dare disobey. The moment before I submerged, I looked up to see that Last Breath was now perched on the ledge itself, its two blue eyes, scanning right to left in my direction, not even a dozen paces away. All I could make out was a large white blur as if he was the color of the moon, only his icy blue eyes were crystal clear.

The cold water enveloped me a moment before his gaze reached me, and it was all I could do not to open my eyes under the water—even knowing it was full of blood—because I felt like I had just kissed death on the nose.

Cain gripped my hand and squeezed tightly, trying to reassure me.

I don't think I ever held my breath that long before. Definitely a record. I even waited until I was seeing stars through my eyelids before risking a breath.

My eyes opened almost immediately as I fought not to shiver. Last Breath was gone.

Cain still made us wait fifteen minutes before we dared risk exiting the pool.

I would have waited thirty minutes without an argument. Hell, I would have spent an hour in that cold water. I don't think I'd ever felt so helpless in my entire life. Not even when I'd had my first run-in with the supernatural as a teen in that dark alley when Claire and I had been assaulted. When Roland had saved us, introducing me to the world of magic.

Speaking of...I decided a girl could use a father figure after an experience like that. Cain didn't argue. Perhaps he needed a father figure, too.

CHAPTER 18

*W*e burst into Roland's church like the dogs of Hell were on our heels, slamming the massive wooden door behind us with a loud thud that echoed through the decrepit building. We were both panting as we leaned our backs against it.

Cain closed his eyes with a relieved sigh. "Too close. Way too fucking close, Callie."

I closed my eyes, too, murmuring my agreement. I had stored some extra clothes and weapons here and knew Roland would have something for Cain to change into. We could dry off, warm up, talk to Roland, and try to figure out what we wanted to do next. Per my new rules, I just needed to focus on two steps at a time—

A throat cleared, making me jump and my eyes shoot wide open.

At the end of the nave, near the pulpit, two men stood beside some lawn chairs and one of those cheap, standing fire pits found at most home improvements stores—but those didn't typically blaze with crimson flames. Only Roland's fire pits did that.

Roland's crimson eyes pinned me to the door like spears, looking a little wild around the edges—flashing from relieved, to suddenly very, very concerned.

Because he wasn't alone. A second man stared at us from across the nave.

Looks like I found my two steps, I thought to myself, climbing to my feet. I straightened my coat and met Cain's eyes, silently asking if he knew the second man. Cain shook his head almost imperceptibly. We made our way to the pulpit, both staring at the fire hungrily. Even if it was wizard's fire, it promised warmth.

"You're alive," Roland growled as we reached the fire, his voice dripping with fury.

I maintained a safe distance from the stranger, ignoring the curious look in his eyes as I turned to Roland. Something about his face told me not to speak anything that I didn't want made public, but I only knew that because I had known Roland my whole life.

"Alive, but cold. Rough night," I told him, voice neutral.

"What she said," Cain agreed, folding his arms as he placed himself between me and the stranger. A sudden shriek from deep within the bowels of the church made me jolt. It sounded like a man being tortured. I arched a brow at Roland.

"Le Bone," he said in a flat tone. "May I introduce Miss Callie Penrose and Cain," Roland said, holding out a hand to us. "And this is Henri Bellerose, the Master Vampire of Paris. He just finished a private conversation with Le Bone," he added with a meaningful smirk.

My skin crawled at that, suddenly realizing—in a vague way—why Le Bone had screamed loud enough for us to hear upstairs. It must have been a very difficult conversation for Le Bone.

Henri smiled pleasantly, nodding at Cain and then me. Those eyes were too inquisitive for my tastes. "A rose by any other name would smell as sweet..."

My eyes narrowed, and I opened my mouth to put him in his place for attempting flirtation, but he waved a hand good-naturedly.

"My name is Henri Bellerose, and you are Callie Penrose," he explained, emphasizing the *rose* in both our names. Le Bone shrieked again, and Henri shrugged innocently. "I wanted to verify the allegations for myself. Le Bone's guilt weighs heavily on his soul, as you can tell by his shameful whimpering. I hear I have you to thank for the evidence," he said, smiling gratefully.

I nodded slowly, careful not to gloat at the psychopath. "Yes."

"Then, *thank you*," he said with a dip of his chin.

Henri was a handsome man with rich brown hair held back in a ponytail. His features were harsh and angular, his jawline sharp enough to deflect a sword, and his eyes twinkled with a gray so pale they were almost white. He was very tall and lithe, like a scarecrow, but I knew it was a deception. Something about him screamed power and strength—like a cheetah. Perhaps not as large and intimidating as his brethren wildcat felines, but as if he lived on the edge, always a breath away from a brutal, whip-quick lethality.

Henri also *knew* he was handsome. He had that French accent that drove so many women wild. It did nothing for me—but maybe that was influenced by the...*shameful whimpering* accent in the background. He looked younger than I had anticipated, but that was often par for the course when it came to vampires. He was probably a few hundred years old, despite his roguish mid-thirties look. From the tightness to Roland's eyes, I also assumed he was quite powerful.

"Shouldn't you be meeting with Haven?" I asked, remembering that Le Bone's primary fault had been *not* meeting with the Master of Kansas City.

Henri smiled in amusement, picking up on my not-so-subtle hint. "I received permission to enter his city, yes. Haven encouraged me to visit Roland's...*church* to see Le Bone for myself."

"He was just leaving," Roland said politely, turning to Henri. "Unless there was anything else you wished to discuss?"

Henri chuckled. "Swiftly done, Roland. We shall meet again to discuss Le Bone's very brief, anguished existence. I implore you to play with him a bit, perhaps see what other activities he had his hands in while here. You will find no repercussions from me. Do your worst."

Roland dipped his head.

Henri smiled wider. "Think on what else we discussed, Roland. We have great plans for you."

Roland's posture grew harder, but I doubted anyone—even Cain and Henri—noticed the subtle shift. "I have no desire for greatness, but I will consider it. I can deliver you to Haven's compound immediately."

Henri held up a finger. "I would like a private word with the infamous White Rose, first, but I will accept your offer, after." I was surprised to hear him use my nickname, but I didn't let it show on my face.

"Callie does as she chooses," Roland replied. "It's safer for everyone." He shot me a questioning look to let me answer for myself.

"I have urgent business with Roland, but I have a few minutes to spare," I lied.

Henri nodded his understanding. "Then let us be brief," he said, indicating for me to join him as we walked down the nave. I felt Roland watching us like a hawk as he spoke in low tones to Cain. I watched Henri from the corner of my sight, wondering why we needed a private conversation. Then again, I figured I had likely brought this on personally by inserting myself into vampire politics with Le Bone, so it would be unwise for me to dismiss Henri's request.

Once again, I was reminded that I really needed to find my purpose in life. Not to continue sticking my nose into business that I didn't really care about long-term. By poking so many hornets' nests, I was drawing unwanted attention—all because the thrill of the initial chase with Le Bone had sounded entertaining and worthwhile. Now, I had to suffer through his boss thanking me. Or threatening me. Only time would tell.

"When I learned of Le Bone's betrayal, I hastened my visit," Henri explained.

I found myself wondering exactly how he had arrived so quickly. Perhaps he employed a wizard to make him Gateways. As the Master of such a major city as Paris, he likely had all sorts of pull and power.

It wasn't beyond the realm of possibility for him to secretly have a few wizards as pets in his basement. I was speaking with one of the big boys.

And big boys liked big toys.

And they played for keeps.

CHAPTER 19

*H*e guided me over to the statue of Nameless, on prominent display near the wall. The Master of Paris dipped his chin ever so slightly, indicating it. "Why do I sense so much anger from this stunning artifact? Perhaps it does not like my presence?" he asked thoughtfully.

He was pointing at the statue. I frowned, not sensing anything of the sort. "Um…"

Henri turned to face me, looking slightly surprised. "You do not sense it?"

I shook my head. "But he was kind of an asshole in the flesh, so I can't say I'm surprised."

Henri's eyes widened minutely, but on his carefully composed face it was a shout. "You…" he murmured, stepping back from the statue and dragging me with him, not even aware he was doing it, "you're telling me he was an actual *Angel*, and not a magical *artifact*?"

I resettled my balance, unhooking my arm from his in case he decided to run. "Yes. We had a disagreement."

"You trapped an Angel because you…disagreed with him," he repeated flatly.

"Well, I technically caught him as he Fell, but that sounds emasculating and inaccurate," I admitted, staring at the statue. To me, it felt inanimate, but my thumb was practically smoking with arctic violence. Nameless wasn't pleased at the discussion. Maybe that was what Henri was sensing.

"Even in Paris, people spread rumors about the *White Rose*, but I never heard anything about *this*..." Henri said carefully. He reconsidered the silver statue, shaking his head slightly. "*Mon Dieu!*" he added as an afterthought.

I was startled to hear my name had spread to Paris, but that last comment made my eyebrows almost jump off my forehead. I didn't speak French, but I knew *Dieu* was the word for *God*. It was definitely not typical for a vampire to be able to speak the Lord's name. And for the first time, I remembered we were standing inside a church. Henri should be bursting with flame right about now. It also told me why the vampire downstairs was still screaming. He was bound on Holy Ground, the very location likely torturing him in steady, relentless agony.

Unless...my actions with Nameless had desecrated the place, which I hadn't thought of up until right freaking now. Holy crap.

The only reason Roland was able to stand inside a church was because Haven had given him an old necklace designed to protect vampires from that very thing. With his background as a Shepherd, we had all been concerned that Roland was very likely to fall into old habits—accidentally saying, "Bless the Lord," and getting smited by a bolt of lightning.

Henri had apparently noticed my reaction, because he carefully reached into his shirt to reveal a medallion. It was old and gaudy, looking as if fashioned during the Spanish Inquisition. "I live in a city full of old churches," he explained. "You'd be surprised how many of us have these, or what loopholes one can discover with enough time and patience," he said gently.

I was ready for this conversation to be over, but I needed to know one thing. Well, it would lead to another thing. Two steps, remember?

"Why did Le Bone dare to act so brazen?" I asked.

Henri's face tightened in annoyance. "When you live as long as us, you learn how important reputations can be. You cherish them, nurture them, protect them. Younger vampires are eager to build their own reputation, to stand up against us older vampires. It seems he let his ego get the better of him, trying to fly before he could walk." Henri turned to me and dipped his head. "And thanks to you, he will suffer for it. You have my sincerest gratitude and deepest apologies for his crimes. As a representative of the Sanguine Council, I also thank you on their behalf."

I nodded politely, but my mind was suddenly racing. Since I was dead inside and had very little innate trust for strangers—especially after my long night—my conspiracy senses began to tingle. If Henri and the Sanguine Council had orchestrated all of this…it was pretty much exactly how I would have planned it. *Establish a common enemy in Le Bone, earn instant trust, sabotage and betray that trust later.* The question was why?

"I take it you had a reason for coming to Missouri," I asked Henri, keeping my paranoia from my voice. "It can't just be about Roland because you had him in your clutches not long ago in Italy. Which means you are here about someone else, or something else. I'd like to know what that is. Now."

Roland was watching us from across the room, likely hearing every word and wondering the same thing. Cain also looked attentive but made a good show of pretending to be focused on the fire. Roland had trained me, so each and every instinct I relied upon was simply a hand-me-down from the older man. If I was thinking it, Roland had already likely thought of it and moved forward a few steps. Then again, Roland had always told me I often came to conclusions ahead of him, even if I typically used more unorthodox methods.

"The Sanguine Council desires a firmer hand regarding Kansas City," Henri replied, seeming to carefully consider his response.

"Then they should be speaking with Haven…not Roland."

Henri nodded. "That was the point of my visit. Haven sent me here, remember?"

I wasn't sure I fully bought the narrative, but I forced myself to nod. Perhaps Haven had sent him here, or perhaps Haven had been *manipulated* into sending Henri here. I'd check Roland's thoughts on the subject. Which meant it was time for Henri to say *night-night.*

"Well, it was a pleasure speaking with you, Henri. I'm sure Haven is waiting, and we know how cranky Master Vampires can get when they stay up past their bedtimes." Because it was some time after sunrise, now.

Henri did not take offense at my dismissal, merely nodded with a warm smile. He either appreciated my candor, or he was secretly considering dismembering me in the basement of the church after his daytime nap. "It was my pleasure. I can now say I have met—and survived—the White Rose," he chuckled, extending a hand to me. I shook it with a smile of my own, sure to make it look genuine. Because there was always the chance that he *was* a good little vampire. Similarly, there was always the chance that he *wasn't*.

And girls should always keep their options open.

Proving Roland had been listening in, I heard a Gateway rip into existence and I turned to find a crimson portal standing open near the fire. A trio of vampires waited patiently on the other side, straightening as if coming to attention. Haven had designated a spot on his property for Roland's Gateways, keeping a small contingent of vampires ready and waiting at all times.

I'd deflected countless requests from Haven about purchasing some of Grimm Tech's portable Gateways—glass marbles Nate Temple had designed that let anyone create a passage wherever they were thrown. They obviously weren't part of the company's official product line—because they liked to toe the line between a legitimate company and a magical armorer for the supernatural crowd.

Like *Air Jordan* sneakers for basketball aficionados, everyone wanted to get their hands on *Nate's Tiny Balls*—as he had named them—and since he loved to rub in the joke, he now only sold them in sets of two, forcing clients to fill purchase orders that stated requests for *a dozen pairs of Nate's Tiny Balls*.

Henri dipped his chin at us in goodbye, and then stepped through the portal. Roland let it wink shut a few moments later and finally turned to us, seeming to quiver with pent-up fury.

"Now, the two of you are going to get out of those wet clothes and tell me exactly what happened tonight," he snarled.

"This church rocks. Get naked and repent!" Cain cheered, holding up a fist.

Roland shot him a very dark look, pointing at the door behind him that led up to the office. "Extra clothes are in the wardrobe. Might be a little vampy for you, Cain, but I don't care. Callie, you know where your extra clothes are." I nodded, leading Cain through the door.

We'd retro-fitted one of the extra meeting spaces into a type of office for me, a place where I could begin accumulating weapons, clothes, and whatever else I might need at a moment's notice. Like a panic room.

For when I needed to suit up to go hunting wabbits.

Or go treasure hunting, apparently.

CHAPTER 20

I huddled under my blanket, shivering despite the roaring fireplace beside us—a natural one this time. Roland paced back and forth, reading a piece of paper and looking haggard because it was after sunrise. Since my phone had taken a swim in the fountain and refused to come back to life, Roland had made me use his computer to login to the cloud and print out the image that proved my wild claims about Solomon's Temple and this quest.

We sat on comfy chairs in a back office of the church to avoid windows and sunlight for Roland's sake. Cain leaned forward, rubbing his hands together to absorb the heat faster. His back was a mess of scars, all neat, shining, silver lines like a geometric mandala of past pain. His bulging muscles only emphasized the scars, and I had noticed him flinch involuntarily several times. Whether from the bone-deep cold caused by our dip in the bloody fountain or from flashbacks of our near encounter, I wasn't sure.

Our escape from the fountain had been excruciating; each rustle of a leaf, crackling twig, gust of wind, or distant voice almost sending us bolting like startled rabbits. I hadn't dared risk using my magic to get us out of there. Not if it would deposit us right back into the fountain. We had kept to the shadows, vacating the park just before sunrise, shivering, dripping, and scared as all hell. We'd quickly found an alley and I had tested making a

Gateway to safety—since I could look through it to make sure it was functioning properly, first. It had shown us sanctuary just outside Roland's church and we had immediately leapt through. I had closed it behind me so fast that I might have even cut off my own foot without caring.

After sending Henri packing, Roland had forced us to take a quick shower, informing us that we looked so cold that even our blood didn't seem appetizing. *Like cottage cheese*, he had told us. He had personally bullied us into the shower together to warm up, and the two of us were so cold that we hadn't cared about nudity, hopping immediately into the shower to be the first to touch—and control—the jets of blessed scalding water. The water had hurt like a firing squad, forcing us to lean our backs against each other and take the abuse until our bodies recovered. Roland had stepped out of view, but hadn't left the bathroom the entire time, using the shower walls to trap us as he squeezed out the events of last night.

Roland hadn't been patient enough to let us get dressed after our shower, throwing blankets and towels at us and commanding us to sit before the fire and print out the picture as he peppered us with questions. Effectively, holding our clothes hostage.

In light of the fountain drama, and the fact that Cleo had used her dying scream to inform me that the Sons of Solomon were definitely not going to leave me alone, he'd agreed that the Michael topic could be put on a shelf. But knowing him, he would have given his right arm to hear every single detail of my meeting with the infamous Archangel.

Quid pro quo, he had refused to talk about Henri or anything related to vampire politics, telling me he would deal with it himself. I didn't like the sound of that but didn't have the time to do anything about it. Not with the Sons of Solomon breathing down my neck.

And Last Breath.

Roland grunted in frustration, snapping me out of my thoughts as he ran his hand through his hair, looking like he hadn't slept in days. I hadn't been kidding about the bedtime thing. I was impressed he was even standing right now. "I've never heard of this Song of Solomon quest. And I definitely never heard anything about this fountain being constructed in Kansas City." He turned to look at me. "In fact, if I hadn't seen this picture, I would be forced to doubt your story."

I frowned at him. "What the hell is that supposed to mean?"

Cain was staring at the fire, unfazed. He'd been quiet for a while, fingering his dagger.

Roland shrugged. "I made a small Gateway to see for myself. There was no fountain."

I blinked at him several times, not sure what to make of that. "When did you look?" I didn't bother chastising him about the danger of his decision because he already knew it and had considered it worth the risk. And arguing wouldn't help me right now. Roland was on the verge of collapsing from exhaustion.

"When you two were in the shower." He stared at me with a troubled expression. "I didn't see any fountain. Just trees. Not even cleared earth. Not even a piece of trash on the ground."

There should have at least been two coffee cups if nothing else, because I had no idea when I had dropped mine. "That...doesn't make any sense. I saw the newspaper, the bus..." I explained the things I had seen, all talking about that park and the fountain. If anything, this only bothered Roland more.

Cain cleared his throat. "You didn't listen to me, Callie. I told you something was off. That place wasn't normal. I could feel it in my bones. And I never saw any of those signs before the fountain. Remember the newspaper?"

I sighed, remembering very well. Cain had seen none of the signs that had led me to the park. "Maybe we stepped through a Gateway of some kind. It would explain why I wasn't able to Shadow Walk us out," I said, trying to think of any explanation that made sense. "You might not have seen the signs, but you sure as hell saw Cleo. You cut her freaking *hand* off. And I warned you to keep an eye on her. I knew something was strange about her."

Cain stopped fidgeting with his dagger and shot me a confused look. "What are you talking about?"

"At the party," I snapped, growing annoyed.

He frowned harder, his forehead wrinkling. "You pointed to a pretty blonde woman. No one else was standing near her. No one," he said with certainty. "I never saw Cleo before she tried to kill us at the park." He lifted his dagger pointedly, the one he had been fidgeting with. "And for the record, there was no blood on my dagger after I cut her hand off. I remember because it shocked the living hell out of me."

101

The three of us were entirely silent for a few beats, not sure what to make of that. I remembered the confused look I had seen on his face right after. He was right. But at the same time, I had seen her blood spray in the air. "You also practically cut a guy's head off, remember? I know he bled all over the pool, because we sat in it for about thirty minutes."

Cain looked at me very seriously, and then pointed his dagger at my torn dress hanging before the fire. I turned to see...what the hell? No blood? That... wasn't possible. It should have at least been kind of pinkish. The dress had been pure white. Instead, it just looked dirty.

I turned back to find Cain nodding at me. He didn't look happy, but he looked determined to prove his point. "Weird, right?"

I nodded numbly, realizing I was staring back at the dress.

"We both went to the fountain, but now Roland can't find it..." Cain said in a low tone. "These Sons of Solomon want to kill you and can apparently stand in a party without being seen." He met my eyes. "I'm not a quitter or anything, but...we're facing long odds."

Roland spoke up. "What about Last Breath? You said he killed these Sons of Solomon. Perhaps he let you live on purpose?" he suggested. Neither of us replied. Last Breath hadn't seemed like the friendly type, so I wasn't banking on him being charitable.

"What do you know about him, Cain?" I asked into the silence.

Cain leaned back, letting out a frustrated breath. "It's all nonsense. He's the boogeyman. Someone dies a gruesome death without explanation? Last Breath. Someone infiltrates a compound to kill everyone inside? Last Breath. I don't have anything solid one way or another. Just enough urban legends to make your hair curl. The only reason I jumped on it is because he's said to be big, a white blur, and has piercing blue eyes. I saw that at the park, and six people silently died in a single heartbeat." He leaned forward, staring at Roland. "Last. Breath."

Roland turned to me, waiting for my input. "I've never heard of him, but I saw the same thing as Cain, and whatever that thing was, it was terrifying. I've never seen anything like it."

Roland sighed. "As much as I hate to admit it, I think I'm quite literally about to fall asleep on my feet, but I need to point out something to you, Callie. Part of this picture makes my skin tingle..." he said, tapping the paper.

I took one look at him and realized he was right. He should have been asleep an hour ago. I got to my feet, tugging the blanket tight around my shoulders as I studied where he pointed.

"Doors?" I asked Roland, not understanding. I glanced back at Cain. "Does that mean anything to you?" Cain thought about it for a few moments before shaking his head.

"It's capitalized every time it is used." Roland had an intense look on his face, looking at me expectantly. "I think you need to go to Abundant Angel," he finally added, eyes discreetly flicking to Cain to let me know why he wasn't speaking plainly. "Fabrizio might know something about these Doors from his time in Rome." That's when it hit me.

Roland had once shown me something in the basement of Abundant Angel Catholic Church. A room full of mysterious Doors hanging from chains. From the anxiety on Roland's face, I wasn't sure he was happy to suggest the idea. I could also see that he wasn't certain it would hold water, but...

I checked the printout again. Every single time it had been used, Doors was capitalized.

"Just a thought. Do you have any other leads?" Roland asked me tiredly.

I shook my head, thinking hard. I couldn't think of anything, and Roland was about to be dead weight, whether he wanted it or not.

"Cleo did mention her dislike of the Vatican. Maybe Fabrizio has some answers," Cain agreed. "Or maybe he knows more about the Sons of Solomon. Secret organizations started with the Church, after all," he said with a wry grin.

He wasn't necessarily wrong.

"What do you know about this quest, Cain?"

It was a long minute before he responded. "Solomon's Temple..." he began, "is a fool's errand. Like the Holy Grail. It only leads to pain."

"But it's *Solomon's* Temple," I enunciated. Then I pointed my thumbs at my chest, careful to keep my blanket in place so I didn't flash them. Both had seen the Callie product line in the shower, but that had been an exception. I wasn't Claire, flashing my goods left and right for a reaction.

"If it were that easy, there wouldn't be a quest in the first place. They would just give you the keys and say *welcome home, Callie.*" He turned a cold pair of eyes on me. "Get any keys in the mail lately?" he asked. "Because that would be super."

I scowled for good measure but shook my head. "No."

"Exactly. It's settled then. We go see the Italian."

Roland scratched at his chin pensively. "A mythical assassin and a mythical quest..." He glanced over at a clock in the wall and his face hardened.

The room was silent for a few moments before Cain spoke. "We should probably get dressed first," he suggested.

CHAPTER 21

I was marginally pissed off that I hadn't left a spare set of my leather, ass-kicking gear at the church, but at least I had my Darling and Dear boots and jacket to wear with my dark jeans and tank-top. I also had the Templar scarf, which could come in handy. I didn't dare make a quick trip home to change, because I wasn't sure using Gateways or Shadow Walking was such a grand idea. Even though the Gateway worked getting to Roland's, I wasn't really in the mood to chance it. I had a sneaking suspicion that it was a very bad idea, in fact…

I had finished dressing before Cain, believe it or not, so I had wandered down into the church proper, finding myself waiting by the Angel statue.

I kept my eyes on the statue, because it was easier than staring too closely at the shadowy ring encircling my finger. I considered my meeting with Michael, trying to decide if this quest had anything to do with learning how to use the Seal of Solomon, and how to get Nameless off my thumb for good. Probability was high that Solomon's *Temple* might have information about Solomon's *Seal*. And that meant I needed to win this trial.

The message had said there were two ways to enter—one on the earth, and one in the mind. As a wizard, I had extraordinary abilities. But where would they best be used? I didn't have the experience or knowledge the Sons of Solomon had, so did that mean I should try to beat them with the land entrance? Or with my magic—a type of mental power—should I try the mind? Maybe their knowledge was strictly of the Earth—old parchments, old locations, and things of that nature. Clues on Earth. Or it could mean their minds were bigger, and that I should stick to the Earth like a cavewoman, hitting rocks with my club until I found the entrance.

I really hoped Fabrizio had something for me. Because the circular arguments were making me dizzy, and I didn't currently have the brain-power for this level of mental gymnastics.

I also thought a lot about Solomon's Temple itself, if it might be the solution to finding my own purpose. It allegedly held all manner of wonders. Probably answers. I realized I was like those people who bought lottery tickets when the jackpot grew ridiculously high, fantasizing about what they would do when they won. I let out a sigh. Real rewards came from *work*.

And somehow, some way, I really wanted to outwork the Sons of Solomon.

Their very name was a lie. *I* was the heir to Solomon's Temple. I had the Seal to prove it. I didn't care how many books they had read about him. I realized I was breathing heavily, so forced myself to calm down. Maybe Dorian and Cain had a point about my wildly out of control anger. After this quest, I might have to look into anger management classes.

"Put your toys away," Roland said from behind me in a stern growl. I glanced back at him, realizing I had both the Seal of Solomon and the silver butterfly Nate had given me in my hands, like I was subconsciously considering asking the man for help—a place to start.

He did have a lot of archaic knowledge, and I would prefer asking him to Fabrizio. But…what if Nate asked to join me?

I didn't want that. I couldn't explain why, but this felt personal, and not just because of my relation to Solomon. No, something else about this whole thing seemed to stoke a fire deep within me. Perhaps it was my fear of Last Breath. Perhaps it was the challenge. Perhaps it was greed, not wanting to potentially have to share the prize with Nate Temple when I won.

I smiled absently, realizing I had phrased it as if it was a foregone conclusion, even though I had no idea where to start.

"You called Fabrizio?" I asked Roland, tucking the Seal and charm into different pockets.

Roland glanced down at his phone, grunted, and then pocketed it. "Yes. He's waiting."

"Good. I guess. Any words of advice? I don't want the Vatican involved."

Roland cleared his throat. "There's something you should know about Fabrizio, Callie..." Roland's eyes grew distant, perhaps respectful, but I also sensed a healthy dose of fear, as if Roland had only just now considered that he and Fabrizio stood on opposite sides of a line in the sand, whether they wanted it or not. That Fabrizio's apparent reputation was now a threat to him personally. "Fabrizio currently has the most kills of any Shepherd. And before you dismiss that, we were very, very close."

I arched a brow. "Oh."

"If anyone knows about Last Breath it would be him. And I really think you should press him on the Doors below the church. As Head Shepherd, he might know something I was never told. But remember, he stands for the Vatican, first."

He didn't sound frustrated or upset. But crimson fire was suddenly crackling over his knuckles, and he didn't seem to realize it. Was he being... protective of me?

"You do care about me, you filthy bloodsucker!" I teased.

He grunted, releasing his power immediately. I sensed a flicker of a smile on his cheeks, but it was soon replaced by frustration. I didn't even have to ask. He wanted to come with me but knew he couldn't. He might be a liability, having to sleep all day. And he hadn't been to the magic fountain. Barring all *that*, he had vampire drama to deal with, even if he denied it to me.

I had known him long enough to realize when he was hiding something.

Cain strolled up, studying us with a suspicious frown. His hand rested on the hilt of the long dagger on his belt, but sensing my attention, he flipped his shirt over it and lowered his hand to his side.

I realized they were both staring at me, waiting for my Gateway to Abundant Angel Catholic Church, where Fabrizio had moved in.

I slowly shook my head. "We should probably call an Uber a few blocks from here, because I think Last Breath can sense travelling. I don't want to invite him into the church by accident."

Cain looked uneasy at the thought of walking the streets or taking a car, but he gave a resigned nod after a moment. "Even if you're wrong, the risk of you being right is too high. He did show up immediately after you tried Shadow Walking."

I nodded. "He didn't knock on Roland's door after my Gateway, but if he sensed Shadow Walking at the fountain, maybe he can also track Gateways. If I'm wrong, you can tease me about it later. Plus, it's daylight. How scary can a walk be?" Cain gave me a frank look, but I ignored it. It didn't need to be said that Last Breath could be standing outside right now, waiting for us to exit the church. But with it being daytime, I was banking on the fact that he wouldn't attack us in the open. I simply couldn't take the chance of inviting him into Abundant Angel by using my magic to travel. Because it would piss off Fabrizio and likely get a lot of people killed if my suspicion was right.

Roland pulled his phone out of his pocket and handed it over to me. "I'll pick it up when you return. It's got the Uber app on it," he said.

And I wanted to kick myself for not even thinking about that. My phone had drowned. Duh.

Roland looked suddenly awkward, dry-washing his hands, and I saw Cain's face stretching into a wide grin. That's when I realized what the situation looked like—a dad sending his daughter off to college, trying to make sure she had everything she needed, and…

He didn't quite know how to say goodbye. It was…cute.

Then he suddenly wrapped me up in a tight hug, which was extremely unlike him. "Be safe, Callie," he grumbled. "I don't know how I would react if anything happened to you. If you don't come back…I may just drown Kansas City in fountains of blood," he promised in a very cold tone. Then he released me and took a step back.

He didn't smile. He didn't smile for so long that my own smile faltered and died.

Cain chuckled. "Maybe I'll just stick around here, then. Papa Roland isn't half as bad as you made him sound. He's positively delightful."

I shoved Cain towards the doors. "Don't joke about that, Roland," I warned him, turning to walk backwards out of the church. "I'm supposed to be the scary one."

Roland didn't apologize or take back his comment. He didn't laugh. He didn't smile. He just stared at me with those damning crimson eyes, and I knew that inside, his soul was screaming. That he had meant every word. I pretended not to feel the shiver that danced down my spine as I stepped outside and the door closed with a solid thud.

"Remember that look I told you he had on his face after you disappeared from the party?" Cain asked cheerfully. "That was it."

CHAPTER 22

$\mathcal{W}$e had walked a few blocks in the early morning light, and as a testament to our crap luck, the sky had opened up into a steady drizzle, getting us wet all over again. At least I was no longer wearing a dress, much more comfortable in my dark jeans, tank-top, and jacket. It was a relief when we climbed into the Uber, because every loud shout, engine backfire, or general street-ruckus had made us flinch, waiting for Last Breath or a Son of Solomon to jump out at us in the middle of broad daylight. Mainly because Cleo had somehow remained unseen at the party, blending in so fluidly that there had been no way to discern her from any other guest.

So, any casual pedestrian could be a threat.

I leaned back in my seat after a few minutes of directing the driver to ignore his GPS unit and take side streets. I realized I had been checking behind us, watching our fellow drivers for a tail. I would have been embarrassed, but Cain looked just as concerned—like we were bugs trapped in a box. We definitely didn't make our driver feel very safe, what with the thick paranoia we brought into the car with us, and I think he was relieved when we suddenly shouted for him to stop by a random laundromat. I hopped out first, but Cain lingered for a few moments before climbing out.

The driver didn't even ask for a good review before he took off.

We leaned against the wall of the laundromat—only a few blocks from our destination—trying to blend in with the foot traffic and get a read on the street life. Cain even lit a cigarette, watching the pedestrians across the street in apparent boredom.

"When did you start smoking?" I asked absently, keeping my eyes on the street.

He grunted. "Off and on for a few hundred years."

I frowned. "Why aren't they dripping wet?" I asked, remembering our plunge in the fountain.

He grinned. "I swiped these from the driver while I was threatening his dog's life if he ever mentioned our fare to anyone," he said in a peppy tone, puffing on his cigarette. "Cigarettes are great camouflage. People see what they want to see. Watch." He exhaled a cloud of smoke towards a couple walking by. They took one look at Cain's cigarette and the smoke, frowned slightly, and stepped wide, not even actually looking at our faces. Cain shrugged, his point proven. "A smoker is obviously *smoking*, whereas two people leaning against a wall with their hands in their pockets are doing something *nefarious*."

I nodded, folding my arms across my chest dramatically. "I thought you were quitting that nasty habit?" I snapped, loud enough to earn an approving smile from another woman walking with her significant other in the opposite direction.

Cain smiled, extinguishing his smoke. "There you go. Quick learner."

I rolled my eyes and began walking, making my way towards Abundant Angel a few blocks away. Almost there. We weren't far from Darling and Dear, but I didn't have time for their nonsense. I also didn't want to run into Phix. The Sphinx thought it was her job to treat me like her pet. If she showed up, everyone would run screaming in fear, and we probably wouldn't be able to talk her out of tagging along...wherever we ended up going—which could be a problem, depending on what Fabrizio said. She was most likely still out on her errand for Darling and Dear anyway, or she would have already ambushed me.

"What if Fabrizio can't help us?" Cain asked. I sighed, not having an answer. Cain patted me on the shoulder reassuringly. "It needed to be asked. I'm sure we would hear from the Sons of Solomon at some point or another," he said jovially. "Then we could just keep killing them until we learn what we need."

I arched an eyebrow at his ridiculous plan. "Let's make that our last option."

He shrugged. "Just spit-balling."

We rounded the corner, coming into more familiar territory. I glanced at Cain, pointedly. "I don't want to talk about it," he muttered darkly, recognizing the area.

"You know, when I first met you, around here, now that you bring it up," I said, pretending not to have heard him, "you seemed to have a lot more skills. You disappeared right before my eyes at Dorian's house, you could conceal yourself, even used a little bit of magic. But back at the fountain..." I trailed off suggestively. "The word *lackluster* comes to mind..."

Cain cursed under his breath. "I haven't been killing as often. It...powers me up. And I may have had a toy or two from Darling and Dear for some of that past stuff. Maybe."

I turned to look at him. "Really?"

"Some idiot girl talked me out of killing things. I've been reconsidering lately, since I'm learning she hasn't been practicing what she preaches..."

I scowled back at him. "Point taken," I finally admitted. Then I patted him on the back. "I'll keep you safe while you figure out how to get your mojo back."

We walked on in silence, and I found myself thinking back on the time I had chased Cain through a nearby alley. It was one of the first times I had used my Silver magic—granting me a strange, wondrously chromatic hue of the world before me. It had broken through Cain's concealment spell, and I'd been able to see a few milliseconds into the future—seeing Cain's avoidance tactics a moment before they had actually happened. I wondered if that form of sight could come in handy now, maybe pick out any Sons of Solomon in the crowd. Maybe even give me a clear vision of Last Breath's true form.

Pedestrians filled the street here, and I realized one was staring directly at me, smiling crookedly as if someone was using him as a puppet. My boots abruptly began to tingle.

I hadn't even noticed that I'd gripped the Seal of Solomon at some point in our walk. Cain hissed at me. "Whatever you're doing, I can *feel* it," he growled in a low hiss. "And if I can feel it, someone else probably can, too!" he warned.

I released the Seal rapidly, but it was already too late. The creepy guy smiling at me suddenly touched the shoulder of a woman beside him. He then promptly shuddered, lifting his head and frowning at me as if wondering why I was glaring at him.

The woman looked up at me sharply, cocked her head, and began to laugh as she strode right for me. "Hello, Callie. I've missed you," she said. My boots were tingling as they faced her, but no longer when they faced the previous guy—who now looked creeped out by the woman he had just touched.

Cain snarled at the woman, shoving me back as he jumped between us.

I wanted to crawl out of my own skin because the toes of my boots pinched when facing a Demon. But they had never tingled before.

"Samael," I breathed, more for Cain's benefit. The Demon I had freed from the Seal of Solomon had found me. But how? Was it from me fondling the Seal or something else? I'd touched the Seal a few times today with no consequence, so what had changed?

The woman continued smiling at me, head cocked oddly as she touched another pedestrian. He instantly reached out, walking through a crowd, and touched someone else.

Who touched someone else.

Then someone else.

Like a line of dominos, everyone began touching a fellow commuter in a dizzying blur so that I couldn't tell where Samael had ended up. I turned from person to person, searching for that grim smile. But everyone seemed confused at their subconscious decision to touch a random stranger, and then confused further to see that everyone around them wore equally confused expressions.

To find yourself in a crowd of alarmed, confused strangers was definitely unsettling. And the crowd was growing as more and more people stopped to see what the traffic was all about.

A small child suddenly lunged out from her mother's side and tackled Cain, hurling him into the glass window of a nail salon behind us with an obviously possessed force. Then she ran up to a pair of old men staring incredulously at the broken window and the sounds of the man cursing and growling within. The child tapped the man on the leg, looking for all the world like she was trying to get his attention.

Then she collapsed in a heap, and the old man looked directly at me, winked, and touched his buddy. You get the picture. A whole lot of bad touching was going on.

The child's mother shrieked in horror, scrambling to her daughter and snatching her up. She ran headlong into another growing swarm of startled onlookers, begging for their help.

The crowd stared from the sobbing child, to me, and then to the broken window, like I'd had something to do with all of it. If I had been feigning confusion like everyone else, I might have fooled them, but as it was...they were suddenly a concerned mob, and they looked on the verge of making a terrible mistake. Attacking me.

All because Samael was a prick, possessing their bodies just to toy with me.

Cain chose that moment to jump back through the window, glass shards falling from his shoulders, his hands and cheeks cut up from the attack. He locked eyes with me. "RUN!"

I did, hating myself for it.

I lowered my shoulder and barreled through the crowd, disgusted at the thought of any of them possibly being Samael in disguise, but I paid close attention to my boots, begging not to feel them tingle—ready to change course at even the slightest sensation. I glanced back over my shoulder to see Cain fighting a crowd of angry men, shouting at them to back down before they hurt themselves. Random outbursts of laughter sprang up from the crowd as Samael hopped from body to body, using them like sock puppets.

I flung a hand back, using the crowd around me to conceal my gesture, and flung magic backwards. A blast of air pummeled everyone to the ground, including Cain, but I knew he would be fastest back to his feet. "Stop fighting and run, Jackass!" I shouted. I saw him jump to his feet and run in the opposite direction from me, fleeing a crowd of angry men climbing to their feet to pursue him.

I heard sirens as a cop car skidded to a stop, two armed officers jumping out to demand what the hell was going on with the brawling pedestrians. One used a bullhorn to order everyone to stand down.

I ignored them, darting through the crowd, flinching at every touch, my heart racing as I studied faces for any smiles. My boots didn't tingle or pinch, but I knew Samael could simply start another chain of touches and end up ahead of me in an instant.

I slowed my pace as I reached the back of the growing crowd, brushing shoulders stiffly against anyone in my way, but doing my best to not draw attention since the police were obviously searching for someone suspicious and I didn't want the crowd turning on me. I finally broke free and settled on a brisk pace, heading towards the church as fast as I could while appearing casual.

"You can't run from me, Callie," a voice said from behind me. I spun, hands out to fight, but the little old lady staring at me from the edge of the crowd didn't move. Just grinned at me with a mouth of missing teeth. The toes of my boots throbbed as they faced her, and I walked backwards as fast as possible, keeping an eye on her hands. "We are family, and blood calls to blood," she said. "But don't worry. I don't want you dead. I want to *thank* you. I also wanted to wish you good luck on your little game. Because if you ever want to face me in the future, you *desperately* need to win. And I so desperately want to face off against you in the future..." The woman rubbed her gnarled hands together excitedly, her tongue lolling out the side of her mouth. "Just think of what good you could do with all that power. The power of the Doors at your disposal. I would offer you my assistance, but you've already got an associate of mine wrapped around your finger. Maybe I'll relay some advice to him now and then..." She cackled loudly, and then turned away, dipping back into the crowd.

I shivered, continuing to walk backwards, keeping an eye on any potential chain of pedestrians who would allow her touch to get ahead of me. It made me look like a crazy person, flinching around people as I practically ran backwards down the street.

I bumped into someone and spun with a squawk of terror, ready to rip their head off.

Cain gripped me by the shoulders, having exited from an alley directly beside me. "Easy, Callie. It's just me."

I wrapped him up in a hug—but only after verifying my boots didn't pinch when facing him—and let out a sob.

He draped an arm around my shoulder protectively and half-jogged me towards Abundant Angel Catholic Church down the block. His other hand rested on the hilt of the dagger at his hip. "How dangerous could a daytime walk be," he muttered sarcastically.

I nodded woodenly, still shell-shocked from Samael's appearance. "I didn't know he could do that," I said. "Why didn't he attack?"

Cain grunted, wiping some of the blood from his cheeks and wrist, and a few more shards of glass from his collar. He just had scrapes, and they were already healing. Figured. Immortals.

"He said he wanted to help me," I told Cain. "That he could get to me through this." I held up my thumb, showing him the ring of shadows.

Cain stared down at it uneasily. "Sometimes Demons lie..."

"And sometimes they don't..." I replied.

And I couldn't take the damned thing off. I hoped the church was strong enough to ward off Samael, or that Fabrizio would have some answers on this damned quest. Some answer as to how we should proceed.

Because the Sons of Solomon wanted me dead.

Last Breath wanted *everyone* dead.

And Michael and Samael seemed pretty invested in me winning.

CHAPTER 23

$\mathcal{T}$he basement of Abundant Angel Catholic Church was much fancier than the actual church above. The basement was also a big fat secret. A hidden keypad camouflaged in the ancient stone walls opened the seemingly decrepit locked hallway door that led downstairs. And my code still worked.

Bad, bad Vatican Shepherds.

As I made my way down the familiar stairs with Cain trailing behind, I couldn't ignore the sense of nostalgia that rolled over me. I'd trained here for more than a decade—learning how to use my magic as well as how to defend myself in the physical arena. From any and all flavors of monster.

Since, you know, pretty much everyone was assumed to be an enemy of the Church. Right or wrong, that was just the way it was. At least initially.

Yet here I was, walking down the steps of a secret military branch of the Vatican in Kansas City with mankind's first murderer. And I was no longer a dues-paying member of the Shepherds. For all intents and purposes, we did not belong in such hallowed halls.

Which was a strange feeling after Roland had spent so long training me here. And now neither of us were officially welcome in the very place we had called home for so long.

We left the stairs to enter a large training room with ridiculously tall ceilings, pillars, targets, platforms, mats, and a suspicious grate covering a large section of the floor.

It was the agility room where I had practiced evasion and maneuvering in my environment. Like a giant clock, the room shifted, adjusted, and moved in ways that forced the practitioner to basically become a ninja or suffer permanent injury. The pillars would rotate, drop, rise, shoot out spikes, and all sorts of other fun surprises. A hacker friend, Othello, had even shown me how to program it to my favorite music playlist—which took a lot of time, but was ultimately worth it. Like a form of meditation.

I'd trained here so often that the room of deathtraps was a pleasant memory. Even when flames shot out where you didn't expect them, or the ground disappeared beneath your feet earlier than you anticipated. Living a few moments off pure reaction and instinct was an adrenaline rush the likes of which I had rarely experienced in the typical aspects of a regular day. But free-running in here had been restricted until I had completed many years of training—when Roland had been confident enough I wouldn't kill myself trying.

We walked on towards the weapons room to find Fabrizio Donati waiting for us.

Fabrizio Donati was a bald, squat man who looked like someone you wanted to have a beer with. He held the title of First Shepherd—the boss of the other Shepherds roaming the world, but also the Shepherd in charge of Vatican City herself. He reported only to the Conclave, a group of seven old, prejudiced assholes who I wasn't too particularly fond of. Despite his other responsibilities as First Shepherd, Fabrizio had been sent to Kansas City to train Arthur, the newest Shepherd initiate since Roland and I were out of the picture.

Arthur was a homeless man I had once run into in an alley and, fearing he had seen me use magic, I had taken him to a nearby café—the same one Cain and I had visited a few hours ago. That moment had changed both of our lives. He had correctly guessed my true name.

To clarify that, I had always gone by Callie since it had been written on the card in my crib when I was found at the steps of Abundant Angel Catholic Church.

It was only years later that I found the crib stowed away in my adoptive parents' garage and, in a fit of teenage angst, I had destroyed the crib...

And found something very peculiar inside the wreckage. I couldn't definitively say it meant anything, but it had been one hell of a coincidence. Needing a bit of magic in my life, I had secretly adopted it—whether true or not. Like believing your real father was David Hasselhoff.

For example.

Although many had tried, no one had ever guessed correctly. Until Arthur, the humble, homeless man. Our friendship had blossomed after that, and he'd told me his own half-forgotten, half-remembered story. And then made me swear not to tell a soul. The jerk.

And it was a doozy. He wouldn't even let me ask him about it in private.

So, we each held the other's most private secret with nothing but our word.

I had been so impressed with Arthur that I had encouraged him to visit Father David at Abundant Angel for a meal, shower, and change of clothes. He had cleaned up so well that he seemed to transform into an adult Hilfiger model in the prime of his life and even weaseled Father David into giving him a job at the church. He'd been here ever since, working in any capacity the church allowed. And now he was Fabrizio's new student, training to become a Shepherd.

Coupled with what I knew about him...it was like watching an episode of the Twilight Zone.

But Arthur wasn't here at the moment, and Fabrizio looked ready to chew rocks.

Under his glare, I very seriously reconsidered my plan of asking for his help. Instead, I pointed a thumb at Cain. "Hey, Fabrizio. This is Cain. He killed a guy once."

"I know very well who he is," Fabrizio said, dipping his chin in a casual greeting.

Cain nodded back and then rubbed his knuckles on his chest as if polishing his nails. "Always happy to meet a fan," he said absently.

Fabrizio's face darkened a few shades right before my eyes.

Before things went sideways, I cleared my throat. "What's new, Meatball?"

He settled his rage fully on me this time, but his voice was monotone as he spoke. "Roland called. Forgot to mention a few things."

I didn't like the crazy look in his eyes. "Oh?"

He nodded. "Might have said something about the fires of Hell raining down upon me if anything happened to you. If you so much as earned a scratch while walking here." He glanced at my fingers. "You didn't happen to get scratched, did you?"

I shook my head silently.

"That's good. That's *really* good. You were supposed to be here an hour ago, by the way. That was another thing Roland warned me about. I think the consequence he gave me for that one was that he would personally turn me into a vampire and *then* kill me, just to guarantee that my soul went straight to Hell." He paused meaningfully. "Something along those lines."

Cain let out a single-note whistle that sounded like a bomb dropping from the skies.

I was shifting from foot to foot, both in shame and anger. It wasn't like it was my fault, but it also wasn't Fabrizio's fault that Roland had set such parameters. "I'm—"

"There's more," Fabrizio interrupted coldly. "In case I didn't fully comprehend the situation, Roland went on to tell me that he would next drown Kansas City in rivers of blood so deep and turbulent that the entire Conclave and every Shepherd would be needed to stem the tide of his wrath." Fabrizio was clenching his fists at his side as he paused. "All of *that* from a man I call a friend. Because of *you*."

Cain was silently mouthing the threats as if trying to commit them to memory for later use.

I lowered my eyes, facing Fabrizio. "He only told me he had called you…" I whispered. "I'm sorry you had to hear that from your friend, and I'm sorry for being late." I clamped my mouth shut, knowing that excuses needed to wait a minute, or twenty. Until he calmed down. I wasn't sure whether to be angry at Roland or…heartbroken.

Fabrizio let out a quivering breath, closing his eyes for a few moments. "I'm just glad that you're okay, Callie. I'll admit, I've known Roland for a very long time, and I've never heard him sound like that. Say things like that. He also doesn't make empty threats. When you didn't show up on time, I very seriously considered calling the entire Conclave here. The only reason I didn't was because I knew Roland was asleep and that your chances of survival between his church and mine were all but a guarantee." He paused, watching me intently. "Then I heard from Arthur, who was walking the streets in search of you. He caught the tail-end of your *walk*. And the aftermath with the police."

I grimaced. "Would it make you feel better if I told you that what happened on our walk was totally unrelated to Roland's threats?" I asked hesitantly.

Fabrizio—calm, solid, and a man of many laughs—looked like I had just punched him in the forehead. "Samael was in *addition* to what Roland was concerned about?" he asked in disbelief.

I nodded.

"What the *hell* have you gotten yourself into, Girlie?" he rasped, reverting to his nickname for me. I let out a breath of relief to hear him say it.

In answer, I held out the picture of the message at the fountain and told him the story.

Fabrizio walked over to the bar and uncorked a more than half-empty bottle of wine as he listened. He poured himself a liberal glass, not even asking if we wanted one. After I'd finished speaking, he stared down at the picture, reading it over and over again.

Cain eventually cleared his throat. "Roland mentioned you knew about some big D's..."

Fabrizio frowned at the bizarre statement, looking up. Cain was grinning from ear-to-ear, but it didn't look like the Shepherd had caught the joke.

"The Doors are all capitalized," I clarified, shooting Cain a dark look. He tapped his wrist and then shrugged, reminding me that time was of the essence. He had a point.

Fabrizio was already staring closer at the picture, his face paling. Bingo. Then he looked up at me. And when I say looked, I mean *looked*. "I need to show you something. Only you."

Cain instantly jumped to his feet, all traces of humor gone as he began shouting at Fabrizio, his fists clenched at his sides. "Oh, no you don't! I'm going with her, even if I have to tag along after her like a lost puppy. I will *not* lose another—"

He cut off abruptly and we both turned to face him, startled by both his explosive outburst and the fact that he had so urgently cut himself off. He still had his mouth open, and his face was beet-red. I'd given him hell before, but I'd never seen him embarrass *himself* so greatly.

"Another *what*, Cain?" I asked, frowning.

My last question snapped him out of it. He closed his mouth, breathing through his nose. I folded my arms, waiting. Seeing I wasn't going to drop it, he finally let out a long, uneasy breath. "Sibling," he all but whispered, staring down at his feet. "I was going to say *I will not lose another sibling*. I know we aren't blood, but I guess I kind of see you as—"

I tackled him hard enough to make him grunt since he hadn't been looking up to see me coming. We hit the mats and I planted a big, fat kiss on his forehead, blinking back my tears.

Not because he had called me sibling. He'd said that casually at the café. But this time, he had said it with *significance*, meaning it so strongly that it had caused him to react in a storm of rage.

And that was very important to me. It had meaning.

It meant he had unshouldered his lifetime baggage over his brother, Abel. Abandoned his guilt, truly, not just on the surface. He never would have reacted like that without coming to some internal decision that he was now ready to have a sibling again. A *real* sibling. Not a friend he had promoted to *sis* or *bro*.

Which was a huge fucking leap, people. Imagine that. From *his* shoes.

And per Dr. Michael, I also needed a family. Maybe I needed Cain as much as he needed me right now.

Cain struggled instinctively until I gave him another wet kiss on the forehead. Then I squeezed him into a tight hug, and he finally let out a hesitant sigh. When I felt him squeeze me back, I knew I had broken through the last of his defenses. That my gesture had welded a little bit of his soul back together—given him that reassurance he needed.

A *sibling's* hug. A *sister's* hug.

He had needed that hug for millennia, folks, but had never let anyone close enough to offer it. To grant him forgiveness for his past crime with Abel.

I climbed back to my feet and stared down at him, wiping away my tears and sniffling. He propped himself up on his elbows, grinning happily.

Then I kicked his elbow out from under him, knocking him onto his back. He gasped in surprise, glaring up at me in confusion.

"Sisters suck, Cain. You just made the biggest mistake of your life." Then I grinned at him, before rounding on Fabrizio. "My brother is coming with me, Meatball. Deal with it."

Fabrizio was watching Cain in amazement, picking up on the deeper meaning in what had just happened. I snapped my fingers to catch his attention.

He visibly started, looking embarrassed. "Right. The Cursed Doors... they started appearing the night you were found on the steps of the church."

CHAPTER 24

I realized I had sat down. I didn't remember doing it, but Cain was kneeling beside me, glaring at the Shepherd. He also had a hand on my shoulder. Fabrizio seemed oblivious, his eyes distant as he shook his head, murmuring to himself.

"Hey!" Cain snapped angrily. "This isn't a monologue."

Fabrizio froze, looking down at us with a frown. "Sorry. It's just…I can't help but wonder if this is fate…" he said softly. "That if you hadn't gone to Rome, I never would have met you. If Roland hadn't become a vampire, I never would have become First Shepherd, and I never would have been sent here." He met my eyes. "I wouldn't have been here to tell you the truth about the Doors. And I wouldn't have been here for Father David to confess his strange secret."

I felt goosebumps on my arms, wondering what the hell he was talking about.

"I'll try to tell it all in a way that makes sense. Bear with me, because I'm only just now seeing it in its entirety," he said, seeming to gather his thoughts.

I leaned into Cain as he sat down beside me, and we waited for Fabrizio to speak.

"Like all good stories, there was a storm," the First Shepherd said, smiling sadly. "And those Heavenly labor pains gave Abundant Angel her first child. You. Father David was battening down the hatches for the surprise storm when he heard a baby's cry and a banging on the front door of the church. He opened it to find you."

"I was there, along with two other Shepherds. Three Wise Men, as it were," he chuckled sarcastically. "We were passing through on an assignment, chasing down a dark wizard." I kept my face neutral but felt like I had just been slapped. Was he talking of my mother?

"You were here? You saw...me?" I whispered, my fingers shaking.

Fabrizio grunted affirmatively. "Yes. A bawling, white-haired babe. But we were Shepherds, not babysitters. Much too serious to give you anything more than a passing glance. We were more concerned with the bolt of lightning that Father David swore struck the church and killed the power," he said, mocking his younger self. "We went off in search of the circuit breakers and made a discovery. Father David had told us to enter the only door on the right side of the hallway to find the circuit breaker. But we found *two* doors on the right side of the hallway." he said, pointing in the direction of the door we had used to enter this very basement. My eyes widened in disbelief and he nodded slowly. "We explored this new door while Father David cared for the bawling babe."

He looked up at me apologetically, and I realized I was breathing faster. Cain placed an arm over my shoulders, squeezing tightly.

"Neither that door, nor the levels below the church, *existed* before that night..." he whispered, holding his hands up to display the training room around us. "We, of course, assumed it had just been missed—the church built atop ruins that had somehow been overlooked, but Father David was adamant about it. Finding a broken wall that led to a secret level was one thing, but finding a perfectly-functioning door that no one had never seen before?"

He shook his head and I found myself—against the impossibility of it all —nodding my agreement.

"That's when we found the lower cavern with the *Doors*. There were only three, then, one for each of us. We debated back and forth and ultimately decided to enter one. My fellow Shepherd, Anthony, stepped through one of the Doors and we waited to see what he found on the other side." He paused, his throat dry. "We waited a full day, but he never returned. My second brother decided to go after him, to save him. I waited three days, but neither returned. And every time I stepped away to sleep or eat, a new Door appeared until the cavern contained a dozen of them. I locked the place down and instantly called the Conclave to investigate—to update the prison cells we had found below, just in case. We spent weeks fortifying this place from attack, warding it from whatever occupied the other sides of the Doors. We sent more volunteers through the Doors, trying all of them. Some volunteers were armed to the teeth, some naked, some were wizards, some Regulars, some were women, some men. We tried everything." He met my eyes, his own haunted. "None ever returned."

I realized Cain was actually supporting my weight, now.

"We locked the area down for years, accepting our losses and hoping to find answers back in Rome in the Vatican archives. By then, you had been adopted, and no one ever connected your arrival with the phenomenon, so transfixed with the Doors and secret lower levels that a baby on the steps of the church was dismissed over the supernatural danger below."

"As above, so below..." Cain murmured under his breath, sounding shaken.

"To this day, no one has connected you to the Doors. But they also do not know about your lineage, your relation to *Solomon*."

"I'm not following," Cain said.

Fabrizio leaned closer as if he'd been waiting for it. "Before I went searching for the circuit breaker, I was out patrolling for that dark wizard in the rain. But I glimpsed something else entirely—reminding me of a drunken bishop's wild story I'd once heard and hadn't believed. That Solomon's Temple was guarded by a fearsome white nightmare with blue eyes of fire. I saw proof of it that night outside of Abundant Angel. It had no interest in me and vanished mere moments after I saw it. But the three aspects are now clear to me. The Last Breath had come to Kansas City. The same night as the Doors. The same night as *you*, Callie..."

I was shivering. Not in fear, but entirely overwhelmed. It was...*impossible*.

Cain cleared his throat. "You mentioned Father David telling you a story about that night..."

Fabrizio nodded uncertainly. "I do not know exactly how it fits in, so I left it for last. Father David kept this secret close to his heart for your entire life, Callie. He feared that, with all the hubbub about the Doors, and the Conclave and Shepherds running around the church in a panic, his story very likely could have brought you to harm. Even if just from fear. But seeing me—one who had been there that very night—back in Kansas City again after so many years reminded him of his lie of omission. He made me swear on my eternal soul that I would not tell anyone but you. If I thought you could handle it..."

I nodded, feeling numb.

Fabrizio took a deep breath, as if hesitant to continue. "Father David swears on the Bible that a Demon attacked the front door of the church the night you were found. And that, more than anything in the world, it wanted *you*. It screamed, and railed, and demanded to see you, scratching at the door and clawing at the steps. But it never entered, and when Father David checked the next morning, there were only faint scratches on the doors and steps, deep enough to be attributed to a stick in the storm, but definitely not a Demon. He even believed that it could have all been in his head, that fear overtook him as a result of the night's many other surprises. That is why he confessed to me. He did not know if what he heard was real or an imagined fear. But he repeated one thing several times, his reason for keeping this secret." He took a breath. *"No child should ever feel alone.* He thought the Shepherds would turn on you for the mere coincidence of it all, and so he refused to tell a soul. And back then...we were so afraid...I'm not sure he was wrong..." Fabrizio admitted with a guilty look.

I didn't respond. I didn't even look at either of them. I just sat there feeling numb. Long enough that I started to feel a faint flicker of fire inside me. A growing hatred. The beginning of a storm. And I wasn't quite sure what I wanted to do with it. So, I nurtured it in silence, focusing on my breathing.

Cain spoke, sounding eager. "Fuck the Demon. Can't even claw a door properly."

I turned to him and smiled, feeling suddenly anxious to move. To do anything but sit still. "Thank you."

He nodded matter-of-factly, turning back to Fabrizio. "If that Last Breath guards Solomon's Temple and appeared when these Doors did, the same night a descendant of Solomon is left on the steps of this very church..."

Fabrizio nodded, speaking the thought that had just entered my mind. "You might have your path to Solomon's Temple..."

I wasn't sure if it was the path of the mind, or the path of the Earth, but I knew it was one of them. "Show me these Doors." I eyed the weapons on the walls. "I think it's time we arm ourselves."

Cain was nodding. "And if Fabrizio can guard access to the Doors from the church, we don't have to worry about the Sons of Solomon chasing after us."

Fabrizio nodded, but held up a finger. "There is the question of *why* they hunt you. They should have more pressing matters to attend with the trial in play. Unless they know of your lineage, or think you have something they need. Knowing that answer may give you what you need."

I thought about it, frowning. The Seal of Solomon in my coat suddenly felt like a mental lead weight. I held it up for them to see. "Maybe they need this?"

The two men stared at the Seal for a time. Cain finally shrugged. "I mean, it makes sense, but if they know you have it, why wouldn't Cleo have asked for it when we were at the park?"

"She must not have known," I said, shrugging.

"Back to the original question, then. Why hunt us down?"

We considered it in silence for a few moments. Finally, I shrugged. "It doesn't really matter, does it? All that matters, is that they want to kill us, and Last Breath wants to kill everyone playing the game. Which makes no sense, by the way. If he works for the Temple—which is hosting this whole trial—why kill the participants?"

"Maybe he is protecting the one participant who *matters*," Fabrizio offered gently.

Cain frowned thoughtfully. "That actually makes a lot of sense. He didn't kill us this morning. He could have, but he didn't."

"Let's consider that a happy ending, but plan for the worst," I said, eyeing the walls of weapons all around us.

Fabrizio smiled at my interest. "Perhaps the Seal of Solomon will grant you some protection, but I always like to have a good knife, or seven, on me." He snapped his finger at a new thought. "Oh, natural items only. We tried sending a video camera through and it exploded. The equivalent of an incendiary grenade," he added meaningfully.

I shrugged. "Magic is fine, right?"

"As far as we can tell. The wizards didn't burst into flame."

"They just never returned," Cain added grimly. "Perhaps their explosions were on the other side."

I scowled at him. "Gee. Thanks for that lovely image."

He shrugged, not looking the least bit ashamed. "Call 'em like I see 'em. We're very likely committing suicide by stepping through. No use in sugar-coating it. And your magic was wonky this morning."

"No one is killing me but myself," I said defiantly. "That will show them."

Cain grinned. "Word." I checked myself to make sure I had no electronics on me. I set Roland's phone down, realizing I was embarrassingly low-tech. Othello would have been ashamed.

Then I made my way around the room, debating. I didn't know what I would find on the other side, but it was smart to plan for the worst. I'd learned firsthand that mortal weapons were the great leveler. Using magic was cool and all, but most wizards never anticipated a dagger coming for their sclera while having a magical standoff. Like throwing dirt in someone's eye in a knife fight. I also didn't want to overburden myself in case we needed to move quickly.

I settled on a few wooden stakes with silver tips, and a gleaming *katana*. The blade had been designed to excel when victory depended heavily on rapid response times. The curved Japanese sword was just under two feet long, and the hilt was long enough to use with two hands for extra strength. I scooped up the belt-like sash, also known as an *obi*, and tied it around my waist. I tucked the katana through the sash with the sharpened edge of the sword facing up. The *wakizashi* that paired with the katana was identical in all aspects, merely shorter in length. Even though the two were typically worn in pairs like the ancient Samurai had done, I left the smaller blade on the stand, deciding to respect the fact that, traditionally, only Samurai had earned the honor of wearing them paired together—the *daishō*, they called it.

Samurai were honorable, noble men, devoting their life to being good. And right now, I didn't feel like being honorable or noble. In fact, I was pretty pissed off. More secrets about my past, and an asshole assassin forcing me enter into a game, so he could try to kill me for entering. And the prize was something that had belonged to my ancestor, so why was I even competing for it in the first place? It should have just been handed to me as an inheritance.

I tucked a few wicked throwing knives into my boots for good measure.

I didn't go overboard because I also had a new Big Brother to back me up, and he was formidable. An Incredible Cain. I turned to him, expecting to see a metal porcupine of death.

My hopes were dashed almost immediately.

He had chosen two long daggers. I noticed one sheath was empty on his belt. "At least grab one sword," I chastised. "Haven't you done this before? You're going to embarrass me if we find ourselves in a sword fight."

He smirked, holding up a finger. "I do have one more, now that you mention it."

He knelt on the ground and closed his eyes as if praying. He began murmuring under his breath, and I shot a look at Fabrizio. The Shepherds shook his head curiously, watching Cain's suddenly religious side come out of the closet.

Then Cain let out a deep breath and placed his right hand over his left forearm and squeezed. After a moment of intense pressure, I saw blood dripping from between his fingers. I gasped, taking a step back, resting my hand on the hilt of my katana.

Then Cain began to pull at something and I almost vomited as he withdrew a curved ivory bone from his very flesh. He gritted his teeth, grunting in pain as the blood flowed faster. Finally, he pulled out a curved bone dagger with a serrated edge.

I blinked. Was that...

Cain finally opened his eyes, letting out a forced breath. "This is my blade. There's no other like it," he said with a weak grin, climbing to his feet.

I stared. Wow. It was the blade he had used to kill his brother, Abel. Since we were about to potentially commit suicide and I had only gallows humor on the tip of my tongue, I risked an inappropriate observation. I turned to Fabrizio. "Maybe he's born with it. But maybe it's Abel-line."

Fabrizio blanched, shaking his head at me.

Cain grunted. I risked a glance at him and found him fighting to hold back a smile. "Okay. That was pretty good," he finally admitted. "And what the hell? If you can't joke about it after this long, when can you?"

I grinned. "Let's do this. Show us the Doors, Meatball."

We followed Fabrizio into an elevator and Cain patted my shoulder. "Think this will work?"

I thought about it and finally let out a sigh. "It's either this or wait for the Sons of Solomon to catch me outside. Or Samael. Or Last Breath."

"And it does seem oddly coincidental about these Doors, almost like they were made for this very moment."

I gave him a serious look. "That doesn't mean we have a free pass. Otherwise there wouldn't be a game, as you told me earlier. Like it or not, this is a challenge. We need to be ready for anything."

Fabrizio typed in a code on the electronic keypad and the elevator began to move. He gave Cain a distasteful look. "You're going to need to hold my hand when we step off this elevator."

"Yeah?" Cain said, ignoring my laugh.

"Or the wards will incinerate you." The First Murderer stiffened.

"Oh. Then I guess we're *those* kinds of friends, now..."

I laughed even harder.

CHAPTER 25

*C*ain and Fabrizio stared up at the hundreds of doors hanging suspended by chains before us, still holding hands. I wished I would have at least brought Roland's phone down this far to snap a picture.

"You can stop holding my hand, now," Fabrizio muttered.

"You sure?" Cain asked doubtfully. "I can still feel them probing me," he said, shivering at the way he had described the sensation of the wards, as we walked through the stone passageway on our way to this cavern. Luckily, Roland had previously added me to the VIP list, so I had access to this area without any hand-holding.

"The wards cover the halls, not this place. We didn't want to place them too close, just in case they reacted with…whatever these are," he said, gesturing at the doors.

Cain very slowly unclasped his fingers, holding his breath. When nothing happened, he let out a sigh of relief. I chuckled, staring up at the doors, recalling the first time I had been here.

The stone cavern was huge, climbing high above our heads. They resembled doors from all time periods, eras, and styles; some made of wood, stone, marble, glass, and even metal. As I scanned them, none particularly stood out because of how varied they were. Well, except for the beaded curtain one. That looked sinister. I spotted a charred, blackened door.

Fabrizio noticed my fixation and gave me a nod of confirmation. So. That was the one they had sent the video camera through.

"Roland told me a different story about that door. Something about a welcoming committee waiting on the other side."

Fabrizio's lips tightened. "That is the official story, yes," he admitted guiltily. I grunted, once again reminded that the Vatican was not to be trusted.

Dozens of the doors spun lazily from their chains at different speeds while others remained entirely static.

No torches lined the walls, but the room was illuminated somehow—kind of like how some nights weren't as dark as others, even though the moon wasn't entirely visible. Just a pale glow reflecting off the chains, doors, and stone walls. Cain murmured something unintelligible, shaking his head. "That's a lot of options to choose from…" he said dubiously.

He wasn't wrong. I picked out a few doors wrapped in glowing, golden chains with locks that prevented them from opening, recalling Roland's explanation—likely another lie fed to him by his lords and masters.

Huge runes were carved into the floor, and I once again studied them, recognizing them as Enochian script—the language of the Angels. I didn't see any that looked like my name or some other obvious clue as to what I needed to do next. No *welcome home* mat or anything.

I turned to Fabrizio. "I assume everything else Roland told me was a lie —about these leading to repositories all over the world. Even other realms."

Fabrizio hung his head. "Since it was impossible to move them in any way, we locked up the Doors that appeared on their own," he said, pointing to those wrapped in chains. "Then we hung a hundred plain doors from the ceiling to fill out the space, knowing that if anyone opened one and stepped through the empty space we could just say *we lost the ability to use that one.*"

I cursed under my breath, hating that Roland had been suckered in by the Vatican. That I had been right to distrust them and not have blind faith in them. "How considerate of you."

Fabrizio's face darkened as he slowly rounded on me. "I lost many friends to these fucking Doors, Callie. Remember that. If I can save a life by fucking lying a little, so be it. But tell me what you would have done differently before you tar and feather me," he said, fists clenching and unclenching at his sides.

I let out a frustrated breath and finally nodded in what vaguely passed for an apology.

"Do any of them actually work?" Cain asked.

I found myself nodding. "Roland told me one led to Rome. We almost used it to attend the trial with Paradise and Lost. When I first met you."

Fabrizio nodded. "That one actually does work, but it took many years to perfect, and only works on those granted access. Blood, sweat, tears. It has to be keyed to the individual."

I scowled. "So, that is why you had Roland give you samples of my essence. To help pull off your trick." I took a deep breath, closing my eyes. "I get it. I'm not happy about it, but I get it. And no, I can't think of anything else I would have done in your place," I finally admitted.

The devious scheme was actually very clever. Have all the Shepherds provide their essence, so the door would work. And if that door worked, then all the other stories must be true as well. *Don't forget about the dangerous ones, they will kill you. And we can't tell you which ones are the dangerous ones. Above your pay-grade.*

I glanced at Fabrizio. "What if someone—hypothetically—chose to ignore your warnings and test out a door, somehow disproving your claim?"

I scratched at my arm absently, concealing my thumb from view. It hadn't been particularly cold recently, but it had most definitely turned warmer than usual at some point in the last few moments. And such a change felt as significant as if it had caught fire compared to its usual constant chill. Was Nameless reacting to a man of God? Or maybe, just maybe, it had something to do with the big Enochian script three feet away.

Fabrizio smiled humorlessly. "Someone like you, for example," he said drily. "The ruse would likely be up. They would continue testing doors until they got to the wrong one and disappeared forever, I would imagine," he admitted. *"Lead us not into temptation...* Which is why we threaten excommunication and execution for any who dare attempt to use a door without permission. For extra protection, we warn that using the doors could unlock the door from the other side, allowing whatever lives there to cross over here into our fortress. Even the ballsiest of Shepherds doesn't want to be responsible for letting a monster into their own church."

I grunted. He had a point. Ultimately, they would be hunted down or test the wrong door and die. Fear was the great motivator. Either way, problem solved.

"What about these runes on the ground? What are they? I can sense their power," Cain asked. Since everything I knew had been a lie, I waited for Fabrizio to preach some gospel on the matter.

Fabrizio studied them with a shiver. "Those are *very* real. Protection runes cast by all seven of the Conclave." He was silent for a moment. "But who knows if they would protect us from whatever lives on the other side? None have returned to let us know, so we simply did our best."

I studied the doors above us, trying to find some pattern. I counted the ones Fabrizio had pointed out, those wrapped in chains. Twelve. I scanned the other doors, analyzing them thoroughly—at least those I could clearly make out.

The shadow ring around my thumb throbbed colder for a moment and I pointed. "That one goes to Rome," I said, not entirely sure why—whether it had been me or the ring dictating the guess. That alone made me shiver, remembering Samael's comment about influencing me through the ring.

Fabrizio was staring at me. "Did Roland tell you that?" he asked very softly.

I shook my head, not meeting his eyes. Instead, I studied the castle-like door with the metal rivets across the beams that led to Rome. There were several other similar ones that physically matched, but something about this one…I could almost hear singing as I stared at it, like a choir.

I finally shook my head and looked away. Cain was frowning, eyes darting from me to Fabrizio, wondering exactly what had just happened. His hand also rested on the hilt of the bone blade in a familiar gesture. I wasn't sure if he was aware how much his face transformed when he touched it. His features became both more feral and more relaxed.

Like it was a part of him. Maybe it centered him, made him feel complete. I wasn't sure, but I would keep an eye on it. Because even though it seemed to calm him, his eyes also had a dangerously wild look to them.

"I hope you have a ladder or something," Cain said.

I scratched at my arms, feeling like I was overheating.

"Actually…we don't. We used pulleys," Fabrizio said, pointing to an alarmingly weathered setup on the side wall. I didn't feel like trusting myself to them. I stared up at the twelve doors, thinking furiously. Which one? If I could only see them closer, maybe touch them…

My forearms began to tingle noticeably, and my ring of shadows grew colder against my thumb, reacting to whatever had made my arms tingle. I scowled at my appendage. On principle, I wasn't pleased that my body could have an argument with itself when I didn't even know why. It was ridiculously unfair.

"Which door?" I mumbled to myself, my lips suddenly feeling numb.

Cain asked Fabrizio something about Last Breath, but I was too focused on the sensation rippling through me. The cold, the heat. Back and forth, back and forth…

"…maybe a lion of some kind. I know how ridiculous it sounds…"

My teeth began clicking together as my whole body shuddered. I was squeezing my arms, now, and realized I was staring at the shadows in the cavern, feeling slightly nauseated. I touched my forehead and felt it was slick with sweat. Fabrizio suddenly stood before me, looking alarmed as he touched my cheeks. I was simultaneously sweating and freezing. "Callie, are you feeling okay?"

I shuddered again, my vision beginning to tunnel as if I was dehydrated and had stood too fast. Cain began to growl from where he stood near the pulleys, but I wasn't sure if it was because he sensed something or if he was just reacting to my apparent meltdown. My thumb suddenly froze, and I gasped as my vision shifted into a world of chrome shades.

One Door among the twelve seemed to glow like polished silver, brighter than the rest, which merely looked gray and dull—still metallic, but not as brilliant. The hundreds of other doors were simply a weak, pale gray.

I pointed at the polished Door, my arm shaking with cold. I realized I was gripping the Seal of Solomon in that fist. The door began to rattle and dance on its chains, tugging and popping the links as if something was trying to break free from within. Cain and Fabrizio began to shout in alarm as the Door abruptly snapped free, molten shards of hot metal chain zipping out in every direction, splintering any adjacent decoy doors to shreds or igniting them in flames. The Door crashed to the ground about three feet in front of me, landing perfectly on its edge, even embedding an inch into the stone, but not damaging or impeding the door itself. The rock floor around it singed upon contact—even one of the powerful runes the Conclave had spent so much time finger-painting was destroyed.

"I think we know what her silver ring does now," Cain told Fabrizio.

I shifted my hand to touch those golden chains and they puffed to vapor like smoke.

It comes. RUN! Nameless screamed from within the furthest corners of my mind, making my thumb bone ache at the sudden arctic chill.

I heard a metallic screech—like nails on a chalkboard—from down the passageway. The elevator. Someone was scratching at the elevator. I locked eyes with Fabrizio—his face now just a tapestry of chromatic hues. He looked shaken, alarmed, and furious. No one but Fabrizio and Roland had the code to the elevator for this floor, and I hadn't heard the elevator *leave* our floor.

"Run…" I heard myself whisper, repeating Nameless' internal warning. But I realized that it was hopeless. The only way left to run was down the passageway…

Towards the scratching sound.

We were all staring at the passageway, Cain gripping the hilt of his bone knife with a permanent snarl, his lips pulled back to reveal his teeth. Then I heard the sound of rapidly scratching claws, as if something was running towards us on all fours.

Cain appeared to be frozen, his body bending low as if to crouch at half-speed, even though my movement felt entirely normal. Cain's mouth began to open as if he was roaring, but in slow motion.

A ball of flame gradually flickered to life in Fabrizio's outstretched hand, proving that something funky was happening with reality. Just like when Michael had abducted me, time had abruptly decelerated.

Then it hit me. I'd seen my vision do this before. When I'd been chasing down Cain through an alley so long ago. The Silver. *Time* hadn't slowed, my *perception* had quadrupled.

I flung out my hand, sending a swarm of Silver butterflays down the passage, hoping to deter the attacker long enough to get Fabrizio out of here. I heard a feral, coughing snarl—not sounding remotely affected by the strange distortion to time—as I ripped open a Silver Gateway directly behind Fabrizio. The runes at our feet suddenly flared in warning, smoking at the use of a Gateway in such a heavily warded place.

Shit. Forgot about the Conclave's finger-painting.

Fabrizio's pulse throbbed in his neck about once every ten seconds, proving the time distortion for everyone but myself and our attacker. I hoped it also delayed the defensive runes.

I grabbed Fabrizio and shoved him through the Gateway, having no idea where I had just sent him. Because Silver Gateways were based on need, not rational thought. It had to be better than his current location. Next, I released the Gateway, grabbed Cain, and then jumped through the open Door, ramming my shoulder into it like I was a one-woman SWAT team raiding a known drug house. I caught my thumb on the frame and it flared with pain, but I bit back my cry.

At the last moment, I glanced back at the passageway to see a four-legged creature stalking towards us, its head hanging below its shoulders like a stalking lion. Or a tiger. It was still just a white blur, although I would recognize those flaming blue eyes anywhere.

Last Breath. I took that as a sign that we were on the right path.

And that we were about to pay dearly for it.

If the creature had opened the door to get down here in the first place, I knew our security wasn't going to hinder it. How it had even found the church, or that I was in it was a mystery.

Was it tracking my Seal? Had it sensed the Fallen Angel on my finger? Or something else? It had killed those Sons of Solomon earlier, but had looked directly at us in the fountain and hadn't attacked. Had it not seen us? What had changed?

It stared only at me, completely ignoring Cain and the rest of the cavern.

I fell through the Door, shoving Cain ahead of me, and then stared back at the figure hunkering low as if preparing to leap at me. The time distortion definitely wasn't impacting Last Breath. Those twin blue flames were not pleased.

The Door slammed shut and we landed on cold stone in a strangely familiar place.

CHAPTER 26

I panicked for a moment, eyes flicking about the room for any sign of Last Breath, but we were entirely alone. Cain grunted, rolling up to his feet, spinning back and forth with wild eyes, not understanding what had just happened—or comprehending our current location.

We were in the cavern of Doors we had just left.

But with a few differences. No runes decorated the floor, and only three Doors hung from the ceiling. There were no pulleys on the wall. The Door we had just exited clicked shut high above, at least twenty feet in the air. I was suddenly thankful we hadn't landed on our necks from such a height. In fact, I didn't even feel a bruise from our fall.

And more importantly, Last Breath had not pursued us. I could make out a faint hymnal song in the air, like it was being carried from far off in the distance, but I also sensed that it was the place itself—part of the air, not truly a song being sung in the distance. It was powerful, like a flavor of magic.

Cain gripped my shoulder. "What about Fabrizio?" he demanded. "He's a sitting duck back there!" he hissed, panting. "Who attacked us?"

I squeezed his arms reassuringly, trying to calm him. He hadn't seen me send Fabrizio through the Gateway. Because his sense of time had been messed up.

"Easy, Cain. *Easy.* Take a deep breath. Fabrizio is fine. Last Breath came for us, but I sent Fabrizio to safety. Last Breath did something to you guys to mess with your sense of time," I said, not knowing for sure whether it had been Last Breath or myself.

Cain took a deep breath, closing his eyes for a moment as he lowered his dagger. He finally shook his head. "Okay. I heard the claws on stone, but never saw anything. Did you get a good look at Last Breath this time?"

"Maybe…" I said, pursing my lips. "He looked like some kind of cat. Or a four-legged creature with a long tail, at least. It was still hard to tell. But it was definitely Last Breath. Same blue eyes. But wherever we are, it didn't follow."

Cain nodded jerkily, eyes darting about the room in newfound recognition. "What happened to the other Doors?" he asked anxiously.

"We went through a Door and ended up here. It's the same cavern," I told him, studying the room. My pulse suddenly began to quicken, and my stomach dropped. "I think this is…the night the Doors first appeared…" I whispered, suddenly realizing what that meant.

The night I had been left on the steps of the church.

Somewhere high above me, baby Callie lay crying in a small crib on the steps of the church, terrified of the lightning and rain. My vision seemed to rock, and I almost lost my balance. Cain caught me immediately, following my train of thought and knowing my sudden reaction for what it was.

A grating sound made us flinch, spinning to face an attack, imagining the worst horrors possible in this strange…dimension, or plane of existence. Was this real? Or a dream fragment of some kind?

A black quartz obelisk—flecked with metallic veins of silver and gold—rose from the floor, dust and gravel crumbling until it grew as tall as a man. Then, silver script flared into existence across its surface.

Well met, Traveler. You have taken the first step towards the treasure trove of knowledge I have amassed. Know that you are firmly on this path, now, and the only way outward is onward.

Cain shot me a brief, incredulous look, lowering his dagger, but we didn't dare risk missing the rest of the message, because the first lines were already fading as the message continued, only showing several lines at a time.

You have chosen the path of the mind—the tougher, more arduous path—over the path of the Earth. This implies you seek more than material wealth, which is commendable, but with greater rewards comes greater risk. I do not envy your decision but applaud your fortitude.

Cain shot me the frankest look of accusation I think I had ever seen. "Shortcut my ass," he muttered, folding his arms.

"Shut up, Cain," I snapped defensively. "The magical rock phallus is talking." But part of me also wanted to throttle Fabrizio's neck as well. Of course, a magical Door hanging from a chain in a mysterious cavern had been a terrible idea. It made so much sense in hindsight. But we'd really had no other choice.

Knowledge requires sacrifice—ironically, memories. The mind of man can hold only so much information, after all. A grail can only hold so much water before overflowing. Only so many thoughts can fill a man's mind.

But in a thought lies the keys to existence, to life itself.

For what is existence, but a single thought from God?

I shared a look with Cain. The magical rock phallus was deep. *Existence was nothing but an errant thought of God?* Wow. That put things into perspective.

Doors will litter your path, and behind each is a different gift. An immediate gain or a delayed gratification—but either gift requires a sacrifice, a memory. There are no single correct answers to this quest, as it is tailored by God and his Angels to each Traveler. An immediate gain may sometimes be the wisest choice over a delayed gratification. Likewise, a delayed gratification may sometimes be the wisest choice over an immediate gain.

Your choice is to find the right Doors that lead to your ultimate desire—knowledge or power. Truth or fiction. Behind each choice is a consequence. But consequences are sometimes known as penance, so be steadfast. Momentary failures might be required for a future gain. Yet momentary successes might be required to prepare you for a future loss. To earn you enough to pay a future price for something you covet most dearly.

Behold the lesson of Free Will, in all her glory.

Godspeed.

The words slowly faded from view, but we continued staring at the obelisk for a few more moments, wanting to be certain no additional advice was forthcoming. Nothing else appeared.

"Well, at least it wasn't ominous," Cain finally grumbled.

I nodded in agreement. But there wasn't any use complaining about it. We were stuck here, wherever *here* was. I took a nervous breath and made a ball of flame in my palms, ready to extinguish it in an instant if it set off any alarm bells. It worked, and nothing deadly happened. Then I tried creating a Gateway the size of my fist—only big enough to see through—thinking of the steps of the church above. It worked, about a gallon of rain pouring through the opening from the storm outside.

I released it with a nervous laugh. It really was the same night. It had to be!

Cain grunted from a pace away, pointing down at the ground. A skeleton sat propped against the wall. I frowned, thinking furiously. Then it hit me. "Is that…Fabrizio's friend?" I asked in a whisper.

Cain knelt down and used his dagger to shift the man's threadbare shirt. It revealed a cross hanging on a chain around the skeleton's neck. He glanced up at me with a somber look. "It seems plausible."

I crouched beside him, flipping over the crucifix pendant. The initials *A.D.* were etched into the back. I stared at them for a long time, thinking of Fabrizio's story. This had to be Anthony. I hesitated for a moment before lifting the pendant from the skeleton's neck. Thankfully, it came free without knocking Anthony's skull off, and I placed it around my neck, so I wouldn't lose it. I turned to Cain with a shrug. "Maybe I can give it to Fabrizio. Put his mind at ease. At least for his friend Anthony…" I said, thinking of the other Shepherd, Luke.

Cain nodded. "What do we do, now?" he asked, tucking the blade into his belt.

"I think we should go check on the…baby," I whispered. "It will at least confirm if we're here the night all this happened."

Cain nodded, but in his eyes was an obvious concern. Was my head in the game, or was I too close to this world around us? I took a deep breath, trying to center myself.

I honestly didn't know the answer, but I could almost hear a baby crying —like a chorus between the verses of a faint hymnal song woven on the fabric of the air.

CHAPTER 27

I opened a Gateway again, this one large enough to step through, and stared out at a dark city street. Rain pelted the pavement and the skies exploded with light that threatened to strike any number of the tall buildings around us and was accompanied by great thunderous booms. I saw a billboard advertising a new movie titled *First Knight*.

The sight struck me like a blow to the jaw. It was a new movie about the abduction of Guinevere, featuring Sean Connery as Arthur and Richard Gere as Lancelot. From the mid-90s. I peeled my eyes away from the billboard, feeling strangely uncomfortable for some reason. It was important somehow…

We really were here in the past; the night I had been left on the church steps.

In fact…

I could hear myself crying in the darkness. Me as a baby.

Rain pelted down, hard enough to attempt to wash Original Sin from the streets of Kansas City, Missouri.

Hard enough to terrify a small baby girl as she was abandoned to face a dark, terrible world without her parents—the two people in the world who should have protected her, kept her safe, loved her, taught her to overcome her fears, comforted her with her first broken heart, taught her to drive her first car, guided her through her first use of magic, perhaps even take her to church.

But none of that would ever happen.

Because they loved their babe *too much* to hold her close to their breasts.

Loved her *enough* to leave her—cold, crying, soaking wet, alone in a world that wanted to destroy her very soul, and gobble her up.

For God so loved the world, that He gave His only begotten Son...

I spun frantically to stare up at the Church. Thunder and lightning cracked across the sky, chaotic enough to reveal long, demented arms of light connecting with each other, growing and snaking and expanding from one to the next in seconds-long explosions of raw power. The very ground shook like there was a succession of mortar shells striking the earth.

And I saw two shadows slip from the front steps of the church, racing away into the darkness. One supported the other, seeming to force the other to run from the steps no matter what it desired.

And above the baby crying, I heard the anguished sound of two parents doing their best to hold themselves together—soul-deep sobs sounding like they were being torn into thirds.

"My parents..." I rasped, blinking heavy tears from my eyes.

Then they were gone, before I could even think to consider chasing them down, to stare into their eyes for the first time, to tell them that I had *made* it.

That I'd fucking conquered this thing called life and that I...

Understood their decision.

Then another thought hit me.

"The Demon," I breathed, suddenly remembering Father David's story about the Demon that had attacked the door to the church. What if it had been Last Breath?

What if he was the Demon? What if this place was different than the one I knew? What if the only reason Father David had opened a door to see the baby was because...

Someone had battled the Demon long enough for Father David to *hear* the baby crying in the first place. That someone had defended the baby long enough for Father David to save her.

What if *I* needed to save *myself*?

Cain cursed as I bolted away from him, towards the front door of the church, to the tiny, fragile crib I could see sitting on the top steps.

I never ran so fast in my entire life. Never. I needed to save the baby. To save myself.

But...

I suddenly realized that I also needed to *see*. To see *myself*. To try and administer all the love of the world in a single glance.

To give that sweet, terrified, innocent, forgotten and abandoned baby the armor she would need to *fight*.

To stare into those baby blue eyes and tell that tiny, terrified child that she would grow up safe with a family who loved her more than anything else in the world.

That the raging storms that now terrified her would soon become a favorite pastime of her new daddy—that he would hold her in his big, strong arms to watch the infamous Midwest storms with her, sipping hot cups of cocoa with tiny marshmallows as they sat on a rickety porch together, huddled under a warm blanket...

That her new dad would love the Kansas City Royals slightly less than he would love her, which was saying a lot...

That her mother would get really sick one day, but that it would be okay. The world would keep turning, just with one less laugh to echo across the mountains and the oceans and the fields...

That she would meet a Man of God, and that he would teach her wondrous, magical things...

That she would befriend a snarky blonde-haired stick of a girl who loved teddy bears and animals of all kinds, and wanted to take care of them...

That she would save a heroic, downtrodden, forgotten man living in an alley, and help him remember his own magical story, rekindling the fire of his very soul and giving him a purpose...

That she would meet a dangerous, wild boy in St. Louis who she would like very much, and that his lips would taste like licorice and mint...

And that, no matter what happened, she would grow up to become a woman of value and virtue—protecting those who needed her help, and picking up soldiers off the field of regret to return them to the front lines refueled with an unquenchable passion back in their hearts...

Yet she would also become a woman of violence and vice—willing to do wrong in order to do right—a woman to vanquish the wicked demons of the earth, the hypocrites in power, ripping off masks of deceit to show the world the truth, wielding despair like a blade to terrify Saints and Sinners alike.

I wanted to tell that baby that I *loved* her, that I would *always* love her, and that she was *worth* being loved...no matter how dark the world seemed.

The front door of the church opened, and I screamed as I saw Father David stare down at the crib in disbelief, but the thunderous booming of the storm drowned out my desperate plea.

"I need to *see* her!" I screamed, sobbing and tripping as I ran. "I need to *hold* her!" I gasped, stumbling and slipping through a puddle.

But the thunder muted my screams, seeming to laugh at my need.

Father David scooped up the crib, scanned the street quickly, and slammed the door, never noticing me waving my arms, screaming, shouting, bawling my fucking eyes out.

Cain was roaring behind me like a caged lion, but I couldn't hear his words over my own ragged shout as that door slammed shut.

"NOOOOOOOO!" I screamed, reaching the steps. I ran up them two at a time, and finally slammed my fists against the door, hammering as hard as I could. "I need to see her! I need to hold her!" I shrieked, repeating the pleas Father David had not heard. "To tell her it will be alright!" I sobbed, my throat raw, my vocal chords shredded so that I could no longer recognize my own voice.

Thunder rolled in one continuous boom, like a train derailing from the tracks to strike an oil rig in a plentiful oil reserve and set off a chain reaction of explosions from deep within the earth.

The doors would not open.

I beat at them, railed at them, gnashing my teeth as I screamed.

They. Still. Did. Not. Open

My fists suddenly erupted with Silver claws, and I tore at the door, screaming at the top of my lungs to give me the baby, to let me see her, that she was mine to protect.

Like a mother should have done.

My claws scored, scraped, ripped, and scratched at the wood...

But the wooden doors were as hard as stone, my claws not doing the damage they should have. I pummeled at them, fueling my claws with as much Silver magic as I could hold, the world suddenly a palette of quicksilver in my eyes.

"I NEED THIS! SHE NEEDS MEEEEEE!" I screamed into the thunder and lightning and rain. The Silvers were based on *need*.

"I. NEED. YOUUUUUUUU!" I roared, my voice hoarse and animalistic.

Because I had never needed something in my life so badly.

Just one look, eyeball to eyeball, to tell that child that it would all be okay someday, that she didn't have to be scared, didn't have to hold onto her nightmare about this very night—one that had plagued me for so many years until I came face-to-face with the Demon, Johnathan.

The doors didn't budge, and I fell to my knees, dragging my claws down the wooden door the whole way, weeping in defeat as the rain relentlessly soaked me.

Cain finally caught up with me, and I heard one word through the thunder. "*...Demon!*"

My tears vanished in an instant—having momentarily forgotten all about the Demon, about Father David's story about this very night, about the Demon threatening the church itself.

And my fucking heart...

Lit.

On.

Fire.

No Demon was coming within reach of this door. No matter *what*.

I lifted my eyes, rain and tears pouring down my cheeks as I slowly held up my claws to look at Cain. He was staring incredulously at the door, shaking his head, mouthing something I couldn't make out through the thunder. Then his eyes fell to my face and hands, widening in shock. I glanced down at my hands and saw the Silver tears falling from my eyes. Like when I had bound Nameless to my thumb.

I stood to my feet, dismissing his concern. "Where is the fucking Demon?" I snarled, staring out at the streets. I imagined a dome of air above me, and the rain abruptly stopped pelting us, hitting my magical umbrella instead. The only way a Demon was coming near these doors was over my dead body.

Cain gripped my arms, his face frantic. "You're not listening! *You* are the Demon!" he hissed, shaking me violently.

I jolted as if he had slapped me in the face. The dome of air protecting us from the rain disappeared and I saw Cain pointing at the door to Abundant Angel Catholic Church.

I turned to find faint, scored lines marring the wood—the destruction, the scratches in the steps…just like…

A Demon had been clawing at the doors, demanding to have the baby for itself.

My legs gave out and Cain caught me, wiping hair from my eyes as he squeezed me to his chest tight enough to restrain me and almost hurt me, murmuring something else unintelligible through the raging storm. I sobbed, jerking my head back and forth in horror, unable to make sense of it all.

How? If we were here now, and David had seen the claw marks in the wooden doors…this wasn't some reflection, some memory, some hallucination of that night.

This. *Was.* That. Night.

Or Father David wouldn't have ever had the story to tell.

And if, in the real world, Father David had ever decided to share that particular story with me—about a Demon clawing at the doors to the church, desperate to get its hands on me as a baby…

Well, something like that could have ruined an impressionable girl's life. Make her feel like she was innately bad. Or that she needed to turn bad. Like a bitter apple.

Turn a potential Saint into a definite Sinner.

I straightened my legs, shaken by the revelation, but also accepting it. By not telling me—or anyone else—sooner, Father David had saved my soul.

Just like a Man of God *should*.

I just hoped that if this was reality, that I hadn't changed anything by overacting my part. That if I survived this quest, I wouldn't return to find that I was an entirely different person—that my actions here, now, had changed the sequence of events—that Father David had instead informed me of the Demon on the church steps when I was only a child, turning me into an entirely different person.

I lifted my eyes to see a white form of shifting fog standing beneath an overhang for a bus stop. Blue eyes stared back at me through that fog, and I imagined them winking. "YOU'RE *DEAD*, DEMON!" I roared instinctively, loud enough to feel like I had torn something in my vocal chords. It was all this fucking creature's fault. Cain grabbed me as tightly as he could.

I began struggling and fighting, trying to jerk free of Cain's grasp, but he held me as tight as a straightjacket.

"No, Callie. It's what he wants! It's a trap!" he growled, squeezing me tight against his chest until I was spitting and screaming like a wet cat.

But he hadn't seen what I had. The Door *behind* Last Breath, and it was glowing Silver. "Let me GO!" I roared, my throat feeling bloody and shredded.

"Not like this! You're crazy right now! Your arrogance is going to get us both killed! This is about more than your ego! More than your pride! More than your self-esteem!" he yelled in my ears.

"That's it!" I snarled.

And I flung my arms out, sending Cain skidding to the ground, his back slamming into the steps of the church. I stared down at him, panting, trying to remind myself that he was a friend, family, not a foe. I glanced back to see that Last Breath hadn't moved and, for all the world, looked to be smiling at me. Taunting me.

I turned back to Cain, forcing my breathing to slow, my head to clear. "You're right. I *am* arrogant, but that can be a strength, too." I offered him my hand. "Get up, Cain. The fucking Door is behind the bastard." I was still furious, but I had it under control, able to think clearly again. Barely.

He flinched, staring out to find I was telling the truth. "Oh." Then he grabbed my hand and pulled himself to his feet. "Yeah, okay..." he said apologetically.

"Get ready to run right behind me. I'm going to smoke this son of a bitch," I swore out loud. I took a deep, calming breath. Then I let a slow smile creep over my face as I met Cain's eyes. "And for the record, I have so much self-esteem that I *sweat* vapor...and it's about to open that fucking Door," I snarled, pointing at Last Breath in a direct challenge.

Then I was running, my smile stretching wider as Cain coughed up a laugh, suddenly catching the word-play of my statement.

My hands hung down at my sides as I ran, hissing as each drop of rain made contact with my Silver claws, forming my own little clouds of vapor as I rushed Last Breath. I leapt at him, fully intending to tackle him through the Door, impaled on my claws.

He lunged into the air to meet me, his paws extended to reveal massive, curled silver claws. And for a single moment, I got a clear view of him.

I stared into those glacier blue-eyes of the white lion and I laughed.

My claws struck his throat, shearing some of his white mane.

His claws raked across my cheeks.

Cain's weight hitting my back shoved us both through the Door.

We were all screaming in one fashion or another as the Door slammed shut behind us.

CHAPTER 28

I struck a lawn of fresh-cut grass and tumbled head over heels, Cain's weight grinding me into the grass with each flip, both of us still screaming as my claws ravaged the earth. I lurched to my feet, claws out, snarling as I searched for Last Breath's corpse.

I was about to skin the damned cat and make a new scarf.

All I heard was a mocking purr, slowly fading away.

A beautiful, warm sun shone down on us, and my clothes were not remotely wet. I blinked rapidly, squinting at the bright, pleasant day. Birds chirped from nearby trees, and a faint murmur of song could be heard in the breeze—like the soothing hum of a child.

I couldn't remember why I was here. Why Cain was here. Just a rage that made my arms shake. Rage at Last Breath. I had stabbed him in the throat with my claws, and I remembered the lion's own silver claws raking my cheeks.

Silver claws…

Cain stepped into view, staring at me nervously as if fearing to see severe wounds. But he blinked rapidly, wiping at his eyes as if he didn't believe what he was seeing.

He reached out a hand and plucked something from my cheek. I felt him pull a long strand of something that had stuck to my skin. He held out a strand of silver foil. I reached up and found two more that I pulled off. They went down my cheeks and even over my eyes.

Right where Last Breath had scored a hit with his claws.

I stared at Cain, not understanding.

"His claws didn't harm you. They just...left silver streaks on your cheeks..." he said, almost to himself. I glanced down at my hands to see more of the silver foil on my palms and shirt, but these were silver drops. My tears. Cain noticed them, too, and looked on the verge of losing his Biblical shit.

"It's my thing," I told him, shrugging. "Well, the tears anyway. I'm not sure about Last Breath's attack. Those should have ripped my face off..." I thought about his silver claws, and my own silver claws, frowning.

Were we...the same somehow?

"He is a lion," I heard myself explaining, trying to make some sense of it all. "And he has silver claws like me..."

Cain was nodding but didn't look particularly pleased about the news. "I saw. But what does it mean? And why are we at the Vatican?"

I flinched, looking past his shoulder at the familiar buildings behind him. I looked left and right, and then spun in a slow circle. He was right. We were in Vatican City where I had first met Fabrizio and the other Shepherds. Where I had met the Conclave. But...when were we here this time? Was this also some past event? Like the church had been?

I didn't see anyone walking around us, no nuns, or Shepherds. No one. But the place didn't necessarily feel empty or anything. Not sinister, just an unusually low-key day at the Vatican.

Cain placed his hands on his hips, glaring at me. "We need to talk about your apparent demonic P.M.S. loss of control of back there," he said, pointing at the now-empty space where we had fallen through the Door.

I wilted guiltily, the memory coming back to me in bits and pieces. I had felt so raw, so emotional, almost primal. I hadn't taken a logical, rational step until the end. Just reaction, wanting to give that baby—me—the weapons she would need to defend herself.

But my form of support had been as a raging demon, likely only *adding* to the fears and terrors that would sit with that baby for decades, until she learned to overcome her fears, when a Demon named Johnathan would come knocking on her door.

I locked eyes with Cain and, sensing no one was around, I sat back down in the grass.

He studied me warily, a disappointed look on his face let me know he wasn't won over by my act and that we were still going to talk about it. Then he sat down beside me, waiting.

"I don't know what came over me. I just reacted. Knowing what I know now, how much fear and loss I had as a child, what I had to grow up with on my conscience. I just wanted to give that baby a role model, a kiss of encouragement. A hug from a stranger that, even if she couldn't ever remember that moment specifically, she might remember someone squeezing her with so much love that she could never forget it. Even in the darkest of days to come, that someone loved her."

Cain shook his head slowly at the insanity of it all. But I also saw compassion in his eyes. "This place is...cruel," he finally said. He waited a few moments before continuing. "But we have to keep our heads straight, Callie. I think it's all part of the test. To push us, to break us, to find out what matters most to us."

I nodded in understanding. "I know."

"You also made Father David's story come true. *You* were the Demon he heard outside the church..." he said in a very soft tone.

I shuddered with disgust. "But what does that mean? Is this place real? Some memory shard? Some twisted hallucination?"

Cain thought about it for a long time, finally shaking his head. "I don't know. But I do know that this seems to be some extravagant way to test our desires, our fears, our very *selves*," he said, enunciating the last word. "And we have to remember that. Each Door is a lesson, a choice, and the obelisk said there were prizes and prices for each one. We have to keep our goal intact."

I nodded in silence, gathering my thoughts. What was our goal? What was *my* goal? Had it changed? Why was I really here? For the treasure of Solomon's Temple? Because I'd been invited to play a game? Because I was related to Solomon? Was I here for answers or riches? Power or knowledge?

For others...

Or myself?

Cain was watching me thoughtfully. Seeing me finally focus on him, he let out a faint smile. "You fucked that pussycat up, by the way," he said. I fought the grin struggling to break through, but finally relented.

Cain burst out laughing, slapping his knees adamantly. "You are one crazy bitch, Callie. Crazy as hell," he wheezed, wiping tears from his eyes. "Do you have any idea what you *looked like* on those church steps? It was terrifying, and I don't scare easily. I've been respectfully concerned about others before, sure, but actually bone-deep scared?" he chuckled, shaking his head. "I wouldn't have opened those doors if Abel himself had come back from the grave to beg me," he whispered after a few moments. He grew silent as if the admission had only just been realized. Then he grunted. "Yeah, not even then," he finally reaffirmed.

"I'm not quite sure how to take that," I said, frowning.

"Oh, since you are on my side, it's a big damned compliment," he said, holding out his hands with a *don't shoot* gesture, grinning wide.

"Okay. I can be the boogeybitch if it makes you sleep better at night. What are sisters for?"

He smiled—but in a way I wasn't sure I had seen him smile before. A soul-deep acknowledgment of my meaning, not just a topical agreement to my words. "Sister from another Mister," he said in a serious tone.

"So, your Sis needs to dial back the crazy—"

"Easy there, Sis. No need to be hasty. We might just need some of that crazy soon, but it could use a tight leash," Cain corrected.

I nodded, rolling my eyes. "Fine. Calculated crazy. Got it." I scanned the Vatican grounds, searching for a Door, but I didn't see one. "What are we doing here? If this quest was designed to make us react, we need to approach it with clear goals. The point of all this is to reach a final destination, not wallow in our passions—our fears, loves, victories, or losses. We need a compass."

Cain nodded. "The first Door took us to the church the night the Doors first appeared. The night your own story all began. But why that moment? Was it because there was something you needed to see, or did it just want to mess with your head?"

"I think we need to decide what Last Breath is really doing here," I said. Cain frowned, looking puzzled, so I elaborated. "He essentially led us to the second Door, and it's fair to say he forced us through the first Door back home."

Cain considered that and gave a hesitant nod. "Maybe. If that's true, is he helping guide us or is he misleading us?"

I nodded seriously. "I'm pretty sure he's not helping. He clawed my face."

"You stabbed him through the jugular, first. Maybe he's dead."

I shook my head, recalling the purring sound I had heard upon landing in the grass. "I don't think so. His claws didn't hurt me, so maybe mine didn't hurt him. We both used Silver claws."

Cain stared down at the silver foil in his palm, nodding warily. "Good point. If I was making a quest, a challenge to give people the option to find my secret stash of stuff, and I made a guardian to protect it..." Cain said, pointing out facts. I waited for more, but Cain finally muttered a curse. "I don't know where I was going with that. Is Solomon trying to prevent us from getting there or is he helping us? Why have this challenge in the first place if he *doesn't* want us finding it? And if he *does* want us to find it, why hassle us with Last Breath?"

I let out a sigh, thinking. "I don't know, but those are just symptoms. The main purpose is to see if we are worthy of his Temple, right? So, he has safeguards to cut the wheat from chaff. To sort out the bad apples..."

Cain grunted. "Always apples with you. It's like a constant kick to the groin, you know."

I smiled. "Sorry." I had an idea. "Keep an eye out. I don't want the Shepherds seeing us and deciding to attack before asking where our access lanyards are. I need time to think about this."

I closed my eyes and took a deep breath, thinking about everything all at once. I imagined a feather floating in my mind, one coated in silver, despite my initial attempt to make it black—as I was used to doing when I meditated. It had been doing that lately. I ignored the anomaly, not wanting to waste time forcing it back.

I fed every thought, fear, concern, desire, and wish into the feather, watching as a wind seemed to make it ruffle as it slowly rotated in the center of a black field of nothingness. I focused on my breathing, dredging up anything else currently on my mind. My memory of the first Door we had gone through and participating in Father David's story about the Demon outside the church.

I thought about Samael. The Sons of Solomon. Archangel Michael. Roland and Henri. Boiling cauldrons of danger in Kansas City. Events I was only just beginning to hear about in Boston with Quinn MacKenna. Trouble in St. Louis with Mordred hellbent on destroying Nate Temple in his quest for Camelot. I thought about every single thing happening in my world.

And everything that personally bothered me. My own lineage with

Solomon. My parents. The Shepherds. Not knowing my purpose anymore, where I belonged, where I fit in. Why I woke up every single day and put on my boots. I knew I wanted to help people, that was pretty obvious.

But *how* did I want to help people? Putting out fires was great and all, but what was my ultimate purpose? Without an overarching cause, I was always reacting.

I was destroying rather than uniting. Destroying bad things, sure, but when the threat was gone, and it was time to pick up the pieces...

I wasn't doing anything with the people I had saved. I was just letting them continue on with their day, likely guiding them right back into some other monster's mouth.

I didn't want to work for the church. Mainly because I didn't want to be bound to a group of men I thought were flawed—not in their faith, but in their applications of it.

I didn't want to be a part of the Academy—the ruling body of wizards—but I had never had any interaction with them in the first place. What I had seen and heard from others was that they were no better than the Shepherds. They meant well but had deep seeds of corruption planted in their midst.

I didn't want to ally with the vampires or werewolves, although I was friends with quite a few of both.

The bears were better, more noble, but I wasn't really a part of them. I was a good friend but would never be part of their Cave. And maybe they didn't want me to be anything more than a friend held at a close distance. Definitely not to use them as a tool to promote my own agenda.

Whatever that was.

I wanted good. Safety. Protection.

But...I believed that some of the so-called monsters of the world weren't that bad. They were actually kind of good.

Overall, the Shepherds definitely didn't share this opinion. Maybe that was my reason for not wanting to be a part of them. The fact that they had left Roland out to dry the moment they realized he was no longer able to be the poster boy of their cause.

But I wasn't important enough to start my own...what, a gang? An organization? Maybe a church or open up shop as a private detective. *Callie's Angels*, I thought to myself, playing on the concept of Charlie's Angels. I let the errant thought drift and fade away.

The long and short of it was that I didn't have the answer. And right now, I wasn't necessarily looking for an answer. That wasn't how meditation worked. It wasn't a cosmic fortune cookie machine where you pop in twenty-five cents of focus, twist the dial, and receive the keys to the kingdom.

No.

Meditation was about viewing *processes*. You tossed in the parts and watched the gears of the machine of life begin to rotate, searching for meaning and purpose to the function. In that act, perhaps you could see a place where your unique gear could fit, improving the overall mechanism.

Problem was, maybe I had the answers to life right in front of me.

I just didn't know what my gear looked like. What shape it was. What my *self* looked like.

I was, figuratively speaking, a red-hot mess.

Cosmically speaking, I was a Zen-hot mess.

Would the real Slim Callie please stand up?

But who was Callie Penrose?

I pondered that very carefully—in an abstract manner. I imagined inserting myself as a cog into the mechanism of life in my mind's eye. I shaped my cog like a Shepherd, watching the possible futures. Then I tried as a wizard. Then I tried as a Nephilim. Then I tried as a figure in Nate's life, with no specific purpose of my own.

That one made me growl in disappointment. That wasn't going to happen. I would only meet Nate as an equal, never a pawn.

I tried reshaping my cog many different ways.

And I found no answers. Bits and pieces of each attempt were pleasant and worthwhile, but primarily worthwhile for others, not me. Not fully.

I felt resistance—pressure at my internal frustration—so I released the construct, the machine vaporizing to nothing, leaving only the white rose on the black background.

Wait…

My heart began to race, realizing that a white rose was *not* the chosen imagined construct for myself. It was a black feather. No, a *silver* feather…

My focus vibrated warningly, threatening to fall apart. I relaxed all strain and control, letting my subconscious do as it would. After a few flickers, a white rose slowly rematerialized before me. I studied it absently, careful not to look too closely at the new addition to my meditation.

It meant something.

What had changed? I was still the black feather, and still the silver feather. I could see them occasionally flickering into existence, superimposed over the white rose, as if all three belonged.

Then I noticed the faint outline of feathered wings arcing out to either side of the rotating rose and feathers. I felt strain again and relaxed my mind, allowing myself to become a casual observer in the halls of my own mind.

The image abruptly clarified.

Wings hung on either side like they belonged to the center apparition. The rose and two feathers. The wings glistened with a bluish, white glow, sometimes seeming to be made of feathers and sometimes like dry ice and chips of floating stone.

This was entirely strange. The whole point to meditation was to have one rock-solid focal point. But my focal point was shifting all over the place, changing, morphing, growing *wings* for crying out loud.

It had to symbolize my own inner struggle—that I didn't know myself. Which likely had to do with Dorian Gray's ever helpful comment. About how everyone he spoke to was terrified of me. That he was even terrified of me. That they had taken to calling me the White Rose in fear.

There were so many loose ends in my life.

Heaven wanted me. Hell wanted me. The Shepherds wanted me.

They also *didn't* want me.

My parents loved me. My parents abandoned me.

I wanted to do good things. But I was willing to do *bad* things to attain those good things.

I wanted to know more about my past. But I was terrified to learn anything more about my broken childhood. My broken family. But I was forming a new family of friends. Of brothers and sisters bound by more than blood.

And some of them were monsters.

I liked a guy—really, really liked a guy—who was, on the best of days, an incredibly dangerous person. He also wanted to do good things and had definitely done bad things in order to achieve the ends he sought. And...I probably would have done the same in his shoes.

But from the outside looking in...

I wasn't sure if we could be seen as the good guys. Maybe we were actually the villains.

I'd trapped a freaking Angel on a ring around my thumb. How was that a good thing? Even if he had Fallen, there were already rules and precedents in place to handle that kind of thing.

And none of them included some upstart wizard in Kansas City kicking the doors down to keep the Angel for herself.

I realized, suddenly, that this had always been my cross to bear. It was such an epiphany that it almost broke me out of my meditation. I very calmly relaxed again, focusing on the shifting image before me in a very unspecific way.

Look, meditation was tough. Take my word for it. If I say I focused in an unfocused way, I know what the hell I'm talking about.

I heard Cain grunt and realized I had spoken the thought out loud. My entire construct wavered—on the verge of collapse—but I gripped it defiantly for a moment, enough to solidify it again, like I was righting a wobbling canoe. Then I set it back adrift. It settled, flickering slightly, and I let out a deep breath of relief.

I didn't dare risk snapping out of my meditation because, as bizarre and conflicted as my thoughts were right now, they were just thoughts, and fuel for my focus. I fed them—the fading sounds of Cain beside me, the chirping birds in the trees, and the sensation of warmth from the sun—into my construct. The shifting-winged-double-feather-white-rose-chi symbol that represented my rock-solid understanding of myself.

Just trust me.

The totem began to shift and pulse as if breathing, pleased that it was allowed to *be* without my interference.

I thought about the quest, the Doors, Cain, Last Breath, the Sons of Solomon back on Earth, how I was going to choose the next Door, what was motivating my choice in the Doors, and what I was willing to do, what price I was willing to pay, what I really wanted from all of this...

Everything and everyone were focused on one single place...Solomon's Temple.

It was said to house all the riches of the world. All the knowledge of existence.

I realized I didn't really care about that. Power sounded nice, but only insomuch as I could utilize it for good in the world—to right a wrong.

Knowledge was the same. If it helped, great. If not…I didn't really care. I wasn't like Nate, who loved learning things for the sake of learning them.

I realized that I wanted, more than anything, to make sure no more little girls were left on the steps of a church, all alone, without parents, in a world full of monsters. That without evil, none of that would have taken place.

The little girl would have lived to see her parents' faces.

The focal construct burst into flame, the rose and feathers and wings igniting like a magician's flash paper, knocking me out of my meditation as surely as a bucket of cold water had been dumped down my spine.

I opened my eyes, panting to see Cain staring over my shoulder. "Oh, good. You're done braining. We have company." I turned to see three Shepherds approaching at a swift jog about a hundred yards away, coming from the building where I had met the Conclave. The official headquarters of the Vatican Shepherds.

I climbed to my feet, facing them directly. I kept my hand free of the hilt of the katana at my hip, momentarily surprised to find it still there and not wedged in the grass from my fall. Cain had his bone dagger sheathed at his belt, but I shook my head pointedly as his hand drifted closer to it.

"Let's see what they want, first," I said under my breath.

Cain was frowning at the approaching Shepherds. "Since when did Arthur become a Shepherd?" he asked warily.

I turned to see Arthur leading two other Shepherds my way. His face was hard and uncaring.

"The Conclave awaits you, First Shepherd Penrose," he said formally, lowering his eyes. Beckett Killian and Claire Stone dipped their heads as well. Like we were not close friends, but an unquestionable command structure. And apparently, I had broken the glass ceiling. First Shepherd…

I shared a long look with Cain, but his faux façade of serenity was a gentle reminder that this place wasn't what we thought. Maybe it was real, maybe it wasn't.

But me being the First Shepherd pretty much confirmed that it was a nightmare.

CHAPTER 29

*T*he three Shepherds led us into a familiar room to face the Conclave of milky-eyed wizards who essentially ruled us. None of them looked familiar to the ones I had met in the past.

But...I couldn't really remember any of the faces I had seen during my last visit with the Conclave. The more I stared at the men before me, the more familiar they became, and I could faintly recall private discussions with them from previous weeks when we had formulated our attack plans for the Knights Templar, led by Olin Fuentes.

Malachi, the head of the Conclave cleared his throat, looking like he had been healed of the wound that had almost killed him a week ago. The room wavered for a moment, but I ignored the dizzy spell as I focused on my long-time mentor.

"Congratulations on your victory over Olin Fuentes and the Templars. I trust you brought proof?" he asked with a bureaucratic smile, letting me know he didn't doubt me and this was just a formality.

I reached into my pocket and pulled out a silk pouch full of werewolf fangs. I rattled them in my fist, then handed them to Claire. She didn't meet my eyes as she accepted them and took them to the table for the Conclave to inspect. She returned to my side, eyes downcast.

"Thank you, Miss Penrose. You fill our hearts with pride," Malachi said.

I nodded humbly. "I couldn't have done it without Shepherd Killian's assistance in locating their hideout, or Shepherd Stone smoking them out with the frontal assault."

Malachi nodded. "They will be rewarded for their contribution, but at this time I want to extend an honor that none have ever received. The Spear of Longinus that you entrusted to us has been restored." He stood, and lifted a long, white spear from the table that I hadn't noticed until now. My fingers itched hungrily but I kept my face calm.

Cain murmured something behind me, and it sounded troubled, but I held out a hand to calm my old friend. I'd told him—at least a dozen times— not to speak before the Conclave.

"Please accept this weapon and know it will be of great aid against Hell's Horsemen of the Apocalypse, led by Nate Temple and his ilk."

I nodded grimly as I approached, feeling a flush of anxiety that I kept hidden from my face. "I will end the plague of Horsemen, as the Vatican demands," I vowed.

"We know, Shepherd Penrose, we know. You have always acted in the best interest of the Church. We have faith in you," Malachi said, a hidden smile on his face as he motioned to a door on my right.

I hesitated, my hand almost touching the spear. His milk-white eyes— like all the other members of the Conclave—had briefly flickered darker. My fingertips tingled this close to the Spear, eager to snatch it up. *So close...*

Cain was suddenly behind me, and I heard other members of the Conclave grumbling about the break in protocol. I glanced over at him, ready to chastise him for the disrespect in front of my superiors. "Get back in your place—"

Cain was pointing at a door to the side of the room. I glanced over to see a strange, Silver door that hadn't been there a moment before. I frowned, puzzled.

Then I heard the clanking of chains on the other side of the room. I turned to see Nate Temple, bleeding and shackled, a leather gag over his mouth to prevent him from speaking, from Singing, shuffling out from...

A *second* Silver door.

My world rocked suddenly, and my hand grasped the Spear. I gasped as power flooded into me, rocking me back on my heels. Cain caught me, supporting me so I didn't fall. My eyes settled on the Conclave who were grinning wickedly, pointing at the shackled wizard.

The Horseman of Hope.

"Execute him, Miss Penrose," Malachi snarled acidly.

I flinched at the tone, turning to meet his gaze. But...his face was calm and composed, not matching the tone I had just heard. And the other members of the Conclave weren't grinning. In fact, they looked terrified to be so close to the bound man.

What was happening? I felt so strange...

Like this was some dream. Some nightmare.

A familiar voice whispered in my ear, but it was all I could manage to hold the Spear in my palms without unleashing a torrent of power that would likely kill us all.

"You love him..."

I gasped as if he had just stabbed me in the kidneys. Did I love my enemy? Nate Temple had torn the world apart with—

Wait, no he hadn't. He'd been the only one standing up for mankind, hadn't he? I glanced back up at Malachi, shaking my head in confusion. His eyes flashed from white to black, his face contorted from malicious grin to somber frown, back and forth, too fast to be real. Which meant...

The world flashed Silver and I shuddered at what I saw. Demons had possessed the majority of the Conclave. I glanced back to find the same with Claire, Arthur, and Beckett.

I reached into my pocket, feeling something that reminded me of a kiss, for some reason. It was warm in my hands as I wrapped my fingers around it. My hand latched onto something else, and I pulled both items out. A silver butterfly charm and a black feather with a red orb at the tip.

I lifted my eyes, time still moving slowly thanks to my Silvers, and glanced at Nate Temple.

His eyes were chaotic storms of white and gold. Not a sliver of black to them.

I took a deep breath, ignoring the hubbub of the Shepherds slowly advancing, sensing that something was wrong. I flung out my hand, hurling the silver butterfly at Nate Temple's face.

It struck his mouthpiece, tearing it free.

At the same time, I lifted the feather and shouted a single word as the world snapped back into real time. "GRIMM!"

A black bolt of lightning struck the center of the Conclave, tossing their bodies outward or incinerating them on contact. The room erupted with shouts and screams as a black unicorn appeared in the center of the rubble of bodies and the remains of the wooden desk where the Conclave had sat. He met my eyes and they were white fire, his silver hooves pawed at the floor, flames licking at the carpet and catching the rubble on fire. His coat and mane were long, black feathers with red orbs at the tips.

Grimm abruptly impaled Malachi in the forehead with his horn and a demon attempted to flee his body, snarling and cursing as it erupted in black flame, cast back to Hell.

I pointed my spear at Nate Temple without breaking eye contact with the unicorn, ignoring how close that gnarled, bloody, black horn was from my throat. "Save him..." I pleaded.

Grimm snorted, his nostrils flaring with deep, inner flames, and then he galloped past me, scooping up Nate Temple and shattering his chains in one swift swipe of his horn. Nate's hands came free and the room erupted with chaos as balls of flame roared through the air, walls of thorns rolling over any survivors. He opened his mouth and...men of the cloth burned.

Claire and Beckett died horribly, impaled by wicked black thorns as large as spears.

It was over before it had even truly begun, only the gasping death throes of those too stubborn to die quickly remained. Nate and Grimm stared warily at Cain and I, ready to react at even the slightest provocation. I met Nate's hard eyes and gave him a very faint smile, my heart fluttering at the chaos and destruction flickering in those depths.

Because in that chaotic storm of madness...

On his lips...

Was the Song of Creation's Chaos.

I settled the butt of my spear on the floor and gave Nate a careful curtsy. Then I grabbed Cain by the shoulder and shoved him towards the Door that Nate had exited from as a prisoner.

Malachi shouted out behind me. "Traitor! You have doomed the world!" But as a complement to his voice, I heard a mad cackling sound, and I saw a double-vision of a demon crouched atop the table, his head bobbing up and down as he clapped his slimy, scaled hands together. "Enjoy the Spear, White Rose, it's whispers are so sweet it chills my blood."

I ignored it, racing through the door, gasping in confusion but also a supreme sense of accomplishment. I had done something right. Nate Temple was no enemy. He was my friend.

"Fuck this place," Cain growled, tucking me close as we fell through the Silver Doorway. He was careful to keep the Spear out of the way, but he kept right on with the cursing as we fell into darkness.

CHAPTER 30

I sat in a booth across from Cain at a greasy diner. The adjacent table of twelve was cheerfully singing a birthday song to a child who cared only for the birthday cake and candles placed directly before him.

Cain stared back at me, his face aghast. "Callie!"

I nodded. "Yeah?"

"Put the goddamned Spear away!" he hissed, leaning forward. I flinched to find I was holding the Spear of Destiny propped up beside me on the floor. I focused on it furiously, wondering how no one had yet pointed it out. It winked out of existence a moment later, just as the waitress rounded the corner, meeting my eyes.

"Oh, I didn't see you there, hon," she said with a genuine smile. "Sorry for the noise. Coffee?" she asked, holding up a pot in her hands. I nodded woodenly, and she deftly poured us each a cup.

"Just the coffee is fine," Cain said hurriedly as the waitress pulled out a notepad to take our orders. I mumbled my agreement and she shrugged.

"The coffee is free—"

"Perfect," Cain interrupted impatiently.

The waitress narrowed her eyes. "*If* you order," she added, frowning. "Let me know if you change your mind," she sighed. Then she left to check on the birthday party. The kid was crying about wanting a larger piece, and

166

then crying harder when he was told he was supposed to share the rest of it.

Cain leaned forward, wrapping both hands around his mug of steaming, black tar heroin. I took a contented sip, meeting his eyes. "What. *The fuck.* Was that?" he hissed.

I shook my head, feeling on the verge of hysteria. I remembered being in Rome only a few minutes ago, fighting for my life against a possessed Conclave. I had watched my best friend die, and I had felt *nothing*. And...I couldn't remember how we had gotten there. Or what the fight was about. Couldn't even remember ever being a Shepherd...

"Where are we, Cain?" I whispered nervously, dialing back my paranoia and deciding not to share it with Cain. He was already on the edge and didn't need a shove. Especially since I was on the edge with him and we were holding hands.

"Let me hold the doors, my dear. It's chilly outside," I heard the waitress say from across the room. We both glanced up sharply, something about her words catching our attention. She was holding the doors open for a little old couple shaking snow from their boots. I frowned, not recognizing them. Then my eyes settled on the doors and I felt a slight pinch between my eyes.

"It's cold enough outside to rob me of my last breath," the old man chuckled, thanking the waitress, and ignoring his wife's indignant squawk at such a macabre joke.

I gasped as my coffee slopped over my wrist, the memory hitting me like a truck. We were on a quest, a game. The Song of Solomon.

"Last Breath," I said, turning back to Cain.

"Doors," he hissed back, his eyes wide. Then we were both scanning the room, searching for any sign of threat. But it was an entirely normal diner, no danger. No lion ready to rip our faces off. No Silver Doors. Just us and our coffee. Then I focused on the faint singing I could hear in the background, as if it was coming from outside. That was familiar, too.

Cain noticed my attention. "Yes, the bloody screaming."

I frowned. "It's a song," I argued. "Why does it sound familiar?"

Cain looked uncertain all of a sudden, almost fearful. "Because we heard it the moment we stepped through that first cursed Door. Maybe it's the Song of Solomon. The tortured screams of Last Breath's victims," he grumbled. I had no idea what he was talking about. I heard no screaming, only the sweet, distant melody.

Like an upended box of puzzle pieces, snippets of memory began falling upon the rickety card table of my consciousness—some right-side up, others upside-down. I had watched Claire *die* in Rome, and I had felt *nothing*. How was that not sociopathic? Even now, I felt more alarmed at the realization that I hadn't felt anything than the fact that she had died. She was my best friend. Something was very, very wrong.

It was as if once I stepped through the next Door, some thread was cut, leaving me with little to no memories of what had happened prior, fully immersing me into the new fabricated reality.

But...

I had been holding the Spear a moment ago. The one the Conclave had given me. That was real, or I wouldn't have been clutching it in this diner. Did that mean Claire really had just died?

Cain was watching me, nervous of whatever he saw in my eyes, and holding out his hands for me to calm down.

"None of that was real...Rome, the Shepherds, none of it," I told him forcefully.

He nodded very slowly. "Obviously..."

"Then why was I holding the Spear a minute ago? It's different than...I remember," I finally said, pushing through the mild headache caused by the thought. "It really has been modified somehow, but I don't think in a good way," I told him. "Almost like it's rigged to break..."

Cain's eyes widened. "Shit. Are you sure?"

"You told me to put it away, so no, I'm not sure. But it felt...off."

He scratched at his unshaven cheeks, thinking furiously.

Now that I was aware, I thought back on how we had started this quest. It was difficult to draw to mind, but it finally hit me. I remembered talking to an Angel, but not how I had gotten there. Then there was the fountain, Roland meeting with Henri the vampire, and Fabrizio.

But for the life of me, I couldn't remember any specific moments before that.

Which was strange. I could remember all sorts of things from months ago, years ago, even my childhood. But I couldn't remember very much over...what, the last week? I remembered paying my phone bill a while back, but that had been due two weeks ago. Had something vital happened in that period? Something I needed to know right now? Some clue?

"Choices," I murmured, catching my breath. "We're looking for—" I cut off abruptly, not wanting to say it out loud in front of all the patrons, but Cain nodded, understanding that I had been about to mention Solomon's Temple. "The rules said something about choices. Back there in Rome, I made a choice," I said.

Cain was nodding. "The Spear?" he asked thoughtfully. "Or Nate?"

I thought about it, wondering. "I don't' know. It was almost like a dream of what could have been if I became a Shepherd. That it would someday put me on a path against Nate…" I offered hesitantly. Then I shrugged. "What do you think?"

Cain shrugged. "You're the brains of the operation. I'm just the muscle."

I thought about that and considered the fact that he might be wrong. "You seemed more clear-headed than me. At least back there. I got wrapped up into the experience. It felt so real…"

Cain frowned. "Maybe because it was about you becoming a Shepherd? The experience had nothing to do with me," he said, thinking out loud.

"Does that mean we're going to run into visions of your future, too?" I asked.

He thought about it. "I don't know. Maybe? But this whole thing seems centered on you. You're the one who saw the signs leading you to the fountain, not me. I didn't even believe you, remember?"

"Good point, but you're here, now. Maybe that's all that matters."

Cain shook his head, growing more confident. "I think I'm just here as your support. The first vision also had nothing to do with me."

I leaned back in my seat, shaking my head. "Well, what the hell do we do next? Do I keep getting new tests? What am I supposed to do to find the Temple? Self-reflection won't get us anywhere. This isn't a vision quest. My Spear is *different*, Cain. That's not a hallucination. At least, I don't think it is," I admitted, wondering if even this moment was some imagined dream.

Cain thought about it. "Maybe it is a vision quest. To hand over Solomon's Temple seems like the kind of thing that would require a background check."

"Then why did it just show me a potential future—"

I blinked, cutting off my chain of thought. Was this about me trying to find my purpose? My future path? Did the Temple want to see what kind of person I could become? What kind of person I *wanted* to become? "The obelisk did say that each quest is tailored to each individual…"

Cain nodded, sipping his coffee.

"But in the moment, I couldn't remember any of that. It was all so real…"

Cain grew silent, not having an answer for a few moments. "Maybe that is my purpose. To center you…" he offered, but he sounded doubtful. "Maybe you should have taken someone else with you for this, Callie. I'm not exactly a moral compass."

I grunted, realizing that I was smiling. "I don't know…maybe you are. Not necessarily moral, but you care for me quite a bit. You want the best for me. You offered to go on this stupid quest to help support me."

Cain was shaking his head, looking exasperated. I figuratively rolled up my sleeves, feeling more confident in my assessment despite his denial. Time to pull out the big guns.

"I know you, Cain…I've seen your heart," I said softly. He flinched as if I had hit him.

"Yeah?" he asked, lowering his eyes to his coffee. "It's black. Like my coffee."

I nodded, reaching my hand out for his. "But it's *there*. You really care for me. You really do see me as a sister…"

His scarred hands seemed to shake at the accusation and he didn't speak. "Just because I care for you doesn't mean I'm the right one for the job."

I smiled warmly, squeezing his hand. "You're all I've got, idiot. Do you see a line of people behind me?" I asked him with a stern look.

He grunted, and finally met my eyes. "I'll try my best, Callie."

"Good, because my next plan was to poke you with my broken Spear until you agreed."

He grunted uneasily, not at the threat, but in self-doubt. He took a deep, resigned breath and nodded one time. "If I'm your Plan A and poking me with the Spear is your Plan B, I really hope you've got the rest of the alphabet laid out…Sis," he said, as if testing out the word. I grinned happily. "Now, when do we get to kill some shit? I'm good at that part."

I scanned the room. I was actually getting tired of this quest, and we had only just begun. Because Cain had a point. I just wanted to fight something directly. No more games. I wanted an enemy, or if we were going to keep playing games, I wanted to know what it was all for.

I didn't care about the Temple. Not really. I cared about the chance to learn something about my history. About the Seal of Solomon—in order to keep it safe and not let more demons out like I had the first time I wore it.

Solomon's Temple could have been a broom closet for all I cared.

Because if it had answers to those two things, I would have been a happy girl.

I didn't need a palace or armory of weapons or treasure.

I just wanted this to be over, to at least know for certain this game would give me what I sought. Because if I won and didn't get those two things, I was liable to burn Solomon's swanky Temple down to the ground, cooking hot dogs over the smoldering rubble with Cain.

If I got those two things…was I finished? Was that all I wanted? A few answers and then to bow out of the constant fighting, the Demons, the Angels, all of it? Take my ball and go home?

I still didn't have the answer to that—what I wanted to be. What I wanted to do.

I scanned the room, hoping my anger would draw out Last Breath for disrespecting his sacred game. It didn't. Neither did any Doors suddenly pop into existence.

I sighed and took a deep breath, focusing on need. Nothing happened. I pulled out the Seal of Solomon and felt everyone in the diner suddenly turn to look at me, all conversation ceasing like they were of one hive mind. Even the faces on the *television*—a kid's sing along program of some kind featuring grown men in bright-colored track suits singing with a giant puppet—stared at me as if they could see me. My skin was suddenly crawling.

"Erm, you might want to hurry it up. They look angry," Cain murmured, his hand slowly shifting to his belt in case they all attacked at once. I focused on need again, not need for the solution to this quest, but the need to learn more about myself, because so far everything seemed to be aimed at teaching me something.

Even if I was a terrible student and hadn't fully understood the lessons hurled at me.

It was kind of like when you walked into a room and suddenly everyone grew quiet. It was fairly obvious everyone had been talking about you, even if you didn't know what they had been saying. Yeah. This quest felt like that. The not-so-subtle lessons were the specific rumors floating around about me, and the quest itself was the room of back-stabbers.

So, I focused on me—my flaws, my strengths, anything that made me passionate or made me care. And the room transformed into a quicksilver tapestry, the people now like a crowd of life-sized Silver Surfer action figures. And two Doors glowed brightly.

As luck would have it, they led to the restrooms.

Cain grunted, looking back only briefly to follow my line of sight before checking on our fellow patrons again to make sure we weren't about to be jumped. "We have to choose one?" he asked. "What kind of backwards truck-stop quest for knowledge is this?" he demanded.

I sighed. "Are you familiar with the buddy system?" I asked, standing and holding out my hand, still keeping an eye on the motionless chrome people watching us.

Cain grunted and let me help him to his feet. "It's a mystery to us menfolk."

"Prepare to be enlightened," I told him, leading him towards the women's restroom. "Also, you're not supposed to be in here, so act sneaky," I added. I placed a palm on the door and felt my hand grow warm. I took a deep breath and pushed.

This time, the door sucked us inside like we had been flushed down a toilet, and I could have sworn I heard maniacal laughter in the distance.

CHAPTER 31

I opened my eyes to see Cain sitting across from me, sipping a scotch. He looked momentarily startled, sniffing at his drink, but then his eyes settled on Roland Haviar sitting beside him. Roland held a wine glass of blood extended out, awaiting Cain's glass for a toast.

Cain's confusion evaporated, and he smiled, clinking glasses. "To another day in the land of the living," he said, continuing a conversation that I couldn't quite recall. Maybe I had dozed off again from the pain medication.

Roland turned to me, frowning at my hand. I blinked to realize I held the Spear of Destiny in my fist, propped up as if I anticipated needing it to stoke the fire before us. "You don't have to carry it around like that, Callie," my old mentor chuckled. "It's not like you will ever need it. Hang it on the wall where it belongs. Let everyone see the source of our Salvation. The reason the war never touched us. The only reason we survived when the world broke in two."

"I know, but I like holding it," I said, suddenly remembering. I had taken away the Spear of Destiny, refusing to let either the Angels or Demons lay claim to it. I'd used the power of the Spear to make a safe-haven for my friends—a place where the war could not reach us. Beyond our dome of safety was only death and destruction, now.

"I'll let that joke go. Too easy," Claire said from the couch beside me, grinning.

I rolled my eyes at my best friend. "Has anyone seen Nate? I wanted to talk with him."

The room went as silent as a speech at a funeral wake. I frowned, looking over at Roland. His smile had evaporated.

"Nate Temple died twenty years ago, Callie..." Claire said in barely a whisper, frowning at me with a concerned look.

"Oh...right," I said, frowning in embarrassment.

Because I remembered. Nate had refused to join us, wanting to fight even though there was nothing to win without the Spear in play. Without all the new Horsemen Riding to battle.

But another thought seemed to be hammering at the base of my skull, giving me a headache. I almost felt like I had a fever. I could have sworn I had saved Nate at some point. Back when I had led the Shepherds. But... wait. Hadn't the Conclave been Demon-possessed? Hadn't *Claire* been possessed, too?

They'd wanted me to *kill* Nate Temple, hadn't they?

I realized I was breathing faster, sitting up straight in my chair on the verge of a panic attack. Was this some kind of sick joke? Why was I sitting here doing nothing? Where were we? Where was everyone else? All my other friends?

"Wait...that's not what happened," I slurred tiredly. "You saw, Cain. You were there."

"Is she teasing us?" Roland asked Cain. My friend, Cain, stared back at me, his face frozen in shock. But not at my comment, as if something I'd just said had concerned him very deeply. Or...had reminded him of something.

"I...think she's kidding," he finally murmured, his forehead furrowed. "We had a long trip back from Rome."

Claire grunted. "You haven't left the Den of Ed in years. No one has. Callie can't even walk!"

I flinched abruptly, each comment striking me like a switch. The Den of Ed...That was a wasteland I had once seen...Why would we live *there*? I never would have named a place after it.

Cain was blinking rapidly like someone had just asked him to solve a math problem in his head. He locked eyes with me, shaking his head in confusion. "The Den of Ed…" he repeated, testing the foreign words on his tongue. "That's not right. That *can't* be right. Apples…"

I struggled to sit up straighter and almost lost my balance, even though I was seated. I stared down at my legs to find two withered old twigs for all the good they would do me. They were essentially just bone. I began sucking in breaths rapidly, hyperventilating. This wasn't right. None of this was right. I couldn't just sit here and do nothing. I began panting harder, shaking my head. "No, no, no, no…"

"Oh, sweetie," Claire said, sounding heartbroken. "I'm sorry. I shouldn't have said it like that. Without your sacrifice, we would all be dead. Please forgive me," she pleaded, tucking a blanket over my legs and patting my bony thighs.

I tried to move them—to even make them twitch—and couldn't. I was gulping air, now, shivering. I had always been a mover—jogging for fun, training with Roland, fighting monsters. I gripped the Spear tighter and it began to crackle.

Roland jumped to his feet. "*Easy*, Callie. Please give me the Spear. If you break it, our defenses will fail and we'll be forced to fight!"

I stared up at my old mentor incredulously. "What…the fuck is *wrong with you?*" I screamed, spittle flying from my mouth. "*Of course*, we should be fighting!"

Cain was nodding, actually leaning forward interestedly, but Claire and Roland looked horrified.

"You robbed everyone, so we wouldn't *have* to fight, Callie. Don't you remember? You brought it all here, taking away the most dangerous artifacts in the world to keep us *safe*. Took them to the one place they couldn't get them." He held up his hands, spinning in a slow circle. "Solomon's Temple," he said. "In the Den of Ed."

Like a pricked bubble, I gasped. Roland looked suddenly relieved. "There, there. Do you remember now?" he asked, smiling compassionately.

I did. I remembered all too clearly. I had robbed Darling and Dear. Robbed Nate Temple. Robbed the Demons and Angels. I had been a thief, and I'd hoarded it all here, in my sanctuary—Solomon's Temple. I'd invited my friends to come live in safety, and closed the doors on any who refused, naming the land around my palace The Den of Ed.

I'd remembered ignoring those who labeled me traitor, coward, thief, and a liar…

Because I hadn't wanted to keep fighting, to keep sacrificing friends to a lost cause.

I'd offered them sanctuary. And most had refused. So *many* had died...

If I had been able to stand, I would have fallen to my knees in disgust of my own inadvertent apathy.

I'd ended the world with my apathy. "They're all dead..." I rasped, blinking back tears.

Roland nodded sadly, and I heard Claire sniffle. "You tried to tell them, but they wouldn't listen. Their loss. We don't need them." Claire nodded her agreement to Roland's claim.

I studied the two, shaking in disbelief. "You have it backwards...They. Needed. US!" I shrieked.

Cain's lips were pulled back in a snarl, not even seeming to be aware of it. I ignored Roland and Claire, and locked eyes with Cain. He nodded subtly.

"Now look what you've done," he abruptly snapped, jumping to his feet. He glared at both Roland and Claire. "You've startled her half to death! You know how she is on her bad days. How much her sacrifice cost her, not just physically, but emotionally! Go get her some tea. Now."

Claire and Roland winced in unison, apologizing profusely. Then Claire bolted from the room as if afraid Cain might chase her with a switch.

Cain rounded on Roland. "Go get her a warmer blanket and tell that infernal screaming to pipe the fuck down!"

Roland had taken two steps before Cain even finished speaking, but my mentor froze at the last comment. He slowly craned his neck to glance back at Cain from over his shoulder, frowning. "What are you talking about? I don't hear any screaming."

Cain didn't miss a beat. "Thought I heard someone shouting in the background. Never mind. It's gone now."

Roland nodded uncertainly. "I'll be right back. Don't let Callie move. You know how stubborn she gets in her fits. She's liable to try to run out of here and break her legs. Or the Spear. I'll call the healer to come check on her, and I'll make sure Claire doubles the pain medication in her tea." He turned to me with a concerned smile. "We'll get you some rest and you'll feel like new in a few minutes." Before I could scream in panic, he was gone, leaving me alone with Cain.

I struggled to stand, suddenly terrified that he was going to help them put me to sleep. The batty, old protector of this wasteland needed her pain medication doubled. What had I done? Why had they let me do it? Had they been that afraid of war to let me commit such an atrocity?

Cain was suddenly scooping me up and I began beating at him, scratching at his face with my free hand, the large Spear too cumbersome to stab him with from this angle. He didn't try to stop me, only spoke in a calm, measured voice. "Sister, if you're in there, I need you to listen up. I see a Silver Door, so I hope you have the Seal handy. Does any of that make sense to you?" he asked, grunting as my fingers scored a sharp line across his cheek.

I froze, staring up at his face from inches away. Silver Doors. That was an escape of some kind, but I couldn't remember where they led. "Cain? Is that really you?" I whispered.

He smiled. "More or less, no thanks to you," he admitted, eyes flicking to my bloody nails. "Unless you're just a crazy old lady who doesn't remember why a Door is significant..." I let out a sob of relief, pressing my face into his unshaven neck, my entire body shaking.

He patted me on the back reassuringly. "I'm so weak, Cain. And they're going to drug me. We have to get out of here before they get back!"

I heard steps outside from the hall and tensed. Cain was already moving, spinning me to face a Silver Door with about a dozen locks and bars on it as if it held the Devil himself on the other side. I was terrified of that Door for some reason. I couldn't remember where it led, or what was on the other side, but I knew it had been a long time since I had fought anything.

What if it led to an army of monsters? I had the Spear of Destiny, but I couldn't even stand.

I took a deep breath and heard an echoing gasp from the entrance to the room.

"What the *hell* are you doing?" Claire demanded, dropping a tray of cups. I heard Roland shouting and boots pounding up the stairs.

Then I felt magic blooming behind me and glanced over Cain's shoulder to see Roland staring at Cain murderously. Crimson power crackled around his fists. "Release her, now, Cain!" he warned menacingly. "If the Spear exits that door, the protection vanishes, and we will all die. I won't let you do that."

Claire stared at us, torn between attacking Cain and saving me, like I was the innocent victim in all of this. Then Roland made the decision for everyone and hurled power at us.

"Go, Cain!" I screamed, slamming the tip of my Spear into the center of the Silver Door as Cain dove for it.

The Silver Door exploded into splintered shards, and monstrous roars suddenly boomed through the opening like we really had just opened the Gates to Hell.

Roland's blast missed us by less than a heartbeat as we crossed the threshold, and I heard Claire wailing in horror. "What have you done? You've killed us all!" What felt like a waterfall of warm oil washed over me, cleansing me of…

Something. I couldn't remember what.

The sound of rushing wind and a demonic laughter filled my ears. I was falling and decided I may as well have a scream. But I fell for longer than I could hold my scream. As I was getting ready for a second scream, I realized I wasn't alone.

Cain was beside me, but he wasn't screaming. He looked asleep.

Knowing we were about to die, I tried to remember something pleasant about my life. All sorts of memories came to mind—some happy, many terrifying or sad. But the strangest thing of all was…

I had no idea why I was falling.

And why was Cain falling with me?

CHAPTER 32

I waited for the moment I would splatter onto cold rocks like a Picasso impersonation, but we began hitting clouds. Frigid, wet clouds. They slowed our descent more than they should have, and we abruptly landed on a patch of cold stone no harder than if we had tripped over our shoelaces.

The laughter had grown increasingly louder as we fell, and I scanned our surroundings in a frantic motion, trying to gauge the threat. I saw that we were on a spit of rock hanging in midair—a bridge of sorts—with no other land in sight.

Cain lay motionless ahead of me; even when I poked his rear with the butt of my Spear, he did not move. I risked a glance down at him, fearing I had used him to break my fall and killed him.

I hissed to find his back a wash of raw, burned flesh—still smoking in places. What the hell?

I poked him harder, seeing that he was breathing. "Get up, Cain. You have to get up," I pleaded, growing increasingly panicked as I swept our surroundings.

Because it was familiar in a strange way. We were on a bridge. A long, thin bridge of stone hanging in midair. We were smack-dab in the center. Well, kind of. The bridge was evenly bisected by a thin line of dark and light. Half of the bridge extended off towards the light, revealing a blue sky and a white throne where the bridge became a circular island of sorts.

The other half of the bridge stretched off into a dark sky, ultimately leading to a black throne on another dark island. Cain lay on the illuminated side of the line, and I was seated on the dark side of the line.

The black throne closest to me was not empty. The occupant was the source of the laughter. I struggled to flip Cain over and was relieved to find that my legs were functional again.

I hesitated at such a bizarre thought. Of course they were functional. Had I hit my head in my fall? Why wouldn't my legs have worked? I shook off the thought and began shaking Cain. He opened his eyes with a gasping groan, sitting up straight. He gritted his teeth at the obvious pain, but he had his priorities straight. They scanned the bridge like a predator until he found the source of the laughter.

His eyes narrowed, and he struggled to his feet. I helped him, using my Spear to help support his bulk. We faced the creature from the center of the bridge, our boots halfway between light and dark. And I knew him.

Samael began to clap as he descended from the black throne, his laughter fading to an amused chuckle. "Well, well, well, look at what the cat dragged in…" he mused, his cloven hooves grinding down upon the stone bridge at the base of his throne. I could hear a faint tinkling of metal as he moved. Almost like chainmail.

I remembered meeting another Demon named Amira in this exact place before. She had taunted me mercilessly, trying to get me to use the Spear of Destiny against her. But each step I had taken closer to the dark throne had weakened the Spear, and each step closer to the light throne had strengthened it. The two bands of black that marked where the Spear had been broken into thirds were slightly brighter than I remember, but somehow also darker.

I tried to step back, knowing that the Spear still wasn't fully repaired, and that we just might need its power to survive the next few minutes against the Greater Demon.

Samael approached, white teeth emerging from his black visage. "Go ahead. You're going to need it at full strength in a few moments," he said politely. "I don't need to deceive you. Not this close to the end of your miserable existence."

I began shuffling back, feeling the Spear of Destiny growing stronger with each step, the fractures rebuilding infinitesimally. Not approaching its original strength, but much stronger than it had been moments ago. Something had happened to it recently, breaking it further, but I couldn't recall what that was.

My mind felt so fuzzy.

But my strength was alive and well. I could feel my muscles twitching in anticipation, ready for a fight. And I could feel the Silvers in my blood, snarling to be let loose.

I studied Samael as he continued his approach, forcing us into a corner —into the light where the white throne sat. He was just a ten-foot-tall figure in black, with a cloak trailing him for about another ten feet, like an ebony bridal gown's train. The only features I could make out were his white teeth, his fiery red eyes, and the strange clinking sound.

He finally reached the line demarking the light and grunted. Then he stepped over it.

Smoke lifted from his hooves and I heard him grinding his teeth, but he kept advancing, more of him entering the light, and more of him smoking as a result. I had never actually seen him before, but I knew him deep in my soul. His very presence was a declaration of his name, no matter what body he possessed.

I stared in disbelief, understanding that the light was torturing him and that he also didn't care. I also noticed that his flesh was made of tarnished silver coins, and his hair and beard were made of scored, tarnished silver chains—the source of the clinking sound. But despite the texture of his skin, his features were...beautiful. Stunningly cruel, but perfect in every way.

His upper body was bare and not as heavily muscled as I would have thought. He was lean and emaciated, but his skin was also flawless, and I got the sense that he was hungry—that he hadn't eaten in a while and would flesh out easily once he fed.

His lower body was that of a goat, ending in cloven hooves the size of my head, and entirely covered in fur made of more chains. His cloak seemed made of patched leather, and I suddenly felt queasy, thinking they were about the right size for scalps.

Human scalps.

Cain began to snarl defiantly, holding out his bone dagger before him in warning. "Leave her alone. You want a fight, I'm right here, Samantha."

Samael rolled his eyes—I'm not sure how I knew, since they were simply orbs of red fire—and continued his advance. "You are already destined to join my brothers in Hell, Cain. Unfortunately, you won't be seeing Abel anytime soon. He got a free pass upstairs."

Cain laughed loudly, straightening his shoulders to shake my arm off and step between us. "You think I don't know that, Samantha?" he scoffed. "That I haven't thought about that every single day since I killed him?"

Samael shrugged, not seeming even remotely annoyed at Cain's nickname for him. Then he glanced over his shoulder, back at the black throne. Lightning flared in the distance, and a steady, rumbling growl reached our ears, revealing roiling clouds as if something was approaching through the sky. The lightning flashed again, and I caught a faint silhouette of a massive figure on a throne, his wings flared out high above his shoulders as if stretching his arms above his head after a long nap.

He made Samael look tiny. To look so large from so far away...I shuddered in horror. I also recognized him. I had seen him twice before while fighting against his minions. This Demon had been a silhouette in their eyes as I watched them take their last breaths after killing them.

I frowned at that thought.

Last Breath...

Samael turned back to us, grinning wide. "He grants your wish, Cain. Thank him, for soon you will serve him." Samael met my eyes for a moment. "I'll deal with you in a moment, girl. Don't worry. I have something special in store for the one who set me free," he purred, his chain beard swinging and clinking as he laughed.

"What do you want, Samael?" I demanded. "Cain is nothing to you. I think you're here for something long, hard, and eager to say hello. But we'll start with just the tip."

He grinned back. "Naturally," he admitted. "I can practically *taste* your hatred, White Rose. It makes this next part so much sweeter."

"Come get it, then," I taunted, tugging Cain back beside me.

Samael sighed. "You do not wield even *half* the power you will need to confront me, Daughter of Solomon. Let alone enough to actually defeat me. Run along, gather some more. I can be patient. Take as much power as you want from the world. Whenever you are content, we will meet. You have but to call out my name." He continued to advance, looking amused at our defiance. I hadn't realized we had continued stepping back, my Spear growing stronger with each step.

But his words froze my bones. Was he that arrogant? Or was he telling the truth? I could sense his raw power. It was enough to make my skin feel tight, almost forcing me back.

"You lie," I snarled, gripping my Spear tighter.

Samael paused. Then he blinked a few times. Finally, he sighed. "Have at it, then, White Rose. I will not move. Do your worst and see for yourself." He lifted his arms and waited.

"I don't see any Doors, Callie..." Cain muttered under his breath. I frowned suddenly.

Doors. This was a challenge.

Icy fingers suddenly danced across my scalp at the realization.

We weren't here to fight Samael. This wasn't real. Or, at least, it wasn't my true purpose. I was on a Quest to find Solomon's Temple. And this asshole was in my way. Maybe I could kill two birds with one stone...

"We just need to stall him long enough to find it," I whispered back.

"That might be a problem. I don't think he was exaggerating about his strength."

"I can hear you, in case you were wondering," Samael said with a chuckle. "And I *want* you to find the Doors, Callie. How else would you get the strength to stand against me someday? The strength to avenge Cain's death?"

We both tensed, expecting an attack, but nothing happened.

Samael grinned. "I'm a Demon of my word. I'll let you have the first punch."

I shared a long look with Cain. Then I scanned the bridge for Doors. There weren't any. Without another word, I drew deep on my wizard's magic, calling up every drop I could muster. Then I fueled it with white light, something I seemed to recall hearing that most wizards couldn't do. Something related to my ties to Heaven—whether through blood or happenstance, I didn't know. Or couldn't remember. I thought I remembered one other person who could do it...

I waved away the irrelevant thought. Regardless, the white tint made for a stronger punch in the magical arena.

I hit Samael with everything I had—one great concussive blast to his forehead with a condensed vortex of power the size of a dime. Cain groaned as I let the power go, almost knocked from his feet. The release of so much power made me wobble on my own feet, seeing stars and feeling as if I was about to vomit. It was all I could to do continue clutching the Spear and not drop to my knees, panting.

My magic hit Samael directly. He didn't even try to block or deflect it.

His beard clinked slightly, and he may have blinked.

Samael stared back at me, nonplussed, his smile stretching wider. "My—"

He had been too busy gloating to notice the Spear of Destiny screaming towards his face.

But he had good reflexes. He batted it away like a pesky fly, frowning at it in annoyance. But all I heard was the echoing splintering sound. Not a final snap of breaking entirely, but the more torturous creaking noise. The broken Spear went flying off the bridge—into the infinite sky. I grabbed Cain by the sleeve and leapt off the bridge, my wings of ice and stone chips erupting from my back on instinct. I tucked them close, increasing my speed as we shot down after the Spear. I managed to grasp it and unfurled my wings, halting my descent and sweeping us back up to rise above the opposite side of the bridge than we had plummeted from.

Something snatched at my wing, shattering it with a squeeze before hurling us into the white throne. I felt multiple bones break, and my wings crunch upon impact. Blood oozed from my lips and my vision wavered to show a stunned Cain at the base of the throne, barely able to see straight as he struggled to regain his feet.

I held the Spear in my hand but gasped to find that it was nearly broken into thirds, the wood bowing alarmingly at the weak junctures so that it was no longer perfectly straight, barely able to even support its own structure. Dropping it may have been strong enough to destroy it for good.

And...I was sitting on the white throne, where it should have been at its strongest. I shambled to my feet, falling down the steps to check on Cain, my broken wing trailing behind me, flaring with throbs of agony as it bumped each step. I gritted my teeth, my eyes watering against the pain as I helped Cain to his feet. He stared back woozily, then noticed something behind me.

"The Door," he whispered eagerly.

"You are free to go, White Rose," Samael growled. "Tuck your broken wings between your legs and run through your precious Door with your broken Spear. I'm afraid Cain won't be joining you. I need you properly motivated to fight me down the road, Callie. I don't want you running and hiding from me when I come calling. Not a second time," he added, chuckling.

"No..." I whispered, shaking my head defiantly. Then I grabbed Cain's sleeve. "You can't have him. If he stays, I stay."

Samael frowned. "Then you both die," he explained, sounding annoyed.

"Just go, Callie," Cain growled, jerking free of my grip.

I snatched back on, harder this time. "No! I'm not leaving you with him!" I hissed.

"Are you certain?" Samael asked, staring directly at me.

I ignored Cain's protests, answering Samael with a resolute nod. "Yes."

Samael let out an annoyed breath. "Oh, well. It probably wouldn't have even been a good fight anyway. I'm just romanticizing it. Perhaps I'll just kill you instead, leaving Cain to eternally wander this place alone, reliving the moment he lost his *second* sibling."

Then, in an absent, almost dismissive gesture, Samael lashed out with a black trident of inky obsidian that was about a mile long. I hadn't even seen him holding it. I snapped my eyes shut, accepting my fate, knowing I could never dodge it in time. I heard the thud of impact.

But...I felt nothing.

I opened my eyes to see that something obstructed my view. Cain stared at me, his eyes wide. Three barbed points stuck from out of his chest, only inches away from piercing the both of us. He coughed up blood and fell to his knees.

"Idiot," Samael murmured absently.

I gasped, following my brother down to the ground. I was screaming in horror, slapping at his shoulders, hitting him, punching him. "What have you done?" I shrieked at him, sobbing over Samael's laughter. This wasn't fair. Wasn't how it was supposed to happen.

Cain gasped in pain, struggling to draw enough air from his torn lungs to speak. "I thought I'd hold the Door open for you...Sis," he rasped. He shoved his bone dagger into my hands weakly. "Take it." Then he coughed up more blood as Samael jerked the trident back from his torso.

Cain weaved back and forth for a moment and finally lifted his hands to my shoulders to support himself. He managed a smile through bloody teeth as I wept, gripping the broken Spear in one fist and Cain's bone dagger in the other, ready to hurl them both at Samael the moment my brother died.

Cain squeezed my shoulders weakly, drawing my attention. "You tried to warn me…that sisters are the *worst*. You were wrong…" he said, smiling weakly. "*Brothers* are the worst. Get out of my room, brat."

And he shoved me.

The motion was so unexpected that I toppled right through the Door behind me, cursing and screaming as I dropped my weapons in an attempt to snatch onto the frame with my bloody fingers—anything to keep me beside Cain for one moment longer, to at least see his eyes close for the last time.

But all I heard was Samael taunting me. "I'll be seeing you soon, White Rose…"

I wished I could have told Cain that I didn't have much longer to live myself, because my vision was already tunneling. I had broken something in my head when I struck the throne.

Something important…

CHAPTER 33

I landed in a pool of boiling water and instantly screamed as my head went completely under, the water scalding not only my flesh, but my open wounds. My sensory receptors exploded with pins and needles and my skin twitched and burned with both fire and ice, tugging and pulling as the conflicting sensations raced from my toes to my ears. My eyes shot open at the unexpected shock, and then they too caught fire as if flushed with acid.

My scalp tugged and twisted agonizingly.

I floundered for the surface, the pain so overwhelming I thought I was about to gasp and suck down the boiling liquid and burn my insides raw. I breached the surface, gasping frantically, realizing that the water was only waist-deep—if even that.

And the air was pure fog and steam.

I stared down at my body as the pain slowly began to ebb and fade. My wounds...

Were gone. Or almost gone. I felt as weak as a day-old kitten, though. And I was wearing only a silver cross for some reason. I wasn't sure where I had gotten it, but it looked old. Its heavy weight stuck to my chest rather than hanging free as I glanced left and right in an attempt to pierce the fog and find out where I was.

Or how I had gotten here. I focused on that last one, gripping the cross in my fingers and squeezing until my fingers ached. Then it hit me.

Samael. I'd fought the Greater Demon...and he'd kicked my ass. Did that mean I was in Hell? It was very hot, but it was also...pleasant. And the water seemed to have healed my wounds.

"Would ye look at that, Aidan," an older man sang in a deep, Irish accent, his face suddenly leaning forward from out of the fog. "Hair as white as a rose."

I squawked instinctively, jumping back a step upon realizing that I wasn't alone and that my nudity was on full display. Where the hell had he come from? And who was Aidan?

And where was my brother when I wanted protection from a creepy old—

Cain...

My legs turned to jelly and gave out as a high-pitched whining sound abruptly filled my ears. Instead of sinking, my rear landed on a submerged bench near the outer lip of the apparent hot tub—the seat low enough to leave only my head and neck above the surface. I tucked my knees to my chest and wrapped my arms around them, hugging myself into a ball as I blinked back sudden tears, resting my chin on my forearms as I pursed my lips to keep from openly weeping.

I no longer cared that a stranger shared the hot tub with me. I didn't care about anything.

Cain was *dead*. He had sacrificed himself to save me from Samael. The demon I had accidentally unleashed upon the world. My only friend in this place was gone. My brother was gone. I had the vague suspicion that other important people had died recently, but all I could think about was Cain. Through my tears, I realized I was actually biting my lips, now, a deep ocean of rage bubbling up within my heart.

Another thought drifted in and out of focus through my warring anger and agony, taunting me, but I couldn't catch a hold of it. It was something about this place—the reason Cain and I had chosen to come here...

What he had died for...

"White Rose, eh?" another man asked from directly beside me, chuckling jovially at my new nickname. I managed not to flinch at the realization that I'd almost landed in this second old man's lap when I had fallen into my seat.

188

That would have started an unwanted party.

"The bloomin' hell did ye come from, then?" he asked, waving a hand to dispel some of the steam between us and reveal a bulbous, red nose and a scraggly beard that dominated a rather small face. He was old and looked wiry—his cheeks were drawn, and sported a long, wicked scar on one side—and his milky green eyes were that of a kindly but crafty grandfather.

"When yer our age, Aidan," the first man piped back up, leaning forward as if to give his friend a hard time, "ye don't question miracles. Ye just t'ank the Lord." He pursed his lips and jerked his chin down, signaling he had stated an unarguable fact. Then he shot me a mischievous wink before leaning back again.

The larger man's cheeks were red, plump, and round above his thick white beard, and the skin beneath his eyes was puffy, giving him a perpetual squint—or a permanent smirk. He sported maybe three hairs on the top of his head, and his skin was windburned from a life spent outdoors. His emerald green eyes were vibrant, and I sensed a ruthless intelligence in those depths. This man wasn't just smart—he was also no stranger to danger. I could tell that he was deliberately orchestrating his body language to assure me he meant no harm, but I could tell there was no deceit in it. No trickery. He genuinely wanted me to feel safe.

"Aye, Paddy," the scrawny man—Aidan, apparently—agreed in mock reverence. "Praise be to Jeezus, and all of that other nonsense."

Paddy rolled his eyes as he grumbled an apologetic prayer that I couldn't quite catch, but his tone made it sound like a familiar curse aimed at the blaspheming Aidan.

Despite everything, I felt myself relaxing. Maybe it was the hot water fusing my body back together. The banter of these two old men—and the utter ridiculousness of my current situation—was even forcing a sliver of a smile to creep over my cheeks, even though happiness was the last thing I wanted to feel right now. I was growing accustomed to the fog, and the two men slowly came into focus without me having to squint.

Paddy noticed my obvious discomfort at being nude in a hot tub with two strange men and smiled disarmingly, pointing out a stack of towels behind me. "We don't bite, child. And Aidan's as blind as shite on a log. Ye may as well be a sheep for all he can tell."

"A shite in shinin' armor, I is!" Aidan cackled, splashing water at Paddy.

"But she ain't no sheep, that's for certain. She's a White Rose! Ye said so yerself!"

Paddy wiped the splashed water from his face, rolling his eyes. "Those must belong to ye," he said, pointing. I turned to see my leather clothes neatly folded up within reaching distance from the pool. The Spear of Destiny rested atop them, and I cringed to see the deep cracks in the haft—the two places where it had once been broken and re-forged now looking hollow and brittle. A flick of the finger might be enough to destroy those weak points.

I turned back to my new pals, frowning thoughtfully. Why weren't they bothered by the fact that I had just appeared out of nowhere? They hadn't asked a single question, taking the whole situation in stride. More importantly, why was I here in the first place?

"Where am I?" I asked, prioritizing my needs. Because wherever I was, I needed power. I needed to go find weapons. Magic. Anything that would give me the strength to crucify Samael—to avenge Cain.

"She speaks, she drinks!" Aidan cheered, suddenly holding a glass of whiskey in his hands.

Paddy nodded his agreement, holding a glass of whiskey in each of his beefy hands. I spotted a bottle resting on the edge of the pool but didn't see a label. "Welcome to Dublin, White Rose," he said, extending a glass my way. "God invented whiskey to keep the Irish from rulin' the world, but we keep tryin' anyway!"

I frowned hesitantly, drinking being the newest last thing on my mind... after happiness.

"No harm in declinin'," he said gently. Something about the look on my face made his own crinkle compassionately. "I have a niece about yer age— pretty as a *red* rose, as a matter of fact—and I would hate it somethin' terrible if I ever saw such sorrow on her sweet, freckled cheeks."

"Aye," Aidan growled, suddenly sounding surprisingly dangerous. "Point out the bastard that set such a fright in yer eyes!"

"We'll roast him on a spit," Paddy assured me in a calm, promising tone.

"Give him a proper kickin', and maybe a few more on the ground for good measure!" Aidan added, sounding like he meant it quite literally.

I accepted the glass of whiskey with an uneasy smile and took a sip, hoping to draw their attention back from what they assumed was a boy problem—but I did find it oddly comforting, their sudden protective streak for a damsel in distress.

Chivalry wasn't dead in this hot tub.

The whiskey hit my tongue like straight smoke and fire, almost making me cough in surprise. It wasn't that it was bad—it was delicious—but I hadn't quite expected such a kick. The burn somehow helped to soothe the pain in my heart at the loss of Cain. I glanced about the room, searching for an exit of some kind, but it seemed I would have to get out of the pool to check because the room was massive, illuminated by dim torches that didn't quite reach the outer walls. Our hot tub was one of a dozen, reminding me of a Roman bath house.

I needed a way out. I needed to get stronger. To avenge Cain. Regardless of why we had ever come here, that was all I cared about now. I stared into my glass of whiskey, imagining it fueling my rage, strengthening me, like lighting a fuse.

"I don't know what yer lookin' for, Lass, but ye should stop and smell the roses, ye should."

I looked up to find Paddy staring at me. "Pardon?" I asked.

Aidan grunted. "Oh, Jeezus, Paddy. This one speaks all proper-like." I turned to Aidan, leveling him with a stern look. "Bugger off, you," he snapped right back. "What the fancy idiot is tryin' to say is that if ye can't sit back and enjoy a point, what's the pint?"

I frowned, wondering if we were having a failure to communicate, his accent throwing me off. "I think you have that backwards. If you can't sit back and enjoy a *pint*, what's the *point*, right?" I asked, switching the words to make sense of his drunken advice.

He snapped his fingers, leaning forward as if he had just trapped me. "Good advice. Ye should take it, White Rose." And then he pinched a piece of my hair, flicking it teasingly.

I stared at him, utterly gob smacked. How drunk was he?

Paddy cleared his throat. "There's a time for fire, and a time for water. A time for sowin', and a time for reapin'. A life of one over the other is a life of pain. Balance, child. Pint," he said, holding up his glass of whiskey as a figurative example. "Point," he said, jerking his beard at my Spear. "Wield them both, child, and then ye will always be content."

"But the world isn't black and white—" I cut off, realizing my argument was only proving his point. "Balance," I muttered, holding up my hand before he could point out my flaw. "Live in the gray."

Paddy nodded sagely. "A life spent at only the bottom of a bottle is no life. A life spent only at the end of a spear is no life." He winked at me mischievously. "But bring a pint down to the fields of war...with ye all covered in blood and whatnot, sippin' a cool lick of whiskey after yer victory..." he sighed rapturously. "What more could ye ask for?"

"Blood and whiskey!" Aidan chimed in, clinking his glass.

"But I just want the world to burn," I whispered, unable to shake the replay of Samael murdering Cain before me. "I want to punish them. All of them. Over and over again...I want them to taste my pain in every fiber of their being. I want their *descendants* to taste that pain as a genetic trait passed down from generation to generation."

I waited for them to gasp in disgust, to chastise me, but I heard only silence. I looked up to find them smiling knowingly. "Scales tip back and forth, leanin' more heavily in one direction at times. Sittin' in perfect balance is boring. It's static. Do ye want a life of standin' perfectly still, too cautious to risk rockin' the boat?" Paddy asked. Then he made an unflattering flatulent noise with his lips and slapped his belly with a laugh.

"As you skip through the castle of vengeance, be sure to whistle a tune and admire the pictures on the walls. Murder a bastard. Bed a fine Irish lad. Light a field on fire. Taste a cake. Croon a song with a child, laugh with a friend. Stop to smell the roses, even when they're splattered with the blood of your enemies," Aidan said, flicking my hair with a finger again.

Paddy took a healthy sip of his whiskey, his deep voice resembling the sound of gravel as a result. "I have never in me life seen somethin' so beautiful as the moment of fierce silence after the storm of battle. The sun risin', the birds chirpin' hesitantly, the laughter of the survivors." He met my eyes. "Ye don't focus on the death. Ye learn from it, to be sure. But what happens *after* a battle?"

I frowned. "I don't know."

"They make *songs*...about *life*," Aidan whispered adamantly. "Songs of joy, of their loves back home. They celebrate."

Paddy nodded his agreement. "Ye can't live a life of war without lovin' somethin'. Without havin' somethin' to fight for. Somethin' to smile about. Someone to drink with." To prove his point, he held out his glass in a toast. Aidan and I complied and took a drink. "And when you do finally get your justice…" Paddy went on, "well, murder would have never tasted so sweet as one fueled by a lovin' heart. Make your rage a shrine to the fallen, beautiful enough to make men weep, cruel enough to make Demons flee. But do a little dance, after, or ye will look like a psychopath."

I was pretty sure doing a dance after making a shrine of my enemies would be the psychotic decision, but I knew what he meant. "You guys are hardcore," I finally admitted with an easy smile. "Cheers." They took healthy drinks, looking satisfied they had taught me something.

I idly wondered where they had come to their conclusion, what with all their archaic *fields of battle* analogies, but what really dominated my thoughts was Samael.

And a healthy dose of rage.

I recalled Cain's easygoing manner, how he had always made me laugh at the worst times, and felt a grin fighting for a place on my cheeks.

Balance. Not just rage, but something to stoke that coal. A cool breeze to make it white hot.

Samael's cruel, vicious laugh, and Cain's dry, sarcastic laugh.

"Who are ye, girl?" Paddy asked softly, studying me with those cunning, dangerous eyes.

I opened my mouth but immediately hesitated. I wasn't quite sure how to answer. Names were such fleeting things, but they were supposed to be powerful, weren't they? They were supposed to mean something.

So, who was I?

I almost told them I was nobody. Nameless. It felt right, but it also felt wrong.

And Nameless made me feel like my thumb was cold. It wasn't right. I dipped my hand back into the water, battling the imagined chill as I thought about their simple question.

What was my name? Who was I?

I knew I wanted to destroy the Demon and that I had lost a brother. But that was it.

I'd had a name, once, but I wasn't sure it still applied. I had discarded it at some point. When Cain had taken his last—

A slow smile came over my face.

"I'm a demon's last breath. I'm a sinner." I smiled at them. "I'm the White Rose."

The last one fit the best, like a tight glove—but they all felt correct to some extent. The two men nodded somberly, sensing the depth to my answer. "And I think I've got some dancing to do." I knew there was more to my name, but I'd just have to figure that out later. After I leveled up enough to defeat Samael.

I cast Aidan a stern look. "Turn your head before your ears curl," I told him, and then I climbed out of the pool, setting my glass down on the ledge. I ignored Paddy's booming laughter and Aidan's standing ovation as I toweled off and dressed, careful not to nudge the Spear. Then I scooped up the Holy weapon with both hands, closed my eyes, and focused on keeping it safe. The Spear winked out of existence, disappearing somewhere within my body where I had been used to carrying it up until recently. Even though I couldn't quite remember when I had pulled it out in the first place.

I paused to find a bone dagger had been tucked beneath my clothes. Cain's blade...

I scooped it up, testing it between my fingers. The hilt was warm, and I pretended the heat was a parting gift from my brother Cain—a reminder to stop and smell the roses, my balance, a loving, comforting hand on my shoulder.

Even though it was obviously only warm because it had been sitting on the warm stone of the bath house.

Two doors lay before me all of a sudden, gleaming silver. Their glow seemed to thicken the steam, obscuring the edges of the room. About six-feet of empty space separated them.

I knew one door represented vengeance.

The other door represented a sister's love for her brother.

I gritted my teeth, lifted my hands, and clapped them together. My fists suddenly glowed silver, and the two Doors hammered into each other with a great gonging sound that made the steam in the air suddenly pulse with agitation.

I placed a hand on the center of the double doors and shoved, flinging them wide open.

"Don't forget to arm yourself, lass," Paddy reminded me.

"With pints *and* points," Aidan added with a wink.

I felt a heavy weight in my pocket and pulled out an unfamiliar silver butterfly brooch that I must have picked up at some point. It made me smile for some reason, like a red-hot kiss in my palm. I pocketed it, deciding to use it—and Cain's dagger—as my pint. Because Cain and that cute butterfly both seemed hungry for blood and laughter.

I glanced over my shoulder, nodded, and then I danced through the Doors.

"Our little psychopath is a' dancin'!" Aidan cheered, clinking glasses with Paddy.

The Doors groaned closed behind me, leaving me to dance in the darkness alone.

CHAPTER 34

I couldn't remember how many Doors I had used, and I didn't really care, to be honest. I only cared that I grew stronger for it—picked up some item each time I went through, some weapon I could use against Samael.

Because I had a very clear list of priorities, and they were the only things keeping me from breaking, from listening too closely to the ghosts of whoever I had once been.

Open Doors.

Gain power.

Slaughter Samael.

Stop to smell the roses.

With each Door, I grew stronger, deadlier, and less compassionate.

And more and more, I discarded pieces of myself—whoever that naïve person had been. But since I kept my priorities at the forefront of my attention, I no longer cared about that. It was a trade-off. Each step through a Door showed me wondrous, terrible things and places and people, replacing who I had been with a new person and a new name.

On a distant level, this troubled me, but I told myself I would turn my attention to it after dealing with Samael. After hurling my silver butterfly brooch through his heart like a bullet.

After plunging Cain's dagger in each of his eyes.

Slowly.

After I made him beg me to do it.

I stared at the white fire crackling before me. The mountain air was chilly up here, but I'd acquired a hooded cloak of living crystal flame to keep me warm—among other things. Strange horses grazed in the skeletal, barren trees just beyond the campfire's light. I could smell hot blood in the frigid air, proving the beasts weren't eating foliage, but something that had once had a pulse.

"Well?" a voice asked, drawing my attention back.

I looked up at the cloaked figure, studying his strange Mask and his strange wings. He was dangerous, this one. Something about him felt familiar, too, but I'd long ago given up on trying to kindle those types of feelings. They just left me frustrated.

And I'd found that when I grew frustrated, I wasted energy killing everything in sight before I moved on to the next Door.

He offered two items to me, both incredibly powerful. But they had figurative chains attached, and I didn't like chains, even figurative ones.

A Silver Door shimmered into existence behind him and I let out an impatient sigh, turning back to his proffered 'gifts.'

I finally climbed to my feet. "I'll find another merchant," I told him, kicking the snow from my boots.

He studied me in silence. "I'm not selling anything, Cal—"

"Everyone is selling something," I snarled hurriedly—feeling angrier than the situation warranted. I didn't know why.

His twin flames for eyes acknowledged my reaction without even a flicker, despite the screaming wind. "Let me know when you change your mind," he said in a tired voice. "When you remember who you are."

Something tried to hold me back, to tear off that Mask and see what tortured soul hid beneath, what cocky bastard dared challenge me with such a simple statement, but I wisely forced myself towards the Door and stepped through before I gave any serious thought to killing him for the comment.

I wasn't sure who would have won anyway. He was incredibly powerful —a wild, chaotic man lurking beneath a calm façade and a Mask. He looked like the type of person to dance at the end of the world.

We likely both would have died in a confrontation.

And that wouldn't have helped me complete my checklist.

But for some strange reason, as I palmed my silver butterfly charm, I imagined kissing him...

CHAPTER 35

I stared dubiously up at the tiny, talking, mushroom-munching bear perched on the boulder atop the hill ahead of me.

"I fail to see how letting you see my breasts will help me kill Samael," I repeated, scanning the peaceful clearing for a Silver Door, growing agitated.

He giggled, tossing another mushroom up into the air and catching it in his mouth. Then he leaned back onto his boulder and closed his eyes with a contented grumble. "What if I said I was a breast whisperer?" he asked, cocking one eye open to peer down at me, gauging my reaction with a strange look on his muzzle. Was he…smiling?

"I'd have a new bear rug to make, Starlight," I growled. I frowned at the last word, not knowing where I had pulled it from or why I had called him that.

His eyes flashed to mine and he opened his mouth, his tongue hanging free as he nodded. "You *do* remember some things…" he mused, scratching a paw at his grey-flecked muzzle. "Looks like I get to show you some pretty twisted shit. Oh, and I don't need to see your breasts. Been there, done that," he added, chuckling.

I glared at him in disbelief. *"Excuse me?"* I snarled. "You most certainly have not seen—"

He flung up a paw and an orb of smoking, golden light abruptly struck me in the face, bathing me with heat. The forest clearing around us suddenly disappeared and I saw a vision of me in a sweat lodge, completely naked, with this exact bear guiding me through some form of meditation. And he most definitely saw my breasts.

Then the vision was gone so fast that I stumbled as I found myself still standing in the clearing. The bear hadn't moved, and the glowing orb hadn't actually harmed me in any way. I stared him in the eyes, not understanding the vision or how I had forgotten such a bizarre event, and definitely not approving of him throwing a ball of light at me.

But what really bothered me was that I apparently knew this talking bear.

He snorted. "Told you. Been there, done that." He suddenly rolled off the boulder, hit the ground with a grunt, and then continued rolling towards me down a small hill covered in flowers. "*Weee…*" he sang, giggling until he came to a stop a pace from my boots, flowers stuck in his fur, but he sat upright with a serious expression as he met my eyes. "Now, do you want me to show you some stuff that you *don't* want to see, or some stuff that you *do* want to see?"

I hesitated, recalling my priorities—to kill Samael. "Stuff that I do want to see," I said, giving the obvious answer.

"That's a really good choice, but I'm going to show you both anyway."

I folded my arms. "Not likely."

"First," he went on as if I hadn't spoken, "you're going to want to take off your new weapons. For your benefit, not mine. They'll mess with the visions—and probably your sanity."

"That's it. I'm going to go find the next Door," I told him, checking the trees behind him. Sadly, I saw no Doors, just endless thick woods.

He sighed patiently, leaning back on his paws. "Like a good little Catholic, you are scared of Relevations."

"I think you mean Revelations," I said, not understanding the reference, but knowing he had misspoken the word.

The bear shook his head. "No. Relevant Revelations. Relevations," he explained. "Those truths that are uncomfortable. The ones inside your own walls—the assassins in the shadows of your own castle. Heard it in a movie, so it must be true." Then he began laughing.

I didn't know what a movie was, but his explanation was bafflingly sane somehow, so I finally shrugged, still not seeing any Doors to take me away from this place. The damned bear must have something I could use against Samael—even if he was overdosing on his mushrooms.

"And you will not touch my things?" I asked.

He held up a paw in a solemn oath. "As a rule, I don't like *things*. Just experiences. I will not touch them, and I will keep them safe for you until you return."

I appraised him warily but saw no cause for concern. He was trustworthy. I simply knew it like one knows water is wet. And his warning to take off anything that might interfere with the visions he was about to show me made sense. I didn't want to overreact while holding onto a deadly weapon.

I took off my hooded cloak of living crystal flame and laid it out on the grass like a blanket, murmuring soothingly to it. The crystal flame listened, reforming into a smooth, comfortable spot for me to rest upon.

Then I stabbed Cain's dagger into the earth.

I slipped off the obsidian halo from my head, ignoring it's incessant whining. I still wasn't entirely sure about that acquisition, what with all the baggage it seemed to carry along with it. Even if it could let me see a God with my own naked eyes.

I set it on the grass, suspiciously close to Cain's dagger, smiling as the whining instantly ceased in fear.

I took off my curled jade earrings and touched them together, surprised at how silent the world now felt—since I was no longer able to hear the thoughts of every living thing. The trees had been louder than I had realized, their gentle humming song like a soothing mantra.

I pulled off the ring of pure white light from my right thumb, and then six other rings that were harder to explain, let alone understand. I knew only how to use them as weapons and hadn't bothered listening to the previous owner explain their other abilities. I shook the pile of rings in my palm, closed my eyes, and blew a faint breath over them. When I opened my eyes, they were gone. Just like the previous owner had told me.

Most of the other weapons I had acquired were unseen—merely in my mind—and impossible to remove. Power. Magic. Spells. Understanding. Stories. Manling Tales. Fairy Tales.

Truths.

I stared down at the bear and nodded my head that I was ready.

"You probably want to sit down..." he suggested.

"I'm sure I'll be fine."

"Cool," he said. Then he leapt up faster than I had expected and slapped me on the forehead with the pad of his paw, knocking me down into the grass.

Instead of hitting the grass, I splashed into what felt like a pool. Then the clearing—and the bear—winked out of existence, leaving me in a void of nothingness. I stared down at my body and was startled to discover that I didn't actually *have* one. I was just...part of the Nothingness. A sentient, voiceless, bodiless void. But I could still recall my purpose.

Kill Samael.

The void shook wildly, and then morphed into a scene that felt somehow familiar.

A strong, older man in a leather coat knelt before a Cross made of red-hot coals. His hands were covered in blood, and his entire body flickered with crimson fire as he struggled to hold the Cross together. He was laughing and crying, tears of blood streaming down his cheeks.

Someone else was laughing and crying as well, a matching harmony to his, but it came from everywhere and nowhere, and felt like it was fighting to stop the man and his Cross.

The image *rippled* like a reflection in a pond and was replaced by another.

Two puppies chasing each other playfully through puddles of blood—jumping, splashing, and barking as their tails wagged back and forth, flinging blood everywhere.

Ripple.

A beautiful Sphinx telling herself riddles in a silver mirror—somehow giving wrong answers but *not* wrong answers.

Ripple.

A wooden Cross Pattée cracking and splintering as the hands of time destroyed it—but new shoots of green leaves grew from within those dead cracks.

Ripple.

Four Masked figures on giant, four-legged beasts confronted each other, their mouths opening as they conversed, but all that could be heard were the cries of the damned and the horns of war.

Ripple.

A never-ending explosion on a field of black that seemed to rip my mind into pieces but was also comforting.

Ripple.

A dog-fighting pit with silhouettes of giant ephemeral and elemental beings placing bets from high above. Four adult dogs hoarded human bones in one corner while four puppies squared off against them, snarling, yapping, and stumbling over their own disproportionately massive paws. But they were growing rapidly, and the adult dogs bared their teeth with seeming alarm.

Ripple. Another vision. *Ripple.* Another vision.

Again and again and again…

With no other choice, I rode the winds of chaos, watching the never-ending explosion of visions—watched as the ripples grew more violent and far-reaching.

CHAPTER 36

$\mathcal{I}$ came back to with a groan, shivering from the experience. One vision especially stuck in my mind, waking my body up like an electric shock.

Samael waiting for me on the roof of a building. But something else waited for me on the roof of the building as well. Something I had once wanted but couldn't quite recall.

On that rooftop was a choice.

I looked around for the bear, ready to demand an explanation—for him to elaborate on the visions. Were they real? Possibilities? Warnings?

But the little mushroom-muncher had left.

True to his word, my weapons and jewelry were exactly where I had left them. I began putting them on absently, recalling the visions and trying to make sense of them, wondering if any of them were immediately relevant. According to the bear, they had all been relevant revelations.

"Relevations," I muttered, setting the black halo on my head. My last item. My eyes latched onto a bent katana in the grass. Perhaps not my last item. But it was a broken blade. And I already had one broken blade.

I pulled the broken Spear out of my body with a familiar gesture, wincing anew—like I did every time—to see it still damaged. Perhaps a broken blade had its uses. Maybe two wrongs could make a right...

I scooped up the katana and stared at it intently, listening. I smiled as it finally greeted me, and then I asked it a question. It practically vibrated with joy—to hear it still had a purpose.

The katana abruptly melted to liquid, splashing the metal all over my hands. I smiled down at it, focusing on it, listening to it, telling it what I needed it to do. It responded instantly, forming into a hovering ball of chrome above my palm.

Then I called upon my old friend, the Silver magic.

The two merged together like love at first sight, growing stronger for it.

Then I glanced down at my broken white Spear and sang a song in a language lost to mankind lifetimes ago.

The silver sphere struck the white wood of the spear and began to glow. I sang louder, sweat dripping from my brow as I fused the silver into the wood, healing it. Why hadn't I thought to do this before?

After an eternity, it was finished. I realized I was kneeling on the ground, gasping. And I held a silver spear in my hand—still as light as the original, but harder than steel.

The Spear was fixed. Forged anew. That hadn't been too difficult.

Now I had something to fight Samael with until I got close enough to use Cain's dagger to carve out his living heart.

I had a bit of Silver left over from the Spear's re-forging, so I flung it at a nearby rock, cursing the tiny bear. But I was also grateful because his visions had shown me where to go.

The excess silver splashed into the rock, creating a Door, but something seemed to be fighting it. I set my shoulders, gripped my Spear, and pulled the last ring from my pocket. The Silver Seal gleamed too brightly. Nevertheless, I set it around my finger and pointed at the hesitant Door, willing it to obey me and serve me.

Because I was a Goddess who demanded respect.

It finally formed into a Door and I nodded stiffly. Why hadn't I used the Silver Seal before? I hadn't needed to wait for Doors to appear on their own, I could have just made my own. I had amassed so many trinkets that I couldn't even recall where I had picked this one up.

I realized my pulse was quickening as I wrapped myself in power, arming myself to destroy Samael before he had a chance at banter. He would only say one thing before he died.

Please.

I took a calming breath and stepped through the Silver Door.

CHAPTER 37

I stepped out onto the roof of an abandoned building in an abandoned city. The same rooftop I remembered from my vision, but Samael was nowhere in sight. Instead, two knights stood with their backs to me—one wearing gold armor and the other wearing silver armor. They were both tall, heavily-muscled men. The golden knight looked to be twice my size, but the silver knight made his fellow look like a gangly teen wearing his father's armor.

Or...they were both actually tiny, highly-insecure men wearing a lot of metal padding.

I had a feeling that I would find out soon enough—the easy way or the hard way.

They were patiently and silently watching a Silver Door before them and seemed to not have noticed my arrival. The sunset sky was a smear of purples and greens like an epic storm was in process, but the air was still and dead. I saw lightning off in the distance but heard no thunder.

The air smelled pleasant—making me smile. Like fresh fruit in a lush garden.

I studied the two men warily, wondering if I should kill them now or wait a few moments. Their armor was ornate and imposing, seemingly designed more for court balls rather than fields of battle. But that could be a calculated deception. Like the jewelry I wore—superficially trite and pretty—their armor could actually be equally dangerous items of power.

Something about them seemed familiar, like I had seen them somewhere before, but I didn't remember them from my visions, and definitely hadn't met any knights in my travels through the Doors.

They continued to stare at the Door with infinite patience. Who were they expecting? Samael? I cleared my throat, thumping the re-forged Spear of Destiny into the floor at my feet. They spun quickly at the noise, but their armor was as silent as silk on silk, proving my earlier thought. No plate armor was that quiet. I had to fight the look of surprise on my own face, marveling at the beauty of the armor. From the front, it was even more impressive.

Their armor wasn't just rich and well designed. They were pieces of art.

The golden knight's pauldrons had been designed to look like a thick, open book resting atop either shoulder. Braided vines held the books in place like restraining bookmarks, stretching on down his strong arms to transform into thicker, older vines. Hundreds of golden leaves grew from the vines, covering his arm in protective, precious-metal foliage all the way to his impressive gauntlets—each big enough to crush my skull with a clenched fist. The gauntlets were segmented and chitinous, making me think of a beetle burrowing near the roots of the vines growing up his arm, but each knuckle was encrusted with a single brilliant emerald.

Enochian script—the language of the Angels—was etched into the entire surface of each gauntlet, and they were both entirely different. For the first time, I felt a shiver of fear, knowing that placing so many runes beside each other should have resulted in nullifying the other runes.

Or they could have produced a blast of destruction that ended the world.

Imagine the moment God realized it had been a bad idea to order Indian curry for takeout.

And that God's green Earth was His Pearly Potty.

I frowned, momentarily startled at the strange thought. Where had it come from? I shook it off as something to do with this strange place and its thunder-less lightning.

Since we were all still breathing, I decided the knight must know a thing or two about runes.

The golden breastplate was one solid piece and portrayed a king with his hands raised in victory. A beautiful palace loomed behind him, but rather than looking designed for defense and war, it looked more like a place of worship and peace. Maybe a temple, then, not a palace.

The knight's metal skirt was a canopy of tree leaves, and the legs were gnarled, ancient tree trunks. Each kneecap showed a life-like human face. One featured a beautiful young woman with thick, flowing hair and the other was a bearded old man with long, knotted, wild hair. The knight's boots looked like a tangled knot of roots—with a single red ruby the size of my fist on the top of each foot.

His helmet resembled a snarling bear with wings at the temples that flared backwards into points. Through the open mouth, I saw only a veil of golden chain links, concealing the man behind. But on the center of the bear's forehead was a silver circle containing a six-pointed star—perfectly symmetrical—with dots between each point.

The silver knight looked almost identical except for his helmet, which was a roaring lion. Instead of flaring wings at the temples, his head was surrounded by a mane of silver hair that looked light enough to shift in the wind or comb with my fingers even though it was also metal. The same star symbol marked his forehead, but in gold, and a similar curtain of silver chain links concealed the man's face.

"You are earlier than we anticipated," the golden knight said in a warm, soothing voice. He waved a hand towards the Silver Door they had been watching, and it evaporated like smoke in a breeze. Impressive.

I thumped the butt of my Silver Spear into the ground significantly, gauging their reactions. They didn't flinch or tense. They were standing near the ledge of the rooftop and I wanted to get an idea of how high above ground level we were, so I began walking towards them, thumping my spear with each step in a steady, ominous beat that produced a faint throb of silver light in a circle around me.

They watched me thoughtfully, not looking the least bit concerned. They were either very brave, very stupid, or very powerful. I was pretty sure I knew which.

I kept a close eye on them as I reached the brick ledge and glanced down. We were about a hundred feet above a narrow, cobbled alley, and across the alley was the back of a decrepit church, slightly shorter than our own building. Once-elegant spires lined the peaked roof, but most of the survivors looked cracked and worn, on the verge of crashing down onto the passageway below. Almost the entire back of the church consisted of one vast stained-glass window.

But not just any window...it was practically a mural—a piece of art in glass form, utilizing every color of the rainbow, so vibrant it almost looked alive.

The church looked on the verge of collapsing in on itself, but that glass window looked as if it would last for eternity. Despite the abandoned city, there was obviously a light on in the church because the majority of the glass glowed enticingly, illuminated from within.

I realized that I was leaning over the edge, feeling drawn to that window, drawn to the story depicted in glass. A crucifix made of red-hot coals dominated the center of the window, held together only by a thorny vine wrapping around it in an upward spiral. A wreath of white roses was draped over the top like a fallen halo.

Or a funeral wreath on a tombstone.

Despite the flaming cross, neither the thorny vine nor the white rose wreath burned.

Just to the right of the center, a man stood staring down at the cross, his back to me so I couldn't see his face.

Just to the left of the center, a small young girl with long pale hair mirrored his stance, much shorter than the adult, of course. The two of them held hands, and where their flesh met seemed too bright to directly look at—like staring into the sun.

At the base of the window were dozens of wicked claws, snarling beasts, and gnashing fangs. The Demons—despite their fangs and claws—were all beautiful. One even looked like Samael, and I noticed an empty black throne hidden to the right of the tangled mass of flesh.

At the peak of the window were Angels, and their faces were scarred, wounded ruins, their eyes pure white. Despite their flaws, they were perfect in every other way, and they were depicted in light, cold colors in the glass.

Each corner of the window was difficult to focus on, my eyes seeming to slip away each time I tried. All except the one in the bottom right corner, suggestively close to the empty black throne.

A man in black rode a black, winged unicorn—an alicorn. The beast's eyes glowed with all the colors of the rainbow, somehow cycling through them one-by-one. Great skeletal wings arced over the man's back, sprouting long black feathers like those on a peacock but with red orbs at the tips.

Unlike a typical feathered wing, there were maybe a dozen feathers altogether, making the wings look impractical and dysfunctional. The eyes of the man's mask glowed such a bright, golden color that I couldn't quite make out the details of the mask itself.

He gripped a coiled, white chain, and a sinister, curved, black blade—looking like it had been taken from a spear-sword—hung from the end of the chain.

I tried again to study the other three corners of the glass window, but could only confirm that they were also masked, humanoid silhouettes riding four-legged beasts. Out of the corner of my eye, the top left figure seemed to flare brighter for a fraction of a second, but when I tried directly focusing on it, I still couldn't pick out any details—seeing only a blurred silhouette. Perhaps the light within the church didn't reach the corners like it did the rest of the window.

I finally leaned back from the ledge, blinking a few times since they felt gritty from scrutinizing the window too closely. The two knights hadn't moved but I abruptly realized I had focused so intently on the window that they easily could have killed me had they wanted.

"Where is my Demon?" I demanded. I'd come here to kill Samael, not to stare at windows or make new friends. I'd seen this rooftop—or one almost identical to it—in the bear's vision, and it had shown me battling Samael. He was supposed to be here. Why else would my Door have taken me here?

A sudden suspicion settled over my shoulders, and I realized I was growling openly. At the knights. With a snap of my fingers, I cast a precise blast of air to knock off their helmets, expecting to find Samael hiding beneath like a bug under a rock. Their helmets evaporated like smoke before striking the rooftop. I already had a second braid of power prepared —a blast so powerful it could level this entire city if I wanted—to rip his face from his shoulders. But my magic sputtered and died as I saw...

Two very surprised, non-demonic faces stared back at me. I knew my own look mirrored theirs. Primarily because the silver knight had the head of a gorgeous white lion. And it seemed obvious that he hadn't been padding his armor. His fur looked as soft as velvet, and his eyes were the color of glaciers—a blue so cold that I imagined a frigid wind hitting my cheeks.

"That was quite rude," he growled unhappily.

"I'm sure she meant it as a polite gesture," the other knight said in a meaningful tone. He was a handsome older man—one of those who seemed to only grow more beautiful with age—and had shoulder-length white hair and a matching, neatly-trimmed white beard. His green eyes sparkled like fresh-cut grass, and his skin was tanned like he either spent every moment of every day outdoors or he had some spice in his veins.

Speaking of veins, his were black, fanning across his face like the roots of a plant. He didn't seem sickly or harmed by it, though. The man just had black veins.

Maybe he had experimented with the wrong Angelic runes on his gauntlets one day.

All that I really cared about was that neither of them was Samael. You would think this would be a relief. That glancing under the bed and not finding a monster was a good thing.

But you would be wrong.

I ground my teeth together. "Where. Is. My. Demon?" I demanded in a clipped tone, squeezing the haft of my Spear tightly, ready to pummel the answer out of them—knocking out tooth by tooth, ripping off fingernail by fingernail, and breaking bone by bone...

As a warm-up to what I was going to do to Samael when I found him.

CHAPTER 38

*T*hey studied me with infinite patience in their eyes, unaffected by my obvious fury. *My* patience, on the other hand, was *not* infinite. In fact, it was so finite that it barely existed.

All I really had left in me was a single drop of tolerance.

And that little sucker had just evaporated. It was time to show them just how powerful I—

"You've forgotten much, haven't you, my child?" the older man said gently. "In your accumulation of power." I blinked at him, caught off guard by his body language, his calm demeanor, and the surprising depth to his question. It earned him a few more minutes of life.

"Sticks and stones may break my bones, but words will never hurt me," I said drily. "Oh, that's right. Sticks and stones can't hurt me anymore either. My accumulation of power has made me invincible."

The man smirked. "We'll come back to that in a few moments."

I frowned at the cryptic comment. "Who are you?" I finally asked, feeling that strange sense of familiarity again as I looked into his eyes. I got the sense that he was the boss of the two.

"Just an old man who likes to learn. You can call me Sol."

"I didn't ask what I could call you. I asked who you *are*."

He smiled, the motion seeming to make his eyes twinkle. "Solomon," he admitted with an easy shrug.

It didn't ring a bell, so I turned to the lion knight. "What about you, pussycat?"

He didn't take offense, but he looked amused by my phrasing. "Richard," he finally shrugged.

His answer made the corners of my mouth twitch as if some inner part of me had heard a good joke, but try as I might, I couldn't find anything funny about the name.

Sol cleared his throat, and I realized I was glaring at Richard, still wondering why I had wanted to smile at his name. "What would bring the most joy in your life? Pretend I am a genie, and that I can grant you one wish."

That snapped me out of my reverie. "I want Samael sobbing and bleeding out on my boots."

Solomon glanced at my boots and nodded appreciatively. "Darling, those are very fancy boots. Are you certain you want to get Demon blood on them? They do look to be one-of-a-kind, my Dear."

I felt my shoulders twitch uncomfortably, but I didn't know why. I masked my reaction by glancing down at my boots for a moment. I couldn't recall where I had gotten them, but they were rather nice. "Maybe not *on* them," I admitted. "Just a figure of speech, I guess."

He nodded his approval, not fazed in the slightest about the topic of Demon blood. "Wise choice. The final location of Samael's gore aside, spilling his blood will make you happy?"

I fought down my instinctive purr of triumph. "You have no idea."

"Then you must be very happy right now," he mused, scratching at his beard with a golden finger. The lion watched us intently, his massive head shifting from one to the other as we conversed. Although I could tell he was incredibly powerful and dangerous, I just wanted to pet that velvety fur and hear him purr. Maybe offer him a tummy rub.

Instead, I squinted at Solomon suspiciously. "I haven't killed him yet. Remember?"

He smiled faintly. "But I know beyond a shadow of a doubt that you have accumulated enough power to achieve that which you said would bring the most joy to your life. It wouldn't necessarily be easy, but the outcome is almost certainly in your favor. Shouldn't that make you happy? To be on the cusp of your life's defining moment?" he asked, smiling excitedly. "What if I told you that I could take you to him right now?"

I practically salivated. "That would make me deliriously happy."

He smiled, holding up a gauntlet as if to beg just a bit of patience on my part. I nodded, deciding he had earned it. If he was telling the truth, of course. "So, right now, you are deliriously happy. Entirely content. You have essentially achieved your life's ultimate purpose."

I hesitated as his specific phrasing. "More or less."

"I am so happy to hear that," he said, even his eyes seeming to smile at my achievement. "What's next, then? You know, afterwards." He noticed the frozen smile on my face and shrugged. "If your life's joy is dependent on his death, then you have no reason to exist after you achieve your goal, correct? Theoretically speaking, of course."

I frowned, not having an argument to such a question. I hadn't even considered it, honestly. I shrugged piously, folding my arms. "Where is my Door?"

He nodded politely. "I must admit that I wasn't actually pretending when I said I could grant you a wish." He held up a finger, stalling me as I opened my mouth to make my wish. "Patience is a virtue. The price of my gift is that you have to listen to me ramble a little bit. Old man privilege."

Richard snorted. "He uses that one often. But it's easier to just let him do it," he told me in a rumbling purr.

Solomon shot Richard a stern look. "Quiet, you." The lion rolled his eyes and folded his arms—again, with no sound of metal on metal. Solomon turned back to me. "As an added bonus, since you've been exceedingly lady-like so far, I'll include another benefit to letting me prattle on. Without my aid, it would take you many months and many Doors to find Samael. My Door is instantaneous."

I sighed in defeat. "Fine. Go ahead, Solomon." I knew the Doors were fickle things, and he was likely telling the truth. For some odd reason, I realized I had specifically angled the toes of my boots to face each of them separately, like a subconscious tic, expecting something.

But nothing happened.

When I looked over at Richard, he was smiling at me. He gave me a thumbs up, of all things.

Then Solomon began to speak, and I turned to listen. "We are not here by coincidence. You arrived on your own rather than through the Door we anticipated," he said, arching an eyebrow to let me know that this was an impressive thing that I had done.

I dipped my head at the compliment but didn't speak, figuring the sooner he finished this little talk, the sooner I could be on my way.

"I am here to offer you a choice. You must decide which leads to your happiness. There is no wrong answer, necessarily, but there are consequences to either option. Each choice will give you some measure of joy, and some degree of pain and suffering. So, heed my words and think twice before answering. I will not attempt to sway your decision, but I will not allow you to choose until I am satisfied you understand the gravity of the situation," he warned.

I nodded, my curiosity piqued.

He lifted a hand in a casual gesture and a Silver Door shimmered into existence a dozen paces away. "Samael waits beyond this Door. His death at your hands is all but guaranteed. Your vengeance will be complete. You will have access to the Doors for the rest of your life, able to find whatever you wish, wandering the worlds for power."

He waited, letting me absorb that. My blood boiled hungrily, and I had to force myself not to make a run for it, even though I knew he would make it disappear if I tried to break his rules.

He nodded his approval, silently applauding my temperance. "Or, that one," he said, pointing towards the church window. I saw no Door, just the ledge of the roof between us.

I turned back to Solomon. "Care to elaborate on *that one?*" I asked, repeating his description. "Because right now, it's rather one-sided."

Solomon nodded, indicating the church. "This one leads to memory and thought. You will remember who you were, and who you are. It will also give you the key to life, but you'll forget it the instant you comprehend it, so we will put that bonus on a shelf for later," he admitted with a tired shrug.

"Why even mention it, then?"

"Just being transparent," he said with a shrug. "I should mention that with your memory and thought intact—remembering who you *were*—this option would grant you an inner power, one that cannot be as easily taken away as your current magical artifacts."

"Maybe who I am isn't that special. I didn't seem to care about that when I came here, or else we wouldn't be having this conversation, right?"

Solomon smirked mischievously. "And do you remember coming here? What you felt? What you sought? Before you confronted Samael, what were you and Cain doing? Because I can tell you one thing—it wasn't hunting down Samael. That was just an unfortunate coincidence."

I frowned uncomfortably. I...had no idea, as a matter of fact. What *had* we been doing?

"If you go through this Door," he said, pointing at it, "you will have the opportunity to hunt down many Demons in the future. Perhaps even Samael's Lord."

"Going through this one will grant you vengeance. You will succeed in killing Samael. After, you will likely feel alone, lost, without a purpose other than the desperate need to accumulate more power as you search for a new purpose to your life. You will find power and will have your vengeance against Samael. But *only* against Samael."

I studied him in silence for a few moments, thinking. "But if I had power, I would have the tools to go after all the Demons later," I argued. "Right?"

"Sure," Solomon admitted easily. "If you remembered to do so..." I cocked my head, not following. "Name one other Demon," he challenged. "One not inside your ring. I'll wait."

I gasped, frowning at the Silver ring on my finger. It *did* have Demons inside. I hadn't cared to study it too closely, only using it for its ability to open Doors. What would have happened had I worn it while fighting Samael? I quickly pocketed the ring, not wanting to wear it any longer.

It also made me concerned about my other jewelry. What dangers lurked with their use that I had overlooked in my quest for vengeance. I...wasn't sure if I had asked anyone.

Solomon nodded. "Power without knowledge is dangerous. To others and to yourself. How about this..." he asked. "Do you remember anyone from your childhood? From your teens? From a few years ago? What is your favorite juice-box? Animal? Color? Best friend? Who was your first kiss? Who was your *last* kiss?" He leaned forward. "I've got an even simpler one...Tell. Me. Your. Father's name. I'll accept any of the three possible answers as correct."

"Four," the lion corrected. "Four fathers."

Solomon sighed. "Right. Four," he muttered. "I always forget that last one."

The lion looked upon Solomon, his face horrified. "He's kind of the most important one."

I fell to my knees as a wave of pain crashed through me. I was shaking my head stubbornly, holding back tears that threatened to spill. I had no idea how to answer his questions. Any of them, and it physically *hurt* to realize this.

How could I not name my own father?

Richard was suddenly crouched down, staring directly at me with his icy eyes. He shook his head sadly, his leonine ears swiveled back. "All that power at your disposal—invincible from all those *sticks and stones*—and mere words hurt you," he said sympathetically. "It must be tough to be so invincible. But…what Solomon is trying to tell you is that it will get even tougher the further you proceed down this path. The more powerful you get, the more pain you will feel."

Solomon nodded sadly, not appreciating that he had been the bully in the example but accepting full responsibility. "On top of these harsh truths, I must heap on another fact…killing Samael will not bring you peace. It will not bring Cain back."

"My *brother*," I corrected in an instinctive snarl, a sudden flare of passion helping me to overcome my anxiety. Solomon shrugged. "You don't know how powerful I am," I told him defensively.

Solomon scoffed dismissively. "Of course I do. I have stood in your shoes. Faced the same trials. Made my own choice. As have countless others."

I blinked at him incredulously. "And which did you choose?"

He gave me an amused look. "If you could recall anything about yourself, you would realize how humorous that question is. You, caring about what others choose or do not choose."

"Am I supposed to know who you two really are?" I asked tiredly, desperately needing to change topics. "Because I don't like your face," I said pointing at the lion. I still felt a vague sense of familiarity about them but couldn't place why. Was this all some elaborate ruse to mess with my head?

Richard glanced at Solomon as if asking permission. The man gave him a meaningful look before slowly nodding. Richard turned back to me. "You may know me as Last Breath."

The familiarity grew noticeably stronger, but not enough for me to understand.

"Like I said, my name is Solomon. I was once a fool. A sage. A wizard. A warrior. A tyrant. A deviant. A saint. A sinner. Some of those still apply, but I'm doing my best."

I glanced over at the stained-glass window, gathering my thoughts. "I don't like that part," I said absently, pointing at the one corner I had been able to study—the man on the unicorn. I felt like I had seen him recently. Had he given me one of my artifacts? I noticed a weight in one of my pockets and pulled out a silver charm shaped like a butterfly.

My hand began to visibly shake as I stared at the charm, but it wasn't any magical power. It was something internal. That charm...bothered me somehow. I hastily shoved it back into my pocket.

Solomon was smiling in amusement at my statement. "Not many people do like him, but he has his uses. He will be important soon. As will others." He studied me thoughtfully, seeming to debate whether or not to say something. I narrowed my eyes in warning and he finally sighed. "Perhaps you could be important, too, someday. If you remembered why."

I grunted indelicately, turning back to the man with the unicorn. "Or I could take him out of the picture," I suggested. Something about him screamed a warning of wild, raw, chaotic magic. A worthy opponent. But also, something more than that. "Maybe after I found just a little bit more power. I could be greater than him, whoever he is."

"Indeed, you could," Solomon said seriously. "You could also be his lesser."

I shot the man a murderous look, but he met my gaze levelly, letting me know it hadn't been a criticism. "The same can be said of anyone, ever. We choose what we become, whether we admit it or not."

I stared back at the stained-glass window, this time focusing on the center. I frowned at the burning cross and the white rose wreath. Then harder at the two figures before it. "I expect this is all some sort of symbolism. That man looks broken, but the girl is even worse—a weak, clueless, little creature. A self-righteous man who once thought too highly of himself and was humbled for it, holding hands with a vapid girl who followed him blindly, never thinking for herself."

The rooftop was silent for a time, so I looked back. The two were staring at me intensely.

"Perhaps she never defined herself. Didn't learn her *I*." He mistook my frown as a lack of understanding, but it was more than that. Those words had sent a chill down my spine. "How can someone say *I love you* if they never defined the first word in the sentence—their definition of self, their values, their ethos?"

His answer only made the chill grow worse, so I redirected my frustration back on the window. "Perhaps," I said. "But it doesn't change anything. Still a stupid girl and a man broken by the weight of his own misplaced arrogance."

I sensed them nodding in my peripheral vision as they waited for me to decide.

"The key to life...but I'll forget it the moment I touch it?" I asked, repeating what Solomon had said.

"Yes. But perhaps you may find it again someday." He waited for any further questions, but finally took my silence as an answer. "Have you decided?"

"You won't try to stop me from using the other Door..." I asked, glancing at the door to Samael. The door to my vengeance. The door Cain deserved.

Solomon nodded. "You could avenge your brother. Then, for many years you could wander the Doors, amassing power for the rest of your days. You will shine like the sun. None would ever dare throw a stone at you—and it wouldn't matter if they tried. What good is throwing a rock at the sky?"

I thought about that. For about a solid minute, almost salivating. I would be invincible.

I didn't look up as I spoke. "But power would be my only purpose."

Solomon was silent for a few moments. "It is almost guaranteed. Risk and reward await you either way. Joy and suffering. The price of free will..." he trailed off sadly.

I stood near the ledge, gripping the Spear in my fist, noticing I was bathed in its Silver glow. I glanced down at my fingers—at my rings. I thumbed the bone dagger on my hip. Then I thought about my other trinkets, realizing they made me feel incredibly safe. I was protected. Almost invulnerable. My entire being crackled with power, but I sensed the truth to Solomon's words.

That power wasn't truly mine. I just wore it. I didn't know why these two even cared about me, whoever I was. I couldn't even recall my own name when he'd asked me. Couldn't even remember my father's name. Just...Cain.

Which made it all so much worse. I was given the option to remember my own name…by giving up on avenging the only other name I knew—my brother.

I sniffled, wiping at my nose as I blinked through tears. "Do you two just stand up here, waiting for someone like me to come along? That's a miserable existence," I whispered, studying the window thoughtfully. Something about that burning cross…it seemed to be dripping blood, reminding me of an elusive dream. And that wreath of white roses…hadn't I seen some white roses recently?

Part of me wanted answers to that damned window. Not for power, but because…it felt like something missing from my life. A curiosity.

I realized that, despite my initial disgust, I wanted to know about those two broken souls. I had enough power to challenge a God right now, but Solomon was right…I felt *empty*. And other than murdering Samael—I couldn't think of a single thing I wanted to do with all my power.

Not one.

"The key to life…" I said again, staring at the man and girl holding hands, the brilliant light where their hands touched.

"A fleeting gift," Solomon said drily. "But you will have your own memories back. The ones you have traded for power." He touched my shoulders gently, the gauntlets feeling like warm skin rather than cold metal. I didn't look up, but I did flinch. "You have tasted raw power. Draped yourself with it. Learned how to make your enemies grovel." I glanced up at him slowly to find his eyes studying me intently. "You could continue on this path, finding more. Or…you could trade it back in. Have a re-do."

I hadn't thought about it like that. I'd come here looking for something. And I'd found it. Well, I'd found *something*. Power. But I definitely didn't feel happy.

If I wanted anything, I had the ability to simply will it into existence. A storm. Rain. Fire. War. Death. But I didn't really care about anything enough to bother with the effort.

None of those thoughts filled me with passion. The fun had been in the chase, not the destination. Here I was, a newborn Goddess, standing on a forgotten roof in a forgotten city.

On the other hand, why would I go back to square one? I'd obviously been unhappy then, too, or I wouldn't have come here searching for something.

Maybe I had taken a wrong turn somewhere. Had I done something wrong? Maybe I had tasted power and been changed. And that mistake had led me on the path to Cain's death.

That thought set my pulse racing. I wanted Samael dead. No question. He needed to die for killing Cain. Wouldn't it be a betrayal to let his murderer walk free—when I had the power to punish him? What would Cain want me to do? As I thought about it, I realized that I had no idea. I hardly knew much about Cain at all. I knew that I loved him as a brother, but...why?

Where had that feeling come from? To know—as an absolute—that I loved Cain as a brother, but to not remember why. That was...oddly disturbing. What if he had actually been a bad man? I couldn't think of one specific thing about him other than that he had fought beside me and sacrificed himself for me. But why had he done that?

That should have been a very easy question to answer. Like...Solomon's other questions about myself.

Shouldn't I know something more about Cain before focusing my entire existence upon avenging him?

And say I did kill Samael...what about after that? I didn't have any friends. No one to tell about my great deed. Cain wouldn't even know I had avenged him.

A new thought chilled my blood. What would Cain think if he saw me now? Would he approve or be disgusted by what I'd become? I honestly had no idea.

All I could say for certain was that he had been my ally, my brother, my compass.

And now he was gone. Neither the Door on the roof nor Door in the window could give him back to me...

I felt so goddamned *alone.*

I didn't realize I had spoken out loud until Richard knelt before me, nodding in understanding. "Through that Door, you will fully forget your memories. But you will have two close friends—revenge and power. After you kill one, power will be your only surviving companion. But you will also have no fear," he offered in a neutral tone.

Strangely enough, that made sense to me. I would have no one who could understand my level of power. They would all be inferior—bugs beneath my boots. If I spoke from the heart about my power, they wouldn't have anything to bring to the conversation. Just...flaccid nods.

They would literally have nothing to share with me that would be of interest.

Nothing that I hadn't already learned without them. Likewise, their problems would mean literally nothing to me, because I would have no basis of understanding for their concerns.

"If you choose the window," Richard continued, "you will never be alone again. But you will know fear—for yourself *and* your loved ones, of which you will have many. At times, you will feel powerless, but you will still *feel*," he said, emphasizing the last word. "There is no correct answer. It is time to choose what you want most in this life."

There were risks and rewards to both. Power after I killed Samael was a certainty.

But the idea of a life of uncertainty made my stomach flutter anxiously, letting me feel something different for a change. Almost…an excitement.

Or I could spend a life chasing more and more power—the thrill in the conquest, but ultimately holding an empty prize since I didn't have anything I wished to *do* with that power. Like a life spent chasing butterflies.

Something about that made me smile and reach into my pocket.

I squeezed the butterfly charm, thinking.

I already had one butterfly. Right here in my pocket. And I didn't think I had obtained it here. It smelled different. Familiar, somehow. And it was just sitting in my pocket with nothing to do. Like one half of a kiss. Why would I want to collect more of these?

Maybe I could do with a little mystery. Some answers.

I smiled at the lion. "Thank you, Dick. What do I need to do?"

Solomon coughed, but the lion narrowed his eyes for some reason. "You fall, or you walk."

Then he stood and walked over beside Solomon, waiting for me to decide.

CHAPTER 39

I climbed up on the ledge, staring out at the window. The ledge was six-feet wide, more of a walkway than a ledge, but even with a running start it would be close.

Because as I made my final decision—to retrieve my memory—I saw a Silver Door between the man and the girl in the window. The Door was both impossibly large and impossibly small. I would have to be very precise.

I let my Spear disappear deep inside me and ran as fast as I could for the edge, leaping into open air.

I flew towards the Door, cringing as I came closer to the window, because they no longer felt like images, but living people. The white-gold hair on the girl's head even seemed to shift slightly from my rapid approach, and the man's shoulders appeared to tighten.

They didn't let go of each other's hands, and the Silver Door grew larger as I neared—hopefully large enough for me to fit through or my suicide would be very disappointing.

The Door did not open as I struck it.

My weight shattered the entire window in an explosion of colored shards of ancient glass.

And in that explosion of glass, I suddenly felt like I had been reborn… given a name. An old name, but a name I knew well. It fit me just perfectly.

Callie Penrose.

I fell into a dark, forgotten church, and found two vampires trying to smash an ornate metal cross with clubs directly before me. They looked up, startled by the cacophony of broken glass and the crazy bitch flying at their faces.

Without consciously thinking, I had drawn two wooden, silver-tipped stakes from my belt the moment I saw them. I proceeded to bury the stakes in their foreheads so deep that I was forced to let them go as I rolled past them. I realized I was smirking at their death throes, but I didn't bother looking back. Grit fell from my fingers, and I glanced down to see my rings of power crumbling to dust.

I shook off the dust and then washed my hands in the vampire blood covering my knuckles, spreading it evenly over my skin like lotion.

Then I walked onward into the church...

Into the darkness of this abandoned, hallowed ground, wondering how vampires had made it inside with impunity.

Only to find two Angels sweeping down upon me from the rafters, their scarred faces a rictus of hatred, elitism, and disgust as they hurled spears at me, skipping allegations to commence with their final judgment.

Which wasn't how it was supposed to be.

My shoulders exploded with fire as wings of stone and ice erupted from my flesh to shield me from the spears. I waited for the two impacts and then swept my wings at the ground to catapult me upwards to meet them midair. Silver Claws bloomed from between my knuckles just in time to impale their heads through the soft flesh beneath their chins—one on each fist. They gasped and struggled, their wings falling slack as I slammed their heads into the ceiling, burying my claws into the wooden rafters so hard that dust rained down.

With a twist of my wrists, I broke off my claws and hurriedly bent the ends so that they were like hooks, leaving the gasping Angels to hang like strung-up fish. I drifted back down to the ground and shook my head sadly at them. "We should have been allies."

Black dust crumbled from around my forehead, and I realized I had lost the black halo crown. And a wave of memories beat at my heart, filling me with an inner fire.

"My father's name is Titus!" I screamed my Nephilim father's name loud enough to shake the walls of the church.

"My father's name is Terry Penrose!" I screamed my adoptive father's name loud enough to crack the pillars holding up the ceiling of the church.

"My father's name is Roland Haviar!" I screamed my mentor father's name loud enough to crack the floor and make me stumble as the church groaned in protest.

My shouts echoed off the walls, but the only other sound was the gasping Angels and my rasping breath. I debated giving an honorable mention to my fourth father. Everyone's Father. The Big Dog. But I was pretty sure the building would collapse at another shout.

I stared up at the ceiling and placed a hand on the Shepherd's Crucifix at my throat—the one that had belonged to Fabrizio's friend, Anthony.

And I knelt, tucking my wings back. "You know who *You* are..." I said respectfully towards the groaning ceiling, dipping my chin slightly. "I'm probably about to make you regret giving me Free Will," I admitted, "but You should forgive me. I know I'm a sinner, but I'm trying to act like a saint."

I thought I heard a rumbling chuckle, but I was pretty sure it was just the church struggling not to collapse in on itself.

I climbed back to my feet and strode on, wondering what other enemies stood between me and my memories. The space ahead of me was now pitch-black, but the light from my brilliant, blue wings of shifting stone and ice illuminated a ten-foot radius in every direction. The ground vibrated in agitation, warning signs that I didn't have long before the church crumbled. The tips of my wings trailed frigid blue flame across the cracked marble floor of the church.

I saw an oval-shaped silver Door in the distance, that looked like it was miles away.

As I moved through the darkness, I came upon two Demons kneeling on either side of my path. They hung their heads subserviently, praying—a sickening, twisted song—and held out their hands, palms down as if to swear allegiance to their dark queen.

"Come, my children," I said, and I placed my blood-stained palms on the backs of their heads. "Father wants a word with you." They flashed with light, suddenly encased in white crystal as I turned them into pillars of salt. I don't know how.

I walked on, not even slowing as I shattered both pillars with mighty blows from my wings.

The jade earrings *cracked* loudly and then fell from my earlobes. They crunched like brittle bones as I walked over them. I didn't look down.

I was too busy smiling as another wave of memories washed over me, rocking me back on my heels for a moment. I took a deep breath and then released it, giving my memories a moment to settle fully into place.

My thumb abruptly throbbed ice-cold and I glanced down to find a ring of shadows now encircling it. *You're back!* a voice gasped in astonishment, the sound solely in my mind.

"Quiet, Nameless," I told the Fallen Angel. "Mommy's busy." I halted my advance as I saw what lay before me.

A gaping, bottomless pit stood between me and the oval-shaped Silver Door. So did the reflection of a friend—not the real thing, since her eyes shone entirely silver.

Phix—the Great Sphinx—was a wildcat the size of a horse, big enough to ride on. Her massive wings were tucked in close as she turned her human head to glance at me. Because, somewhat like a centaur, the majestic creature before me was a cross between a human and a cat, so a human torso rose up from the feline neck—and it was a torso beautiful enough to make a male sculptor leave the love of his life in favor of having the chance to carve this beauty in marble.

Instead of a centaur, I had a *cat-taur*. Possibly a *meow-taur*. I would try out both to see which bothered the real Phix most before officially adopting it. Because I was classy like that.

Phix was beautiful and curvaceous. Worse, she knew it. She managed to flick her long, thick, perfectly-wavy, ebony hair like she was posing for the imagined sculptor. Even her reflection oozed ego-juice.

I had intended to use my own wings to cross the chasm, but...come on. Riding a Sphinx instead? No contest. She crouched down, seeming to read my mind. I climbed atop her back and pointed my finger at the Door ahead. "Good to see you, Phix."

"You will pay for leaving me behind," she purred throatily, but she did arch her back affectionately as I wrapped my arms around her neck in a hug that probably looked more like a choke-hold.

Her words made me tense. "Wait. It's really you—"

She screamed defiantly, cutting me off. Her roar felt like a protective challenge, as if giving a warning to anymore would-be attackers who dared to impede her path. My path.

Then she leapt up into the air. I grabbed a fistful of her hair for support, and she laughed loudly as we raced through the blackness.

The Door didn't seem to grow any larger despite how fast we flew, and I heard the church crashing down to the ground behind us in one rolling, thunderous bell-toll. I squeezed my thighs, urging Phix on faster, growing anxious that the Door still hadn't grown larger.

A gold and a silver knight suddenly shimmered into existence between us and the Door, looking like giants in comparison, thanks to depth perception. They stared at us, unflinching, growing larger at a dizzying pace.

Which is when I realized the Door wasn't far away. And it wasn't necessarily a Door.

It was as tiny as…the eye of a needle.

I gritted my teeth as I recalled the quote from Jesus in the book of Matthew. *It is easier for a camel to go through the eye of a needle than for a rich man to enter the Kingdom of God.*

Well, I wasn't rich, and I wasn't trying to enter the Kingdom of God, but I understood the metaphor. I was paying to play—giving up the powers I had accumulated from the Doors.

In favor of finding myself. Rediscovering myself.

I cast a hurried glare at the gold and silver knight on either side of the needle, and then I slapped Phix on the rump for encouragement. "Fly like a camel!" I shouted, leaning down behind her shoulders and wrapping my arms around her…the fancy bitch had a damned six-pack!

What the hell?

We were both screaming as we zipped between the two knights and hit the eye of the needle at full speed.

I heard a sound as if a treasure chest had been upended as all the powers —both tangible and not—I had acquired in the Doors were instantaneously torn away from me to pay for our passage through the eye of the needle.

My mind exploded with memories, visions, and conversations from my past—heart-aches and heart-felts, tears and laughs, angers and joys, failures and victories, vices and virtues…

And for a fraction of a second, I understood it *all*—the inner complexities of this thing called life, and how all the broken fragments of a stained-glass window fit perfectly back together.

Why all the answers in the universe rested in the space between two palms pressed together.

Between the palms of a noble man and a naive little girl.

Between a man named Roland Haviar and a girl named Callie Penrose.

And…it brought tears of astonishment to my cheeks.

Then it was abruptly ripped away from me, sending my mind reeling. My vision began to tunnel closed as everything around us flared with brilliant white light. But before the world folded in on itself, I decided that *single* moment of enlightenment—even if now gone—had been worth it.

Simply knowing that there was a purpose to it all…

Even if it was tragically malicious and beautifully elegant…

Well, that was more than most people ever learned.

I heard Nameless murmuring another Bible quote to me as I fell into unconsciousness, but something was wrong about it…

Let there be dark…

And there was…

CHAPTER 40

I slowly woke in a vibrating recliner—the warm back of the chair rising and falling with a steady *thump-thump, thump-thump, thump-thump* beat I felt against my spine.

"You live," Phix said. I looked up to see her face only a foot away. I was tucked against her furry body between her paws, and she was purring like a locomotive. It said something about me that I was disappointed I wasn't actually sitting in a vibrating recliner.

I blinked rapidly, studying the white opulence all around me. The ceiling stretched impossibly high over my head. Birds chirped at each other as they flapped from one arch to the next high above. The air was warm, and a gentle breeze brought the smell of fresh fruit and aromatic flowers.

Because we sat on an open-air balcony the length of a football field. The balcony was furnished with pillows, wicker couches and chairs, huge Persian rugs, and columns as wide as a car that held up the expansive roof. I stared out over the black iron railings to see fields stretching as far as the eye could see, a quilt consisting of every shade of green I had ever seen at any paint store. It was breathtaking.

"Better get your legs under you before he sees that you're vulnerable," Phix murmured.

That's when I noticed the arguing voices approaching.

I turned to see a massive, bipedal, white lion walking backwards towards me, fighting an impotent force on the other side like a bouncer at a club. Solomon walked beside him, smiling at me. He wore white linen pants and a loosely buttoned white linen shirt, making the black veins over his wrists, neck, and cheeks really stand out. The dark veins even grew down his chest —an impressively fit chest for his age. The veins obviously weren't a concern to him, more like an embarrassing tattoo from his younger, wilder days.

And I suddenly remembered our conversation on the rooftop. The high-lights, anyway.

The arguing grew louder and my heart stuttered to a stop.

"I've waited long enough, Dick Breath!" a familiar voice snarled murder-ously. "Let me see my gods-damned *Sister*!"

I forgot all about standing, my heartbeat picking back up in a wildly erratic beat. I was shaking, trying to see past the wall of lion.

The beast chomped his jaws furiously at the nickname. "Richard or Last Breath, not—"

But Cain suddenly darted out from under his arms and tackled me into Phix—who hissed indignantly. He squeezed me tightly, laughing and speaking at the same time into the side of my neck. "You did it!"

I was digging my fingernails into his back, shaking in confusion. "H-how," I stammered in a hoarse whisper, my eyes latching onto Solomon. Richard the lion folded his arms with a sigh but seeing Cain and I together seemed to douse his anger significantly, and a smile tugged at the corners of his leonine lips.

Cain detached himself from my fingers with a murmured complaint, but I could tell his heart wasn't in it. His eyes were red-rimmed, and his smile was radiant.

"Apparently, they had a test for me as well," he admitted. "Although no one told me about it ahead of time." He noticed the fast-approaching nervous breakdown on my face and squeezed my shoulders reassuringly. "It's okay. You did it. This isn't a dream. My trial was to prove..." he paused, sucked in a deep breath, and then let it out, meeting my eyes with an inner pride that made my heart melt. "That I could be a good, big brother. That I was willing to sacrifice my life to save my sister."

I lost it. I hunched over, collapsing in on myself, and wept into my hands. The ugly, uncontrollable kind of crying that no man should ever have to see.

Phix hissed at Cain. "Great job, you hairy lummox." She curled a paw to wrap around my waist and tugged me back protectively against her side. Then she began pawing at the floor like cats do, sheathing and unsheathing her claws in a repetitive motion. Except her claws scored the marble floor as she did it.

"No," I mumbled between sobs. "I'm just so..." I trailed off, unsure what exactly hit me the hardest. Overjoyed to learn that Cain wasn't dead. Furious that Solomon had lied to me. Proud of Cain's absolution. Confusion at our location. That Phix—the real Phix—was somehow here and acting overprotective...

I smiled at Cain, wiping at my face. "I'm so proud of you. And..." I reached out and slapped him in the face as hard as I could. The sound rang out like a gunshot, and Richard grunted satisfactorily. I scowled at the lion. "Watch it, Dick. You've got one coming, too, and I feel an army in my fist," I warned.

Solomon grinned. "Friedrich Schiller. Nice."

I gave him a look that shouted he had one of his own slaps brewing. He nodded in understanding, accepting responsibility for his own actions in this.

Cain's cheek was bright red, but he was smiling. "Worth it," he said. And I knew he wasn't talking about the slap. He was telling me that sacrificing himself for me had been worth it—even if he wouldn't have made it back.

I lowered my eyes, trying to regain my breathing. "Thank you, Brother," I whispered. "Now get over here and let me wipe my face on your shirt. It's the only other thing brothers are good for, so you might as well get it over with," I told him.

In answer, he wrapped me up in another hug, petting my hair as he held me close.

I let it all out. All the pain, the sorrow, the relief...and I wiped the results all over his shirt.

"I'm sorry I didn't kill Samael," I told Cain. "But you can bet your ass I'm hunting him down soon," I promised.

Cain grunted. "If you had, I wouldn't be here right now," he said in a soft voice. My eyes widened in disbelief. Then they shot to Solomon, demanding an explanation.

He nodded simply. "The Temple chose to treat your trial like a team effort. By bringing Cain to the fountain, you altered the trial, altered the rules. Without Cain's sacrifice, you would have failed or died—either against Samael or in one of the next Doors. Without your choice to abandon vengeance and power, Cain's death would have been final. The prize demands it," he said, holding up his hands to signify the balcony around us. Then he turned back to me. "But I would have made the same decision were it up to me. Your newfound epiphany to become siblings in all but blood was the perfect test of your moral fortitude, your discretion, and your dignity. You passed and were permitted entrance here."

As angry as I was, I had the feeling he was not lying or being cruel. I shivered, realizing where we were for the first time.

"Solomon's Temple..." I breathed incredulously.

"Welcome home, my great-great-great..." he waved a hand absently, tacking on a bunch more greats. "Granddaughter."

I dipped my head at him, not entirely sure how I felt about calling him family. I hadn't anticipated meeting the bastard. I'd just wanted to rob his house for answers on my past. Which made things awkward.

"No offense taken," he said, smiling directly at me. "Don't worry. I can't read your mind. But your face speaks very loudly."

I decided not to try denying it. The cards were on the table, and after what he had put me through—put us both through—I wasn't too concerned about his feelings.

I turned to the lion, remembering all the things he had done to piss me off. "You, Richard, are a Dick."

In response, he abruptly shimmered, becoming a tall, muscular Asian man...

I blinked incredulously. "You!"

He smirked. "Glad you liked the rosé."

I sputtered, stammered, and then finally took a deep breath. "Why?" I asked him.

"I had to find a way to show you my illusions. The fountain. The Sons of Solomon."

I held up a hand. "The Sons of Solomon...aren't real?" I asked, really considering hitting him in the face. I heard Cain's knuckles cracking, and I remembered how troubled he had been when they hadn't bled on his dagger.

Richard shrugged. "Once upon a time, yes. But they have been defunct for centuries. But people never believe that secret societies fade away, so we just keep using their name, adding to their mystery."

I rubbed at my temples, reminding myself that I shouldn't kill him. Yet.

He went on without remorse. "With the Angels and Samael hunting you at every turn, and Nameless watching your every move, I saw no way to lead you—and only you—to the fountain. But my efforts were in vain," he said, frowning at Cain. "Samael has been—at times—conversing with Nameless. Regardless of how fiercely Nameless resisted," he said, sounding impressed. "It's almost a wonder he ever Fell."

I shuddered at the barrage. To realize that Samael had been tracking me, even if only occasionally, and that Nameless had tried to fight back...I glanced down at my thumb.

And froze.

The shadow ring was gone.

I looked up, my eyes wild. Solomon lifted his hand to show me the Seal of Solomon. Then he tossed it to me, underhanded. "I put him back where he belongs for you. Couldn't have one of them showing Samael where you were. And it will take some time for you to learn how to do it yourself," he told me.

I stared down at the Seal, then at my thumb, shaking my head. It felt... surprisingly empty. I hadn't realized how heavy it had been. "Thank you," I murmured, not knowing what else to say.

At least I had one less thing for Michael to worry about.

I gasped, glancing about for the Spear. "Where is it?"

"Inside of you, of course," Solomon said, smiling at my panic. "But it's resting, like you were a few minutes ago. Try taking it out now and you'll pass out. It needs time to heal. Perhaps a long time. It went through much in the Doors."

I stared at him, suddenly anxious as I remembered Michael's warning. "Is it going to be okay? Is it broken, or did I actually fix it?"

Solomon debated that, thinking hard on the answer. "Only time will tell. But..." he paused significantly, making sure I was paying close attention. "The white blade has found its sheath."

And he pointed directly at me.

Oh.

Well...

"Let's just wait to see what it looks like when it finally wakes up," Solomon smiled.

I nodded, turning back to Richard. There had been only one thing I had really wanted to ask him, and it had nothing to do with the trial. He let out a breath as if knowing my question.

"Why were you at Abundant Angel the night of the storm?"

He stared down at his feet for so long that I began to grow angry, but when he looked back up, I was surprised to see an anguished look on his face. "I was trying to find your mother. She had abandoned the Seal, hiding it in Kansas City somewhere. I could sense that much, but not where she had hidden it....I was chasing rumors the night of the storm, rumors of a powerful wizard creeping through the streets. Because Shepherds were hunting her." he said in a haggard voice.

I almost gasped. Fabrizio. He was talking about Fabrizio. And...my mother had hidden the Seal of Solomon in Kansas City? In the underground cavern where I had found it? That meant...I'd walked in her footsteps.

Richard continued, not sensing my sad, but happy smile. "Constance was using some kind of spell that prevented me from finding her. I didn't even know she was with child, let alone that I saw the baby with my own eyes! Watching as the pastor opened the door and wrapped you in his arms. I had no idea, I was so fixated on finding your mother. That protection that kept her from me, also kept you from me. I only discovered your existence—and the realization that you had been at that very church the same night as me—when you used the Seal of Solomon for the first time."

His shoulders sagged as Solomon stepped up beside him. He also looked pained as he placed a hand on Richard's shoulder. "We saw you outside your own church...the night you bound Nameless. Do you remember?"

I nodded, misty-eyed at the pain in Richard's voice and the look in Solomon's eyes. "Yes." They had been standing on a nearby rooftop.

"That was the first time we realized that our Constance...had a beautiful baby girl. You have no idea how happy that made us. And for us to see you for the first time in a moment of victory. Right after you bonded a Fallen Angel, all on your own," Solomon said, shaking his head in wonder. "Your mother would be so incredibly proud. I know I was."

Richard nodded vehemently. "She would be honored to see the woman you have become. I just wish your circumstances had been different. That we had been able to save you at a younger age. That we could have been there for you."

Solomon smiled suddenly. "Perhaps I could show you your mother's old room..."

My jaw dropped to the floor, but Phix interrupted before I could answer him.

"Not to crash the party, but this place isn't going anywhere. Your tour will have to wait. She really needs to get back to Kansas City to see for herself..." she told Solomon meaningfully.

I narrowed my eyes angrily. Kansas City could wait a few hours. I wanted to get the damned answers I had been seeking after all the heartache I had been through, but Cain met my eyes and shook his head firmly. He looked troubled but was trying to hide it.

Solomon turned to me, the skin at the corners of his eyes tightening. "Ah, yes. I had forgotten about that. Let me just show you how to return, Callie. You just take the Seal, and—"

"Wait. What happened in Kansas City?" I demanded. "Surely it can wait a day or two."

Phix turned to look at me, shaking her head. "Kansas City has waited long enough for you. Because you've been gone for a year."

I suddenly felt very, very cold. *One year?*

I calmly turned back to Solomon, barely whispering. "Can you please show me my mother's room a different time? I need to go check on my friends..."

Solomon nodded sadly.

Because I suddenly remembered Roland's promises to Fabrizio about what he would do to Kansas City if he thought anything bad had happened to me...

There's no danger to the world quite like an angry man of the cloth.

*C*allie Penrose returns in **BLACK SHEEP**... *Turn the page for a sample! Or*
get the book ONLINE!

SAMPLE: BLACK SHEEP

*C*ain stepped up beside me as I stared down from the expansive marble balcony of the fabled Solomon's Temple to the spread of green gardens below. From this vantage, they resembled a patchwork quilt of new life—in a vast array of green shades. Plants, flowers, and fruits that shouldn't have been able to grow beside each other were thriving in perfect harmony, despite all odds. New buds of color peppered the green quilt—

flowers being born in a kaleidoscope of beauty that made any words obsolete. This scene demanded silence. Respectful admiration. Awe—

"It stinks here," Cain grumbled, pinching his nose.

I elbowed him in the ribs, smiling in spite of myself. It smelled beautiful and earthy, the humid, warm air pregnant with life.

"You ready?" Cain asked.

My heart fluttered slightly at the question. Phix had only just told us about how long I had actually been gone during my trip through the Doors —a quest I had undertaken in order to gain access to Solomon's Temple. My ancestral home.

It still felt surreal to be standing here, like I was standing in the heart of the Renaissance—back when all the now-famous art was first being painted or architecture being erected. Like I was the first person to see it all and know what it would one day become.

I had, quite literally, only seen the balcony where we now stood—a massive structure overlooking the gardens. The balcony stretched for over a hundred yards and was filled with all manner of furniture, art, sculptures, and plants; the roof soared high above our heads, supported by gargantuan marble columns.

And this was only one *side* of the *outside* of the vast Temple.

I considered Cain's question pensively, thinking back on my city. Before I had left on my quest, Roland had warned Fabrizio—the First Shepherd— that if anything happened to me, he would drown Kansas City in rivers of blood. He had also sworn that he would hunt Fabrizio down like a dog, turn him into a vampire, and only *then* kill him—just to be sure Fabrizio's eternal soul was damned and black-listed from Heaven. He had warned Fabrizio that only the entire might of the Vatican Conclave and its Shepherds would be able to save Kansas City from his wrath.

Even though Fabrizio was entirely innocent of any guilt—I had just learned that my trip through the Doors had lasted for one year and that most everyone thought me dead.

If one thing could be said about Roland, it was that he was a man of his word. There was a chance that he was still waiting for me, but the more I thought about it, remembering the look I'd seen in those eyes, and his promise to Fabrizio…I didn't have high hopes.

I let out a breath, rolling my shoulders. "We will handle it," I said, more confidently than I felt. I almost didn't want to go back myself. Not because I was scared of what Roland had done.

No.

It was because I was terrified to see what his *actions* had done to *him*—a man of the cloth resorting to violence of the sort that he had previously only reserved for monsters. Except...now *he* was one of those monsters. And the only thing he still seemed to care about was my safety. So I feared that, if he had given up on my return and thought me dead, his actions may have broken something inside him—something he might never be able to recover. In that case, I was the only one who stood a chance of providing any possibility of his redemption—or saving Kansas City.

He needed to see me alive and well, unharmed and whole.

~

*O*n my journey through the Doors, I had seen a stained-glass window on a church. In fact, that window had been what let me escape the Doors to earn the right to enter Solomon's Temple.

And in that window had been a depiction of Roland and a childlike version of me, holding hands before a burning cross, with Heaven above, Hell below, and four haunting figures at the darkened corners of the glass. One of those figures had resembled Nate, I was sure of it, but the others had been only vague silhouettes. Terrifying, frightening silhouettes astride wicked winged beasts of nightmares.

Nate Temple's new gang of Horsemen to balance the Biblical Four Horsemen.

But that was a problem for another day.

Roland, figuratively speaking, had rescued me from the Doors. Now, it was my turn to rescue him—from himself.

Solomon cleared his throat behind us and I turned to face him. He was a roguishly handsome older man with shoulder-length white hair and a well-groomed white beard. His tan skin was a sharp contrast to his white linen pants and shirt, and his green eyes held all the colors of his gardens below the balcony—brimming with life just as vibrant. The one majorly noticeable aspect of Solomon was that a good portion of his veins were black—looking like a root system beneath his skin. Everyone's veins looked that way—you just couldn't normally see them. He didn't seem particularly affected by the veins, so I was assuming they didn't bother him much. Or he had a high pain tolerance.

Richard—or Last Breath when in his lion form—stood in his human form at Solomon's side, hands clasped behind his back. He currently looked like a tall Asian man, heavily corded with muscle and sporting short, black, spiked hair in a messy look. He had the ability to shapeshift entirely into any look he wanted but seemed to prefer this look so far as I had seen.

"Richard will go with you," Solomon said.

I opened my mouth to argue, knowing that having any new faces at my side when I returned to Kansas City might only make matters worse—let alone if Richard shifted into his lion form and was recognized as Last Breath—the creature that everyone had heard so much about when I was last in town. The one everyone had thought to be hunting me.

Richard must have read the uncertainty on my face because he suddenly stepped forward in an almost aggressive manner, causing Cain to growl in warning as he set his feet and his hand shot to his hip where his bone dagger was tucked into his belt.

The dagger he'd used to kill his brother, Abel, so long ago. I placed a hand on his forearm.

Richard lowered his eyes in a submissive gesture, but his voice was anything but as he raised his eyes to meet mine. "I will simply stalk you from the shadows if you deny my aid. My purpose is to keep the Solomon bloodline safe, and thanks to your mother's schemes—hiding your very existence from me since your birth—I have so far failed you in that capacity. I will not let my honor be discarded so easily now that I have finally found you."

My mouth clicked shut, seeing the raw pain dancing in his eyes. He had a point. My parents had concealed my identity with a powerful ward so that those hunting me couldn't find me when they left me on the steps of Abundant Angel Catholic Church as a baby. My mother had fled Solomon's Temple, taking the ancient Seal of Solomon with her, before anyone even discovered she was pregnant, and hadn't been seen since that fateful day at the church where they said their final goodbyes to me.

By coincidence or design—I wasn't entirely sure which—I had discovered the Seal of Solomon in an underground vault in Kansas City. Using it had essentially turned my GPS signal back on, and Solomon and Last Breath had wasted no time in answering the call—in sending me on the traditional quest of searching out the infamous Solomon's Temple, my apparent birthright as his only surviving heir.

A birthright that I had just earned, only to discover Kansas City was tearing itself apart in my absence, and that I didn't have time to explore these halls, get answers to questions about my parents and possibly learn why they had seen the need to hide me from Solomon and Richard, giving me up to be raised by strangers rather than these two.

My mother's actions led a very loud part of me to hold a certain amount of caution when dealing with Richard and Solomon. She must have had a reason to keep me from them. If a magical fortress on a different plane of existence wasn't safe enough to raise me, how could an orphanage or adopted family be any safer?

So...

Part of me wanted answers from these two. Part of me wanted to keep my distance.

"You are our family, Callie," Richard added, in a much gentler tone this time, reading the hesitation on my face.

"She already has a guardian," Cain said, pointing at Phix. The legendary Sphinx—who had been lounging on a nearby fur carpet, cleaning her wickedly long claws with her teeth—paused to look up at us, blinking lazily...lethally.

∾

Get your copy of BLACK SHEEP online today!

∾

Turn the page to read a sample of **OBSIDIAN SON** - *Nate Temple Book 1 - or* **BUY ONLINE**. *Nate Temple is a billionaire wizard from St. Louis. He rides a bloodthirsty unicorn and drinks with the Four Horsemen. He even cow-tipped the Minotaur. Once...*

(Note: Nate's books 1-6 happen prior to UNCHAINED, but crossover from then on,

the two series taking place in the same universe but also able to standalone if you prefer)

Full chronology of all books in the Temple Verse shown on the 'Books in the Temple Verse' page.

TRY: OBSIDIAN SON (NATE TEMPLE #1)

T here was no room for emotion in a hate crime. I had to be cold. Heartless. This was just another victim. Nothing more. No face, no name.

Frosted blades of grass crunched under my feet, sounding to my ears alone like the symbolic glass that one shattered under a napkin at a Jewish wedding. The noise would have threatened to give away my stealthy advance as I stalked through the moonlit field, but I was no novice and had planned accordingly. Being a wizard, I was able to muffle all sensory evidence with a fine cloud of magic—no sounds, and no smells. Nifty. But if I made the spell much stronger, the anomaly would be too obvious to my prey.

I knew the consequences for my dark deed tonight. If caught, jail time or possibly even a gruesome, painful death. But if I succeeded, the look of fear and surprise in my victim's eyes before his world collapsed around him, was well worth the risk. I simply couldn't help myself; I had to take him down.

I knew the cops had been keeping tabs on my car, but I was confident that they hadn't followed me. I hadn't seen a tail on my way here, but seeing as how they frowned on this kind of thing I had taken a circuitous route just in case. I was safe. I hoped.

Then my phone chirped at me as I received a text.

My body's fight-or-flight syndrome instantly kicked in, my heart threatening to explode in one final act of pulmonary paroxysm. "Motherf—" I hissed instinctively, practically jumping out of my skin. I had forgotten to silence it. *Stupid, stupid, stupid!* My body remained tense as I swept my gaze over the field, sure that I had been made. My breathing finally began to slow, my pulse returning to normal, as I noticed no changes in my surroundings. Hopefully, my magic had silenced the sound and my resulting outburst. I glanced down at the phone to scan the text and then typed back a quick and angry response before I switched the cursed phone to vibrate.

Now, where were we...

I continued on, the lining of my coat constricting my breathing. Or maybe it was because I was leaning forward in anticipation. *Breathe*, I chided myself. *He doesn't know you're here.* All this risk for a book. It had better be worth it.

I'm taller than most, and not abnormally handsome, but I knew how to play the genetic cards I had been dealt. I had shaggy, dirty blonde hair, and my frame was thick with well-earned muscle, yet still lean. I had once been told that my eyes were like twin emeralds pitted against the golden-brown tufts of my hair—a face like a jewelry box. Of course, that was two bottles of wine into a date, so I could have been a little foggy on her quote. Still, I liked to imagine that was how everyone saw me.

But tonight, all that was masked by magic.

I grinned broadly as the outline of the hairy hulk finally came into view. He was blessedly alone—no nearby sentries to give me away. That was always a risk when performing this ancient right-of-passage. I tried to keep the grin on my face from dissolving into a maniacal cackle.

My skin danced with energy, both natural and unnatural, as I manipulated the threads of magic floating all around me. My victim stood just ahead, oblivious of the world of hurt that I was about to unleash. Even with his millennia of experience, he didn't stand a chance. I had done this so many times that the routine of it was my only enemy. I lost count of how many times I had been told not to do it again; those who knew declared it *cruel, evil, and sadistic*. But what fun wasn't? Regardless, that wasn't enough to stop me from doing it again. And again. Call it an addiction if you will, but it was too much of a rush to ignore.

The pungent smell of manure filled the air, latching onto my nostril hairs. I took another step, trying to calm my racing pulse. A glint of gold reflected in the silver moonlight, but the victim remained motionless, hopefully unaware or all was lost. I wouldn't make it out alive if he knew I was here. Timing was everything.

I carefully took the last two steps, a lifetime between each, watching the legendary monster's ears, anxious and terrified that I would catch even so much as a twitch in my direction. Seeing nothing, a fierce grin split my unshaven cheeks. My spell had worked! I raised my palms an inch away from their target, firmly planted my feet, and squared my shoulders. I took one silent, calming breath, and then heaved forward with every ounce of physical strength I could muster. As well as a teensy-weensy boost of magic. Enough to goose him good.

"MOOO!!!" The sound tore through the cool October night like an unstoppable freight train. *Thud-splat!* The beast collapsed sideways into the frosty grass; straight into a steaming patty of cow shit, cow dung, or, if you really want to church it up, a Meadow Muffin. But to me, shit is, and always will be, shit.

Cow tipping. It doesn't get any better than that in Missouri.

Especially when you're tipping the *Minotaur*. Capital M.

Razor-blade hooves tore at the frozen earth as the beast struggled to stand, grunts of rage vibrating the air. I raised my arms triumphantly. "Booyah! Temple 1, Minotaur 0!" I crowed. Then I very bravely prepared to protect myself. Some people just couldn't take a joke. *Cruel, evil,* and *sadistic* cow tipping may be, but by hell, it was a *rush*. The legendary beast turned his gaze on me after gaining his feet, eyes ablaze as he unfolded to his full height on two tree-trunk-thick legs, hooves magically transforming into heavily-booted feet. The thick, gold ring dangling from his snotty snout quivered as the Minotaur panted, and his dense, corded muscle contracted over his human-like chest. As I stared up into those brown eyes, I actually felt sorry...for, well, myself.

"I have killed greater men than you for less offense," he growled.

I swear to God his voice sounded like an angry James Earl Jones. Like Mufasa talking to Scar.

"You have shit on your shoulder, Asterion." I ignited a roiling ball of fire in my palm in order to see his eyes more clearly. By no means was it a defensive gesture on my part. It was just dark. But under the weight of his glare, even I couldn't buy my reassuring lie. I hoped using a form of his ancient name would give me brownie points. Or maybe just not-worthy-of-killing points.

The beast grunted, eyes tightening, and I sensed the barest hesitation. "Nate Temple...your name would look splendid on my already long list of slain idiots." Asterion took a threatening step forward, and I thrust out my palm in warning, my roiling flame blue now.

"You lost fair and square, Asterion. Yield or perish." The beast's shoulders sagged slightly. Then he finally nodded to himself in resignation, appraising me with the scrutiny of a worthy adversary. "Your time comes, Temple, but I will grant you this. You've got a pair of stones on you to rival Hercules."

I pointedly risked a glance down towards the myth's own crown jewels. "Well, I sure won't need a wheelbarrow any time soon, but I'm sure I'll manage."

The Minotaur blinked once, and then bellowed out a deep, contagious, snorting laughter. Realizing I wasn't about to become a murder statistic, I couldn't help but join in. It felt good. It had been a while since I had allowed myself to experience genuine laughter.

In the harsh moonlight, his bulk was even more intimidating as he towered head and shoulders above me. This was the beast that had fed upon human sacrifices for countless years while imprisoned in Daedalus' Labyrinth in Greece. And all of that protein had not gone to waste, forming a heavily woven musculature over the beast's body that made even Mr. Olympia look puny.

From the neck up he was entirely bull, but the rest of his body more resembled a thickly-furred man. But, as shown moments ago, he could adapt his form to his environment, never appearing fully human, but able to make his entire form appear as a bull when necessary. For instance, how he had looked just before I tipped him. Maybe he had been scouting the field for heifers before I had so efficiently killed the mood.

His bull face was also covered in thick, coarse hair—even sporting a long, wavy beard of sorts, and his eyes were the deepest brown I had ever seen. Cow shit brown. His snout jutted out, emphasizing the gold ring dangling from his glistening nostrils, catching a glint in the luminous glow of the moon. The metal was at least an inch thick, and etched with runes of a language long forgotten. Thick, aged ivory horns sprouted from each temple, long enough to skewer a wizard with little effort. He was nude except for a beaded necklace and a pair of distressed leather boots that were big enough to stomp a size twenty-five imprint in my face if he felt so inclined.

I hoped our blossoming friendship wouldn't end that way. I really did.

～

Get your copy of OBSIDIAN SON online today!

～

*Turn the page to read a sample of **WHISKEY GINGER** - Phantom Queen Diaries Book 1, or **BUY ONLINE**. Quinn MacKenna is a black magic arms dealer in Boston. She likes to fight monsters almost as much as she likes to drink.*

Full chronology of all books in the Temple Verse shown on the 'BOOKS IN THE TEMPLE VERSE' page.)

TRY: WHISKEY GINGER (PHANTOM QUEEN DIARIES BOOK 1)

*T*he pasty guitarist hunched forward, thrust a rolled-up wad of paper deep into one nostril, and snorted a line of blood crystals—frozen hemoglobin that I'd smuggled over in a refrigerated canister—with the uncanny grace of a drug addict. He sat back, fangs gleaming, and pawed at his nose. "That's some bodacious shit. Hey, bros," he said, glancing at his fellow band members, "come hit this shit before it melts."

He fetched one of the backstage passes hanging nearby, pried the plastic badge from its lanyard, and used it to split up the crystals, murmuring something in an accent that reminded me of California. Not *the* California, but you know, Cali-foh-nia—the land of beaches, babes, and bros. I retrieved a toothpick from my pocket and punched it through its thin wrapper. "So," I asked no one in particular, "now that ye have the product, who's payin'?"

Another band member stepped out of the shadows to my left, and I don't mean that figuratively, either—the fucker literally stepped out of the shadows. I scowled at him, but hid my surprise, nonchalantly rolling the toothpick from one side of my mouth to the other.

The rest of the band gathered around the dressing room table, following the guitarist's lead by preparing their own snorting utensils—tattered magazine covers, mostly. Typically, you'd do this sort of thing with a dollar-bill, maybe even a Benjamin if you were flush. But fangers like this lot couldn't touch cash directly—in God We Trust and all that. Of course, I didn't really understand why sucking blood the old-fashioned way had suddenly gone out of style. More of a rush, maybe?

"It lasts longer," the vampire next to me explained, catching my mildly curious expression. "It's especially good for shows and stuff. Makes us look, like, less—"

"Creepy?" I offered, my Irish brogue lilting just enough to make it a question.

"Pale," he finished, frowning.

I shrugged. "Listen, I've got places to be," I said, holding out my hand.

"I'm sure you do," he replied, smiling. "Tell you what, why don't you, like, hang around for a bit? Once that wears off," he dipped his head toward the bloody powder smeared across the table's surface, "we may need a pick-me-up." He rested his hand on my arm and our gazes locked.

I blinked, realized what he was trying to pull, and rolled my eyes. His widened in surprise, then shock as I yanked out my toothpick and shoved it through his hand.

"Motherfuck—"

"I want what we agreed on," I declared. "Now. No tricks."

The rest of the band saw what happened and rose faster than I could blink. They circled me, their grins feral...they might have even seemed intimidating if it weren't for the fact that they each had a case of the sniffles

—I had to work extra hard not to think about what it felt like to have someone else's blood dripping down my nasal cavity.

I held up a hand.

"Can I ask ye gentlemen a question before we get started?" I asked. "Do ye even *have* what I asked for?"

Two of the band members exchanged looks and shrugged. The guitarist, however, glanced back towards the dressing room, where a brown paper bag sat next to a case full of makeup. He caught me looking and bared his teeth, his fangs stretching until it looked like it would be uncomfortable for him to close his mouth without piercing his own lip.

"Follow-up question," I said, eyeing the vampire I'd stabbed as he gingerly withdrew the toothpick from his hand and flung it across the room with a snarl. "Do ye do each other's make-up? Since, ye know, ye can't use mirrors?"

I was genuinely curious.

The guitarist grunted. "Mike, we have to go on soon."

"Wait a minute. Mike?" I turned to the snarling vampire with a frown. "What happened to *The Vampire Prospero*?" I glanced at the numerous fliers in the dressing room, most of which depicted the band members wading through blood, with Mike in the lead, each one titled *The Vampire Prospero* in *Rocky Horror Picture Show* font. Come to think of it…Mike did look a little like Tim Curry in all that leather and lace.

I was about to comment on the resemblance when Mike spoke up, "Alright, change of plans, bros. We're gonna drain this bitch before the show. We'll look totally—"

"Creepy?" I offered, again.

"Kill her."

$\sim$

Get the full book ONLINE!

MAKE A DIFFERENCE

Reviews are the most powerful tools in my arsenal when it comes to getting attention for my books. Much as I'd like to, I don't have the financial muscle of a New York publisher.

But I do have something much more powerful and effective than that, and it's something that those publishers would kill to get their hands on.

A committed and loyal bunch of readers.

Honest reviews of my books help bring them to the attention of other readers.

If you've enjoyed this book, I would be very grateful if you could spend just five minutes leaving a review (it can be as short as you like) on my book's Amazon page.

Thank you very much in advance.

ACKNOWLEDGMENTS

First, I would like to thank my beta-readers, TEAM TEMPLE, those individuals who spent hours of their time to read, and re-re-read the Temple-Verse stories. Your dark, twisted, cunning sense of humor makes me feel right at home...

I would also like to thank you, the reader. I hope you enjoyed reading *SINNER* as much as I enjoyed writing it. Stay tuned...Callie Penrose returns in GODLESS with her book 7, Nate Temple returns in KNIGHTMARE with his book 12, and Quinn MacKenna returns in HURRICANE with her book 8—all in 2019!

And last, but definitely not least, I thank my wife, Lexy. Without your support, none of this would have been possible.

BOOKS IN THE TEMPLE VERSE

CHRONOLOGY: All stories in the Temple Verse are shown in chronological order on the following page

FEATHERS AND FIRE SERIES

(Set in the Temple Verse)

UNCHAINED

RAGE

WHISPERS

ANGEL'S ROAR

MOTHERLUCKER (Novella #4.5 in the 'LAST CALL' anthology)

SINNER

BLACK SHEEP

GODLESS (FEATHERS #7) — COMING SOON...

NATE TEMPLE SERIES

(Origin of the Temple Verse)

FAIRY TALE - FREE prequel novella #0 for my subscribers

OBSIDIAN SON

BLOOD DEBTS

GRIMM

SILVER TONGUE

BEAST MASTER

BEERLYMPIAN (Novella #5.5 in the 'LAST CALL' anthology)

TINY GODS

DADDY DUTY (Novella #6.5)

WILD SIDE

WAR HAMMER

NINE SOULS

HORSEMAN

LEGEND

KNIGHTMARE (TEMPLE #12) — COMING SOON...

PHANTOM QUEEN DIARIES

(Also set in the Temple Verse)

COLLINS (Prequel novella #0 in the 'LAST CALL' anthology)

WHISKEY GINGER

COSMOPOLITAN

OLD FASHIONED

MOTHERLUCKER (Novella #3.5 in the 'LAST CALL' anthology)

DARK AND STORMY

MOSCOW MULE

WITCHES BREW

SALTY DOG

CHRONOLOGICAL ORDER: TEMPLE UNIVERSE

FAIRY TALE (TEMPLE PREQUEL)

OBSIDIAN SON (TEMPLE 1)

BLOOD DEBTS (TEMPLE 2)

GRIMM (TEMPLE 3)

SILVER TONGUE (TEMPLE 4)

BEAST MASTER (TEMPLE 5)

BEERLYMPIAN (TEMPLE 5.5)

TINY GODS (TEMPLE 6)

DADDY DUTY (TEMPLE NOVELLA 6.5)

UNCHAINED (FEATHERS... 1)

RAGE (FEATHERS... 2)

WILD SIDE (TEMPLE 7)

WAR HAMMER (TEMPLE 8)

WHISPERS (FEATHERS... 3)

ABOUT THE AUTHOR

Shayne is a man of mystery and power, whose power is exceeded only by his mystery…

He currently writes the Amazon Bestselling **Feathers and Fire Series** about a rookie spell-slinger named Callie Penrose who works for the Vatican in Kansas City. Her problem? Hell seems to know more about her past than she does.

He also writes the Amazon Bestselling **Nate Temple Series**, which features a foul-mouthed wizard from St. Louis. He rides a bloodthirsty unicorn, drinks with Achilles, and is pals with the Four Horsemen.

He also co-authors the Amazon Bestselling **Phantom Queen Diaries** with Cameron O'Connell, about Quinn MacKenna, a mouthy black magic arms dealer trading favors in Boston. All she wants? A round-trip ticket to the Fae realm…and maybe a drink on the house.

Shayne holds two high-ranking black belts, and can be found writing in a coffee shop, cackling madly into his computer screen while pounding shots of espresso. He's hard at work on more Temple Verse novels as well as a few entirely new stories outside of the Temple Verse. **Follow him online for all sorts of groovy goodies, giveaways, and new release updates:**

Get Down with Shayne Online
www.shaynesilvers.com
info@shaynesilvers.com

Lightning Source UK Ltd.
Milton Keynes UK
UKHW011830011019
350816UK00001B/125/P